PRAISE FOR NICOLA MARSH

'A heart-warming read from a writer who knows how to deliver a great story.'

Better Reading

'Marsh excels at this sort of small-town romance and she delivers another engaging mix of drama, old regrets and developing relationships.'

Canberra Weekly

'A satisfying read with plenty of drama and a big dollop of romance.'

The Weekly Times

'A beautiful and touching story, underscored by emotional themes, not to be missed.'

Mrs B's Book Reviews

WHERE THE HEART IS

NICOLA MARSH

For every woman who chases a dream

Home is where the heart is and for one country girl, she'll do whatever it takes to save it...

Mila Hayes will do anything to keep her family's farm, including marrying the wrong man. But when the groom backs out at the last minute, and Sawyer Mann, her teen crush and her brother's best friend, witnesses her humiliation, Mila's hopes plummet.

She doesn't believe Sawyer when he says he can help. She's done with short-term solutions. So how will Mila cope when she falls for Sawyer all over again and is forced into making a choice: follow her head or her heart?

Sawyer, now a high-powered land broker who fled Ashe Ridge years ago to escape painful memories, is back temporarily and finds himself unexpectedly drawn to Mila. He kept secrets from her in the past and it pushed them apart. Can he convince Mila this time will be different?

Meanwhile, Mila's grandmother Adelaide, who left her grumpy husband Jack fourteen years ago to follow her dreams, is unsettled by memories resurrected at Mila's wedding.

She's wary of a man tied to this town, but what if he can prove they can build a new future together?

PREFACE

For my readers not located in Australia, I want to preface this novel by saying the story is set in a small country town in Victoria, my home state, in southern Australia.

So the novel is filled with Aussie vernacular, grammar, and spelling.

No worries, hey?

Happy reading,
Nicola

CHAPTER ONE

Mila Hayes took one look at the expression on her groom's face and quashed her quip about how it's bad luck to see the bride in her dress before the ceremony.

Phil Baxter, her neighbour and a man she'd known since she was a kid, looked like he'd been kicked in the balls by his prized ram.

'Is something wrong, Phil?'

A redundant question, considering he couldn't meet her eyes. It gave her time to study the man she was about to marry. For a guy approaching fifty, he'd weathered the years well. While wrinkles crisscrossed his forehead and fanned from the corners of his eyes, his dark brown hair only had a few streaks of grey and he hadn't gained a middle-aged pound. He scrubbed up well too, the tux giving the farmer an air of polish.

'Phil?' she prompted again, and when his gaze finally met hers, Mila's stomach dropped.

He didn't look like a guy about to get married in a few hours.

He looked like a guy being tethered against his will to a ball and chain.

'I'm sorry, Mila.' He reached for her before thinking better of it and thrusting his hands into his pockets. 'I can't do this.'

Mila's heart pounded and her skin grew clammy. This couldn't be happening.

'Everyone gets cold feet on their wedding day, Phil.'

She'd second-guessed her decision to marry a man seventeen years her senior who she didn't love many times over the last three months since they'd decided to seal their business deal via matrimony. But she knew it was the only way to save her farm and family legacy.

Though there was more behind this marriage, and they knew it. Life on a farm could be rewarding but the loneliness... it made her chest ache some nights. Having a frank conversation with Phil, a good friend she'd spent many evenings sharing a wine around a bonfire with, about what marriage could bring to them both had been the best thing she'd ever done.

They'd been realistic during that initial discussion. Feelings may not be front and centre in their marriage, but their mutual respect as friends would make for a solid bond, and if either of them fell head over heels for someone else, they'd figure it out. Whatever that entailed.

But the last thing she expected was Phil to back out on their wedding day. They'd both wanted this marriage: Phil needed more land for his growing sheep flock; she could provide it at a cost. So it seemed logical that once they marry, he helped her financially with as much as he could and she allowed him use of the land to expand his farm and bring in more money.

It seemed like a win-win at the time, with the bonus

of marrying a mate who she liked and respected. She'd never been a hearts and flowers kind of girl—far too practical for that—and marriage hadn't been part of her grand plans.

But necessity had changed all that, and with time, who knew how happy she and Phil could be together? Partners in business and life. It had a nice ring to it.

'Have a beer, Phil. It'll settle your nerves.'

He shook his head. 'It's not that, Mila.' He grimaced and took a step back, like he expected her to slug him. 'I've met someone. On a dating app, a while ago. We've been chatting for months and we finally met in person a few days ago. I think she's the one.'

Mila struggled not to laugh at the irony of her bachelor neighbour, who'd been single for over a decade, meeting someone when he was about to marry her.

'We discussed this, Phil. As long as you're discreet—'

'She's amazing and could be the love of my life, and I want a chance to explore a relationship with her,' he blurted, flushing crimson. 'I don't want to risk something real for a business deal.'

As if sensing a battle, Phil squared his shoulders. 'I know this leaves you in the lurch, but I can still help you financially—'

'That won't be necessary.'

The last thing Mila needed was to be in debt to her neighbour. It would've been easier if she could simply sell him the land in the first place, but some ancient subdivision clause that would cost more money than she had to work around it meant she couldn't. Hence their unconventional marriage deal.

So to have Phil offer her whatever money he could now... no, she'd rather take a bank loan; if they'd approve it, that is. She'd tried, twice, which is why she'd devised her last-resort marriage plan in the first place.

'I truly am sorry, Mila.' Phil shrugged, sheepish. 'I'll make the phone calls now and tell people not to come.'

'You do that,' she snapped, instantly regretting her churlish behaviour when he flinched.

Because deep down, even though Phil reneging on their wedding meant she'd probably lose the one thing that meant everything to her, she was relieved.

Marrying a mate for companionship and sound business practices rather than love had seemed like a good idea at the time when she'd exhausted every avenue to save the farm, but this morning, when she'd slipped into her wedding dress, pinned her hair in a loose up-do, and slathered makeup she rarely wore all over her face, she'd been plagued by doubts that left her nauseous.

What if their friendship soured once they lived together? What if they grew apart rather than closer? What if their marriage ended in a costly divorce? So many 'what-ifs' that left her second-guessing the wisdom of marrying, and now, Phil had taken the choice away from her.

'We're still mates, yeah?' He took his hands out of his pockets and thrust one towards her to shake.

Mila sighed and shook his hand. 'Yeah, we're mates. Though this mystery woman better be pretty bloody special, otherwise I'll cut all your fences and let your sheep out.'

He laughed and she managed a rueful chuckle, despite the panic building in her chest.

Without Phil helping her finance the proposed farm-stay construction that would save Hills Homestead, what the hell was she going to do?

'I better go make those calls,' he said, and she'd never

been more grateful that they'd kept the guest list small, confined to Phil's two best mates, a few farming acquaintances, and his aunt.

Mila had invited her grandad, but he didn't approve so she doubted he'd turn up; her gran said she'd try to make it, but Tally Bay was a long way from Ashe Ridge; and her brother in London had contracted Covid at the last minute so couldn't make the trip.

He half-turned before pausing, his gaze sweeping over her. 'By the way, you look sensational.'

She jabbed a finger at him. 'You don't get to compliment me after ditching me.'

'At least it didn't happen at the altar.'

'Lucky me,' she muttered, her dry response earning a laugh.

'I'll reimburse you for any costs,' he said. 'Just let me know, okay?'

In that moment, the enormity of what she'd lost—namely, a chance to save the place she loved—hit hard, and she blinked away the unexpected sting of tears.

'Go make those calls,' she said, harsher than Phil deserved, and a frown grooved his brow as he cast her a concerned glance.

'Go.' She made a shooing motion with her hands and turned away, waiting until she heard the grumble of his ute's diesel engine before allowing a few tears to fall.

She wasn't this person. She rarely cried, and she'd be damned if she shed tears over a man who'd been smart enough to see the benefits of a marriage based on friendship and for the good of their respective farms, but had fallen prey to Cupid at the last minute.

'Screw this,' she muttered, letting the anger she'd been

keeping at bay flow. It filled her with a distinct urge to smash something.

Her gaze landed on a mallet propped against a verandah post. She used it for hammering in garden stakes. But now, it would come in mighty handy for what she had in mind.

She picked it up, weighing it in her hand, savouring its heaviness. Perfect. Glancing at the arbour covered in Australian native flowers about two hundred metres away, she channelled every inch of outrage and marched towards it, fury fuelling every step.

When she reached the arbour she would've been exchanging vows under in a few hours, she spent a good minute staring at its natural beauty before hoisting the mallet and taking a swing at it.

Those damn tears must've blurred her vision because she missed, and the momentum behind her vicious swing sent her sprawling in the red dirt beneath it, landing heavily on her elbow.

Pain ricocheted up her arm and spots danced before her eyes as she let out a curse. Her day couldn't get any worse.

'Need a hand, Gumnut?'

Hell. It just did.

That voice. The nickname. No way.

It couldn't be.

Then Sawyer Mann chuckled, catapulting her back to the first time they'd met, and she knew this all-round crappy day was about to get a whole lot worse.

CHAPTER TWO

Sawyer knew attending this wedding would be a bad idea. But he owed his best mate Will Hayes, so being his proxy at Mila's nuptials had seemed a small price to pay when Will couldn't make it due to the dreaded virus.

Now that he was here, staring at his mate's little sister sprawled in the dirt as she demolished a wedding arbour, he wished he'd never come. For a multitude of reasons. Most of which he didn't want to acknowledge, because they revolved around a past he'd rather forget. And had tried his utmost to do by moving away from Ashe Ridge and never coming back.

Seeing Mila again after all this time would've been hard. Watching her marry Phil Baxter even harder, which is why he'd arrived a few hours earlier than the scheduled wedding so Mila wouldn't be blindsided by his appearance. While Will couldn't make it, he'd wanted to surprise his sister and had asked Sawyer to be at the ceremony so she had someone akin to family by her side. But if memory served correctly, Mila hated surprises.

She hadn't taken kindly to the tadpoles Will had tipped

into her bath when she'd been seven. She hadn't liked the rubber snake he'd put in her boot at ten. And she sure as hell hadn't been enamoured of Sawyer's offer to be her deb partner in Year 10, which he'd sprung on her the week before when her original partner pulled out.

By the death glare she shot him now as she scrambled into a sitting position, she still wasn't big on surprises.

'What the hell are you doing here?'

She ignored his outstretched hand to help her up and stood, dusting off her dress to little avail. Red dirt streaked the skirt that ended mid-calf and a thin strap had broken, leaving the ruched bodice precariously dipping on one side.

She looked beautiful, with her upswept blonde hair and makeup accentuating her blue eyes and full lips, and his gut twisted with how close they'd once been. There'd been a heart of gold beating beneath tomboy Mila's tough exterior, and she'd been the only one to almost guess his secret back then.

Which is why he'd run as far from Ashe Ridge as he could the day after finishing high school.

'Nice to see you too, Gumnut.'

He made the mistake of grinning and her eyes narrowed to fiery indigo slits.

'Don't call me that.'

'You used to love it.'

'Says you.' She eyed the mallet and for a second he thought she might take a swing at him. 'And you didn't answer my question. Why the hell are you here?'

'Will hated the thought of not being at the ceremony and he wanted you to have a friendly face at your wedding, so he asked me to be here.'

Concern creased her brow. 'I hope he's okay.'

'I spoke to him this morning and he's feeling better. The

usual fatigue and dry cough is lingering, but he's on the mend. Still couldn't travel so here I am.' He flung his arms wide, surprised when her gaze zeroed in on his chest and he glimpsed a flicker of appreciation in her eyes. 'By your demolition job on that arbour, I'm guessing there won't be a ceremony today.'

She slow clapped. 'Way to go with the astute observation.'

'What happened?'

'Phil can't go through with it.' She shrugged like it meant little, but tension bracketed her mouth and her jaw clenched.

The extent of his relief shocked him. He shouldn't care who Mila married, but he did. She deserved so much better than Phil Baxter.

'Want me to beat him to a pulp? Pulverise the dweeb?'

She shook her head. 'Not necessary.' She rolled her eyes and pointed to her left. 'We're still neighbours so it pays to be civil.'

Her nonchalance surprised him. If the love of his life ditched him at the altar, he'd be devastated. Not that he had one of those, and probably never would. He'd have to let a woman get close for that to happen and so far, he'd done a good job of self-preservation.

'At the risk of you picking up that mallet and having a swing at me, you don't seem too distraught about losing your groom.'

'My heart's not broken, if that's what you think.' Her heartfelt sigh made him want to envelop her in his arms. 'Phil and I had an arrangement. Our marriage was predominantly based on business.'

Shock rendered him speechless, and she barked out a laugh devoid of amusement.

'I know it sounds crazy when articulated, but we had a solid plan. I'd give him some of my land to expand his flock in exchange for him funding the farm-stay project I want to build.'

'When you put it that way, ain't love grand,' he muttered, and she flipped him the middle finger.

'Getting tourists to come and stay here is the only way to save Hills Homestead,' she murmured. He only just caught her whispered, 'This place is all I have left.'

His heart twanged and, giving in to impulse, he wrapped his arms around her and hugged her tight. Independent to a fault, she resisted at first, before her body relaxed against his and he tightened his hold.

Resting his chin on the top of her head, he remembered the last time they embraced like this, the day before he'd left town for good. He'd wanted to say so much: to thank her for being his best friend next to Will, to tell her he valued her opinion even when he hated what she had to say, to admit she was the only person in his life who understood there was more to him beneath the clownish surface.

But he'd said nothing and walked away from Mila Hayes without looking back.

Now, with her cheek pressed against his chest, her arms wrapped around his waist, and the faintest floral fragrance from her shampoo tickling his nose, he wondered why he'd stayed away so long.

CHAPTER THREE

'I never should've returned to this godforsaken town,' Adelaide muttered, as her car stalled for the umpteenth time on the outskirts of Ashe Ridge and finally died.

Though it could be worse. At least there was a cottage within walking distance.

She'd call Mila and hopefully get her to delay the wedding. So much for surprising her granddaughter. But it couldn't be helped. At least she'd made it. Almost.

After sliding her phone with its flat battery into her bag and jamming a wide-brimmed straw hat onto her head, she locked the car and headed for the cottage about five hundred metres away.

Her handwoven sandals were no match for the burning bitumen and the hem of her tie-dyed kaftan stuck to her legs as she trudged up the road. She'd forgotten how hot Ashe Ridge could be even in autumn and sweat soon covered her skin.

So much for presenting a cool front when she arrived at the wedding and confronted Jack for the first time in fourteen years.

Seeing her husband would be tough enough without looking like a bedraggled, sweaty mess.

She'd wanted to show him how far she'd come. How living in Tally Bay suited her. How she'd thrived among people who appreciated her, who understood her, two things Jack had never done.

Walking away from Jack Hayes had been the best thing she could've done, and fourteen years was long enough to wait for closure.

She wanted a divorce.

She'd contemplated reaching out to him several times over the years to put an end to their non-existent marriage. But the thought of any kind of contact with Jack, even via lawyers, ruined her mood, and she'd worked hard to achieve Zen.

But a decade and a half was long enough to wait. In a way, she'd been surprised that Jack hadn't instigated proceedings first. He could've reached her any time via Mila or Will, who she spoke to regularly.

Then again, it shouldn't surprise her that Jack was too lazy to get off his arse and be proactive. Her husband had liked being served his dinner at the table, having his bills paid and his life run smoothly. She'd been chef, accountant, nurse, farmhand, mother, grandmother, wrangler, and any other job that needed doing all rolled into one. The one role he hadn't acknowledged her in was wife.

He'd taken her for granted and paid the price.

Not that Jack cared. If he had he would've come after her when she left. She'd spent a few nights at a motel in Kaniva initially, waiting for him to come to his senses and chase after her. He hadn't, making it clear he didn't care if she stayed or left.

That moment, sitting on a worn chenille bedspread in a

motel room that smelled faintly of curry and cigarette smoke, her eyes burning and bloodshot from the copious tears she'd shed, had been a wake-up call. She'd had enough of being Jack's general dogsbody and if he didn't care enough about her to try to convince her to come home, she was done.

She'd taken her time driving from western Victoria to the east coast, spending a night in Lakes Entrance before heading into New South Wales, where she'd stayed at Eden and Sydney before reaching her final destination.

The artistic vibe of Tally Bay, about forty minutes south of its famous counterpart Byron Bay, had beckoned for years and no amount of hinting had made Jack book a trip to the laidback coastal town. She'd contemplated leaving him twice before she finally did and each time she'd researched Tally Bay, knowing she'd love the town if she was lucky enough to visit.

As she'd hoped, the moment she drove into town, a feeling of peace descended, and she'd embraced every aspect of her eclectic new home. She'd stayed in the caravan park initially, to scope out the town, before renting a studio at the back of a mansion owned by an absentee Hollywood couple.

She'd never been more grateful for the nest egg her shrewd mother had insisted she hide away for a rainy day, because it allowed her the freedom to live alone while following her passion: painting.

In Ashe Ridge, she'd never had time to paint. The only time she had a brush in her hand was when Jack insisted she help refurbish the sunroom because he was too tight to pay a local to do the job.

But in Tally Bay, she invested in good-quality paints subsidised by her part-time job in a trendy juice bar and allowed her imagination to run free. Oil paintings, watercolours, charcoal sketches, she'd done it all and had sold enough of her work through a local gallery that catered to tourists to earn a semi-decent living.

Not that the money mattered. She would've happily gone full time at the juice bar if it meant maintaining her freedom, and now it was time to make the break from her past official. Once the ink had dried on her divorce papers, she'd run naked along Tally Bay's main beach and swim at midnight.

The thought made her smile and as she neared the cottage, she took a moment to appreciate its beauty. Sun reflected off the sandstone bricks and the gunmetal-grey tin roof, while an ivory-trimmed verandah ran the length of the front and tucked around a corner towards the back.

Her breath caught as she realised the cottage resembled her dream house, the one she'd pointed out to Jack on their honeymoon in the Adelaide Hills. He'd indulged her, asking how she'd like the interior fitted out and how many rooms she wanted. She'd said she wanted a mezzanine floor to overlook a cosy living room and described exactly how that would look.

Pity when the honeymoon ended, so did Jack's romantic side.

Once they were entrenched at Hills Homestead, the family farm he'd inherited when his parents died, her dreams for a different future faded, obliterated by endless bills and chores and drudgery. And her hopes for the kind of marriage she'd always hoped for— based on love, mutual respect, friendship—faded just as fast.

She'd done her duty and delivered an heir to the farm, but even an amazing son like Cam couldn't appease Jack. She didn't blame her son for leaving town to study in

Melbourne, and when he married a girl with wanderlust in her blood, Adelaide knew she'd lost the one thing that might've kept her in a lacklustre marriage.

Cam and Julie may have hated Ashe Ridge—their disdain more than evident on the rare times they visited—but they had no qualms in dumping their kids on her every chance they got. She'd practically raised Mila and Will, and it hadn't surprised her when Cam and Julie had left to teach children in third-world countries, leaving their own to fend for themselves. Mila had been ten when her parents left, Will eleven, so Addy had waited until Mila finished school before she hit the road herself.

Thankfully, Mila loved the farm, so Adelaide didn't feel so bad leaving her with Jack. Though not a day went by in the ensuing years that she didn't miss her grandkids. She wished she'd been around for Mila and it pained her that she hadn't been tempted to return to Ashe Ridge to be with her granddaughter. But that would mean seeing Jack and too many years had passed by then for the two of them to reconcile.

Mila didn't hold it against her, and they caught up for a girly weekend annually in Sydney. Mila was everything Adelaide wished she'd been at her age: strong-willed, determined, independent. She liked to think Mila got her resilience from her, but in truth her headstrong grand-daughter had probably learned to look after herself because her parents had wanderlust and were never around.

Adelaide blamed herself for that. Maybe her yearning to leave the farm had somehow infiltrated Cam's childhood so he wanted the same. She couldn't call her son selfish for leaving his family behind when she'd done the same.

Her left hip twanged as she stepped onto the verandah, and she rubbed it. Endless hours on her feet while she painted added up at her age and while she considered seventy-three youngish—she still had a lot of living to do—her joints didn't agree.

The cottage had a freshly painted ebony door and a brass knocker that the owner must polish daily to maintain its sheen; she could see her reflection in it.

Taking off her hat and running a hand through her hair, she lifted the brass knocker with her other hand and let it fall. She hoped the owners were home with their cars in the garage because she couldn't see cars in the driveway.

She waited a minute and, heart sinking, she rapped the knocker twice. After what seemed like an eternity, she heard a bolt being slid back and she exhaled in relief. If she could use the owner's phone, she might make it to Mila's wedding on time after all.

However, her relief was short-lived as the door swung open and she locked gazes with the last man on earth she expected to see.

CHAPTER FOUR

As Sawyer's arms tightened around her and Mila allowed her body to relax into his embrace, the emotion of the last hour—heck, of the last year—bubbled up and she couldn't hold it back.

To her mortification, a sob welled in her chest, followed by another, and before she knew it, unwelcome tears had soaked a patch on Sawyer's shirt. Thankfully, he didn't say anything; he just held her, the rhythmic stroking of his hand down her back equally soothing and annoying.

Annoying, because his touch resurrected long-buried memories of her massive teen crush.

She'd been hopeless back then, her skin burning whenever their fingers brushed as he handed her a drink or if he bumped her with his hip, as he often did when they joked around.

Sawyer had been Ashe Ridge's resident clown, constantly making people laugh with his antics. His classmates had loved him for it. The teachers, not so much. He'd never cared, boasting about how he couldn't wait to leave town.

But she'd seen beneath his brash exterior, had seen the flicker of hurt when someone labelled him as *'good for nothing'* or said he'd *'never amount to anything'*. She'd tried to ask him about it once and he'd clammed up, avoiding her for two weeks. It had been just before his final exams and he'd been at Hills Homestead every day, swotting with Will. Her brother had been a brainiac and she'd hoped his diligence would rub off on Sawyer, but Will's best friend had left his cramming too late, and she'd sensed his panic.

When Will ducked out to help Gramps with the tractor, she'd approached Sawyer with the aim of calming him down. But the moment she'd mentioned that ATAR scores weren't the be all and end all, and that plenty of people who weren't book smart went far in life, he'd shut down.

She'd regretted it, because he'd avoided her for the next two weeks. The day after their last exam, Will and Sawyer hit the road—and never returned.

Sawyer hadn't kept in touch, which hurt. She'd hidden her crush well and thought they were friends, even though he was Will's bestie. But she'd got over it. So why was the feel of his arms around her now, and his familiar fragrance of fresh-cut grass and vetiver, making her want to cling to him?

She wasn't the type of woman who needed a man to make her feel better, but in this moment, she tightened her arms around his waist and savoured the rare comfort of being held.

When the ache in her chest subsided and her sobs petered out, she relaxed her hold and eased away, unsure whether to be relieved or bereft when he released her.

'You okay, Gumnut?' Sawyer placed a finger under her chin and tipped it up. 'I have to admit, I've known you for ages and seeing you cry still freaks me out.'

She grimaced, embarrassment scorching her cheeks. 'Sorry about that.'

'Hey, don't apologise. You've had a crappy day. You sure I can't break Phil's kneecaps in your honour?' He chucked her on the chin, making her smile.

'No, I'm not upset about Phil falling for some dating app bimbo, but I'm beyond worried how I'll keep the farm afloat without his financial help.'

'How bad is it?'

The last meeting with the bank manager, a month ago, and the mortgage payments she'd fallen behind on flashed before her eyes, but she blinked them away.

'Bad enough.'

'Anything I can do to help?'

'Not unless you have a few hundred grand floating around so I can complete my farm-stay project and get paying customers to book it out for the next millennium.'

She'd made a throwaway comment, her sarcasm something he should be used to—she'd used it often enough as a deflection technique when they'd been growing up—but she didn't like the speculative gleam in his eyes, as if he'd taken her seriously.

Before he could say anything, she rushed on. 'Anyway, why don't you come inside and have something to eat? There's some catered food that needs to be consumed, frozen, or thrown out.'

Thankfully, he bought her distraction. 'How many guests were you expecting?'

She screwed up her nose, beyond grateful Phil was taking care of calling them. Then again, it's the least he could do, considering he'd been the one to cancel their wedding.

It seemed ridiculous thinking about it now, that she'd

been about to marry her neighbour out of desperation, loneliness, and her obsessive love for this farm.

Her entire life had revolved around this farm once her folks dumped her here, and she loved every inch of the place: the family homestead silhouetted against vast blue skies, the endless paddocks covered in stubby lentil seedlings, the secluded dam, the golden sunsets.

A marriage of convenience, an antiquated notion she'd scoffed at when she'd read romance novels in her teens, seemed a small price to pay for saving her pride and joy.

Losing Hills Homestead, her family's legacy, wasn't an option.

And she'd do whatever it took—including marry for mutual financial gain—to save it.

With that option now off the table, she had no idea how she'd save the one thing in the world that meant everything to her.

'Hey, if you have to think that long about how many guests you were expecting, I'm guessing you didn't send out the invitations?'

She gave her head a little shake. 'Sorry, drifted off for a moment. It was going to be a small ceremony, with guests from Phil's side mainly.'

Disapproval grooved his brow. 'Were you really going through with it?'

'For Hills Homestead, absolutely.'

'But you would've given up some land—'

'A small price to pay to save the rest of it,' she said, her tone unintentionally sharp.

She shrugged. 'I know it sounds ludicrous, but I have my reasons for wanting to hang on to this place at all costs.' She paused and gave him her best stern stare. 'Reasons I have no intention of discussing with you.'

Annoyingly, he chuckled and held up his hands. 'Whoa. No need to divulge your deepest, darkest secrets to me. I'm just here because Will couldn't be.'

'My brother used to eat bugs yet his lousy immune system fails him now,' she muttered, and this time Sawyer laughed outright. 'Anyway, I've over-catered, so come have some food.'

Because if Sawyer was chewing, he wouldn't be talking and asking questions she had no intention of answering. Like why she'd bawled in his arms and the sheer, unadulterated terror that now gripped her at the thought of what the hell she'd do next.

CHAPTER FIVE

Sawyer had never coped well with tears.

When his sisters sobbed over a lost love/crush gone wrong/boy-band breakup, he'd made himself scarce and waited out the tantrums by riding his bike to the other side of town and hunkering down by the river—more a trickle even in winter.

As for seeing Mila cry... it rarely happened. He'd been Will's mate since the first day of Year 5—though he'd known the Hayes kids for years before that because they'd spent every school holidays at the farm—and with Mila a year younger, he'd almost seen as much of her as he had of Will. She'd trailed after them and Will hadn't minded, so he'd put up with it too. Mila had a way about her, a quiet inner confidence, that made him feel settled when he was around her. She was funny too and her astute observations about the kids at school made him laugh.

As for the rest, she'd been the only person to see through him, to recognise that he used humour as a deflection, to wonder if there was more going on, and he'd run because of it.

Though he should thank her, because if she hadn't sown the seed in his head, he wouldn't have got diagnosed at the ripe old age of twenty and changed his life.

'Hope you're hungry,' she said, holding open the back door and gesturing him in.

Seeing her so upset and comforting her in his arms had ruined his appetite, so the sight of the table covered in fancy finger food held little appeal. Entering the farmhouse kitchen had him stepping back in time to the many afternoons after school when he'd run into this warm, cosy space, dropped his bag at the door, grabbed a lamington and a chocolate milk, and raced outside with Will to play cricket in summer or kick the footy in winter.

It had been the highlight of his day and the one thing that got him through the tedious drudgery of being confined in a classroom, being picked on by the teachers because they thought he was lazy rather than stupid and laughed at by his peers because they couldn't tell the difference.

'This place hasn't changed a bit,' he said, when he noticed Mila staring at him with a quizzical expression. 'Brings back memories.'

'I haven't had the time or funds to sink into renovating the main house when I'm hellbent on getting the farm stay up and running.' She shrugged, but he caught the pride in her eyes as she glanced around the kitchen. 'Besides, I like it this way.'

He'd never understood Mila's attachment to this place. Like Will, he couldn't wait to escape Ashe Ridge and he hadn't looked back. But Mila had always been a homebody and she'd loved Hills Homestead with a fervour that bordered on obsession.

Which explained why she'd been about to marry a

sleazy older guy to hold on to it. Anger fizzed in his veins at the thought of Phil Baxter anywhere near Mila, let alone laying a hand on her. Mila may have said it would've been a platonic marriage for mutual financial benefit, but he knew Phil. He remembered the way the older guy would ply women with drinks at barbecues, schmoozing up to them, giving off desperado vibes. And that was before he'd over-heard his sisters Phoebe and Jocelyn talking about how Phil had asked Phoebe out and when she'd refused, he'd proceeded to brush up against her for the rest of the night at the pub. He'd hated the creep ever since.

'Here.' She handed him a plate and proceeded to take cling wrap off the platters. 'We've got lamb and rosemary pies, creamy chicken puffs, asparagus and prawn rice paper rolls, smoky BBQ cheese sliders, turkey and cranberry rissoles, mini fish tacos, French onion potato rostis, and spicy chilli meatballs.'

His stomach rumbled, belying his lack of appetite a few minutes ago, and he chose one of everything before handing her the loaded plate.

She shook her head. 'I can help myself later.'

'Have you had anything to eat at all today?'

Guilt flashed in her eyes as her lips compressed.

'I'll take that as a no, so I'm not going to eat a thing until you do,' he said, laughing when she stuck her tongue out at him.

'You're as bossy as I remember,' she muttered, taking a bite of a chicken puff.

'As I recall, you were the one always ordering me and Will around.'

The three of them had been inseparable in those latter years of primary school, but all that had changed when they hit their teens. Because he saw the way Mila snuck glances at him sometimes when she thought he wasn't looking, and the thought of hurting her... it broke him.

He couldn't do it, so he withdrew a little, kept his distance when all he wanted to do was spend more time with her. If they'd been different people with similar goals, he might've reciprocated her feelings, but with Mila a confirmed homebody and him desperate to escape Ashe Ridge, they were a giant heartbreak just waiting to happen.

'Will mentioned you visited a few months ago?'

'Yeah, I spent three weeks with him in London. He's relishing the city life but he spends a lot of his time at the hospital too.'

'He works too hard,' she muttered, stuffing the rest of the chicken puff into her mouth.

'Yeah, but he loves it.'

He'd always admired Will's drive. Ever since they were kids, his mate had wanted to become a physiotherapist and he'd achieved his dream by working hard at school, getting top marks, and completing his degree at Melbourne Uni before heading over to the UK.

Like himself, Will had never returned to Ashe Ridge, though Sawyer had no idea why his mate rarely visited his family. Sawyer had his reasons for avoiding this town. What was Will's excuse?

'When are you heading back to Melbourne?'

'Tomorrow,' he said, slightly chuffed to see disappointment tugging at the corners of Mila's glossed mouth.

She'd never worn makeup, hadn't needed to with her natural beauty—blue eyes, high cheekbones, heart-shaped face—but he had to admit the stuff she'd slathered on today for her wedding brought out her features in a way that had him struggling not to gawk.

'You really don't like this place much, do you?' She tilted

her head slightly, studying him with an intensity that used to make him squirm—and still did. 'How long since your family has seen you?'

He shrugged. 'I catch up with Jocelyn and Phoebe a few times a year. Jocelyn works in a bank in Brisbane and Phoebe's a pharmacist in Sydney. And Allison's on the outskirts of town, but you already know that.'

'Will might've mentioned Jocelyn and Phoebe when we chatted a while ago. And I wave at Allison when I see her.' She paused, pushing some of the finger food around her plate without eating it. 'I was sorry to hear about your dad.'

'Thanks,' he muttered, the familiar pain associated with remotely thinking about his father making his chest ache.

Henry Mann had been a bastard to his wife and kids, and the best thing the old coot could've done was curl up his toes in a nursing home in Melbourne. Sawyer had been with him at the end, and even then, his father couldn't apologise for being a prick all his life. Sawyer had been relieved rather than sad when the old man had taken his last breath. His father had been dead to him a long time before that, and Sawyer thanked the big guy upstairs every day that his mum had left years earlier so she didn't have to put up with Henry any longer.

'I'd planned on popping in on Allison this afternoon, then hitting the road back to Melbourne first thing in the morning.'

'Definitely a flying visit,' she said, still studying him with that same intensity. 'Do you miss this place at all?'

'No.'

Short, sharp, to the point.

One of her eyebrows arched. 'We had some good times growing up.'

He nodded. 'We did.'

But he didn't want to acknowledge those good times because remembering how amazing it had been hanging out at Hills Homestead with Mila and Will would also mean remembering how shit the rest of his life had been.

He didn't blame his mum for not picking up on his learning difficulties. He'd been the youngest of four kids and even he could see Bernadette Mann had been worn out by the time he'd come along. Jocelyn was sixteen when he'd been born, Phoebe fourteen, and Allison twelve, so he'd been an afterthought or an accident.

Even from a young age, he'd seen the way his dad treated his mum—like an annoyance rather than a wife—and Sawyer had done whatever he could to protect her. Including act like a jackass. Maybe his clownish ways had started then, desperate to make his mother and sisters laugh to distract from the fraught atmosphere whenever his father entered the house. It worked on them, so he carried over his behaviour to school, determined to be seen as the funny guy, the popular guy, the joker, to distract from how badly he struggled to understand the most basic of curriculum.

'Well, if you ever want to take a stroll down memory lane, you know where to find me.' Mila popped a mini rissole into her mouth and chewed. 'Though not for much longer if I can't afford the mortgage repayments.'

His heart sank at the sight of her so despondent and he wished he could help. She wouldn't accept it, but he had to offer once more. 'I meant what I said before, Gumnut. Anything I can do, all you have to do is ask.'

'So you're mister moneybags now, are you?'

He knew she didn't mean to sound so harsh, that she was trying to deflect so he wouldn't notice the sheen of tears in her eyes again. Those damn tears slugged him anew.

'Being a land broker pays the bills,' he said, wondering what she'd think if she saw his bank balance.

The class clown had made good and then some.

With a little careful investing early in his career, he'd managed to buy two rental properties on Melbourne's fringe, as well as the house he resided in when he wasn't on the road, among the leafy streets of affluent Hawthorn.

If Mila needed financial assistance he could definitely help, but her inherent stubborn streak meant she wouldn't accept it no matter how many times he offered.

Unless he took a different approach...

An idea shimmered into consciousness, but he'd have to do some digging before he presented it to her in a way she couldn't say no to.

'Shall we make a toast?' He picked up one of the champagne bottles on ice and waited until she nodded before popping the cork and filling two flutes.

After he'd handed her one, he raised his. 'To old friends.'

'To old friends,' she echoed.

As they tapped glasses, their gazes locked, and Sawyer wondered if contemplating sticking around for longer than a day was the craziest thing he'd done in a long time.

CHAPTER SIX

Adelaide forgot to breathe the minute she laid eyes on Jack after all this time.

Her chest constricted and dizziness swamped her. She clutched at the doorjamb, only to find Jack's arms around her.

'Easy there, old girl,' he murmured, leading her into the welcome cool of the cottage provided by centuries-old sandstone.

The familiar cadence of his voice made her chest constrict further and for some unfathomable reason tears stung her eyes. She'd shed enough tears over this man decades ago. No way in hell she'd cry now.

'Who are you calling old, fossil?'

He chuckled and led her to a suede sofa. As he gently lowered her onto it, Adelaide didn't know what surprised her more: the fact Jack had laughed when he should be ranting at her for abandoning him fourteen years ago, or that the living room resembled her idea of a dream house as much as the cottage's exterior.

The rough-hewn sandstone bricks that comprised the

walls were a perfect contrast for the A-frame wood-lined ceilings and mezzanine. Suede sofas and armchairs the colour of burnt toffee were split by a massive rectangular red-gum coffee table, and a state-of-the-art flatscreen TV perched on the wall above a gas log fire.

How she'd longed for a fireplace like that at the farm, where she hated having to empty ash out of the grate every day in the winter, and the prospect of finding snakes in the log pile outside. She'd asked Jack once, but he'd cited the usual 'waste of money' excuse, adding to her burgeoning resentment.

'I'll be back in a minute,' he said, giving her time to reassemble her wits, and that's when reality hit.

Jack hadn't been pining for her as a small part of her hoped. Oh no. Jack had shacked up with a woman who had the same excellent taste she did.

And she didn't know what made her angrier: Jack moving on—and still looking damn good, with his wavy peppery hair, hazel eyes, perpetual stubble—or her giving a damn.

She closed her eyes, inhaling to the count of four, holding her breath for four, and exhaling to the count of eight, a meditation technique she'd learned many years ago when she first arrived in Tally Bay. It never failed to ground her, but as the sofa dipped beside her and she smelled an intriguing blend of cinnamon and sandalwood, she knew all the deep breathing in the world couldn't settle her.

She opened her eyes to find Jack studying her with unnerving intensity, as if trying to memorise every line on her face.

'Here. Drink this.' He thrust a glass at her and damned if her throat didn't clog with emotion again as she realised he'd made her a manhattan: whiskey, sweet vermouth, bitters, with a slice of orange peel. Her favourite. 'Alcohol's good for the shock. Unless you came looking for me?'

Adelaide couldn't speak until she'd downed half the cocktail in one go, the burn of whiskey a welcome reprieve from the welling emotion. She'd wanted to see Jack this trip, to finalise their divorce once and for all, but she thought she'd have time to prepare for a confrontation. Seeing him here, now, made her head spin. Or maybe that was the manhattan on an empty stomach?

'When's the last time you ate?' he asked, and she hated that he still had an uncanny knack for reading her mind.

Then again, he hadn't done it all the time—if he had he would've known how unhappy she'd been in their marriage and listened to her threats of leaving.

'I don't remember,' she said, barely able to recall her own name considering the shock she'd just had.

'Cheese on crackers okay?' He stood before she answered and walked away, giving her time to acknowledge he hadn't lost his leanness either. Or the butt that had first drawn her attention at a B & S ball in Nhill where they'd first met; a ball she'd attended last minute with a school friend on their way to Adelaide.

She'd been a naive nineteen, her head filled with plans to travel to Italy to absorb the art of centuries; he'd been a brash twenty, cocky about his ability to run the family farm he'd just inherited. There'd been instant sparks—a raging inferno more like it—and she'd spent the night in his swag. And moved to his farm in Ashe Ridge two weeks later.

She thought they'd give a relationship a try for a few months, reluctant to shelve her yearning to paint in Europe altogether, but getting pregnant put paid to her dreams and she accepted Jack's marriage proposal.

'You shouldn't drink on an empty stomach.' Jack re-entered the living room and placed a small white platter of artisan crackers topped with hand cut wedges of brie on the coffee table.

Wow, his new partner must have serious sway over this man, who'd barely hack a slice of cheddar and jam it between two slices of bread to make a toasted cheese sandwich in the old days.

'And you shouldn't ply me with alcohol before checking if I've eaten first.'

Her retort held no malice, and he somehow knew that, because he smiled and her stomach flipped. Purely a reaction to not having eaten for hours and downing half a cocktail.

'You always were a one pot screamer.' He sat next to her again, instantly dwarfing the sofa and making her skin prickle with awareness. 'You looked shell-shocked though, so I thought you could do with a whiskey jolt.'

'Thanks,' she said, embarrassed that it was the first time she'd expressed gratitude rather than making smart-arse comebacks. 'My car broke down half a kilometre up the road and the last person I expected to open the door to this place was you, so yeah, I'm in shock.'

'Eat a few crackers, then we'll talk.'

Impressed by his thoughtfulness, she said, 'Is it okay if I use your phone first? My phone's dead and I want to call Mila, see if she can stall the wedding a little.'

Jack's expression turned mutinous. 'There's not going to be a wedding. Mila called a little while ago. That jackass Phil Baxter dumped her.'

'Oh no...' Adelaide pressed a hand to her chest, her heart aching for her granddaughter. 'He jilted her at the altar?'

'Almost.' Jack snorted. 'At least he had the balls to tell her a few hours before the ceremony.'

He pinned her with an astute stare. 'I thought you weren't coming to the wedding?'

Embarrassment flushed her cheeks. 'I didn't think I'd make it, but I couldn't let that sweet girl get married without me there.'

'Good to see family still means something to you,' he muttered, an angry glint darkening his eyes, and she couldn't blame him.

She deserved whatever he dished up and more for abandoning him. Heck, she deserved the manhattan flung in her face and the crackers dumped on her head for walking away and never looking back.

Though she had her reasons, and if their marriage meant anything to Jack, he would've come after her and she would've told him. Everything.

But he hadn't loved her enough, and she'd given up caring, so here they were, fourteen years later, with a chasm filled with bitterness and retribution between them.

She wanted to say so much, but she settled for, 'We need to talk.'

His brisk nod of agreement was the only sign he'd heard her as he turned away.

Her heart aching for all they'd lost, and the pain to come when they finally confronted their demons, she managed to stuff a few crackers into her mouth and swallow them.

For what they had to discuss, she needed all the sustenance she could get.

CHAPTER SEVEN

Mila should've been grateful Sawyer had stuck around to help remove all traces of her nuptials.

Not that she'd done too much to the house, but she'd wanted Phil's friends and aunt to believe this wedding was real, so she'd draped the verandah in chiffon and fairy lights, and placed Australian wildflowers in beautiful ceramic vases her gran had made many years ago along the railing.

The trestle table where she'd planned to place the finger food had been covered in a heavy ivory damask that had belonged to her grandmother too, and she'd wound vines around more complex floral arrangements made up of proteas, banksias, waratahs, Geraldton wax, pincushions, and billy buttons.

She'd gone to a lot of trouble to make this wedding appear authentic to those who didn't know about her marriage of convenience—namely everyone but her and Phil—and now she felt foolish.

Who had she been trying to convince the most, the clueless guests or herself?

That's the thing about bullishly following a dream, you'd do anything to make it come true—and saving Hills Homestead had become an obsession.

When she'd first proposed the solution to her problems, Phil had laughed so hard he'd almost strained an ab. But when he'd let it sink in, he'd come to see the arrangement suited them both. A forty-nine-year-old single farmer in this close-knit community faced constant scrutiny about his sexuality and speculation about his inability to keep a woman.

In exchange for financial assistance to make her dream flourish, Phil would get the townsfolk and his family off his back—plus a healthy chunk of her land to expand his own farm. Win-win.

So why did she feel like the biggest loser on the planet because she'd been ditched?

She hated to admit it but marrying Phil had been as much about comfort as pragmatism. Their friendship meant a lot to her, and she relished the evenings they'd hang out together, sharing a bottle of wine and a few laughs at the never-ending gossip of a small town. She never felt threatened by Phil. Despite his flirting, he never put the hard word on her or overstepped. They shared a love of schnitties, cold beer, and quiet time under a starry sky. They respected each other and enjoyed hanging out. Some marriages were built on less.

Having him back out at the last minute had wounded her emotionally, not just financially, and if Phil's new relationship turned serious, she'd miss his droll sense of humour and corny jokes more than she cared to admit.

But she'd handled his rejection like she handled the rest of the drama in her life: stoically and pragmatically. Having low expectations meant she'd given up on romance around the time she'd moved on from sneaking her gran's steamy literature from the box under her bed in her late teens.

Unlike Phil, she didn't do dating apps. On the occasional trip out of town, she flirted a little, and if a hook-up opportunity presented itself, she took full advantage. But those 'opportunities' were few and far between, and the last time she'd had sex could be measured in years, not weeks or months. It never bothered her. Until now.

Because for some odd reason, seeing Sawyer after all these years, having him hold her in his arms and comfort her, had her yearning for something that could never happen.

Sawyer was history. Ancient history. She'd be better off remembering that.

Once she'd packed away the rest of the food, freezing three quarters of it because it would feed her for the next month, she finally did what she should've done the moment she entered the house: get out of her dress.

She'd been tempted to rip it off earlier, around the time she'd been demolishing the arbour, but then Sawyer had turned up and she'd forgotten she'd been wearing the thing. Now, as she stood in her plain white cotton undies and matching bra, staring at the crumpled silk streaked with red dust on the floor, she found it symbolic. Her dreams for turning a profit with her farm stay lay in a heap too, unless she could come up with another solution fast.

Not that she hadn't tried already. Marrying Phil had been a last resort and now that option had been removed she couldn't bear thinking about it.

She bundled up the calf-length silk dress with spaghetti straps and stuffed it in the clothes hamper. Not that she'd ever wear it again, but she'd wash it and donate it to the op shop in town. Maybe it would bring the next bride who wore it better luck.

Not that she believed in luck. She made her own, not waiting for a nebulous fate to bestow good stuff on her. Which meant she needed to get her arse into gear and figure out another solution for her financial problem.

'Gumnut, the arbour is down. Anything else you want me to do?'

Sawyer's voice drifting down the hallway had her stepping into jeans, tugging a blue singlet over her head, and slipping her arms into her favourite short-sleeved flannie. Not that she'd been averse to him seeing her in her underwear at one stage, but she'd grown up. Right?

'Be right there,' she yelled, tugging the pins out of her hair and letting it fall, running her fingers through it before snagging it into a ponytail. Her makeup looked even more incongruous now she'd ditched the bridal outfit, but she didn't have time to take it off.

She needed to get rid of Sawyer.

Because the moment he'd asked if there's anything else she wanted him to do, a plethora of possibilities popped into her head, starting with him undressing her, ending with him spending more than a few hours here.

Simply, she didn't want to be alone tonight.

But she wouldn't use him like that. Sawyer may not have reciprocated her crush years ago, but he'd been a friend, a good one, and sleeping with him because she was hurt and lonely wouldn't be fair. Besides, even if she put the hard word on him, he might not want to spend the night.

With a sigh, she pressed her fingertips to her temples. What the hell was she thinking? She needed to thank Sawyer for his help and send him on his way.

She flung open her bedroom door and almost ran smack bang into his broad chest.

'Whoa.' His hands shot out to grasp her arms, steadying her. 'Are you in a hurry to get rid of me?'

'Yes,' she muttered, hating how her skin tingled beneath his touch. 'And stop calling me Gumnut.'

His mouth kicked into the laconic grin that used to set her heart racing. 'You used to love it.'

'When I was ten.'

'You know it's a term of endearment, right?'

'Whatever.'

He laughed and released her. 'You're in a bad mood, but I guess you're entitled, what with being ditched at the altar by Fabulous Phil.'

'I'm devastated by the lack of his financial support, nothing more.'

But he must've heard the hint of vulnerability in her voice, the one she strove to hide every day because deep down she hated being alone despite all protestation to the contrary, because he said, 'I know you're probably exhausted and counting down the minutes until you boot me out of here, but I'd really love to take a look at the farm-stay project you're so passionate about that you'd consider marrying that slimeball.'

She'd love nothing better than to show him her pride and joy, with the first cottage nearing completion and the second well underway, but he was right. She had to get rid of him before she did something totally out of character again, like slide into his arms and hold on tight.

'Phil's not a slimeball.'

'Fine. He's a sleazebag.'

'You're being too harsh, especially considering you haven't seen him in years.'

He rolled his eyes. 'I doubt he's changed. Leopards, spots, and all that.' He grimaced. 'That guy used to be a ladies' man.'

She didn't want to admit that she enjoyed Phil's light-hearted flirtation because it distracted her from how damn lonely she was, and his lingering glances were the closest thing she came to feeling appreciated as a woman.

So she deflected. 'Come on, I'll give you the grand tour, then you're out of here.'

'When you put it like that, how can I refuse?'

They headed through the kitchen and out the back door, where Mila veered left, following the path behind the main shed. She'd purposely chosen the expanse of land to the west of the shed because it afforded guests privacy, out of sight of the main homestead.

Her ancestors had been clever in laying out the farm. The homestead and adjoining land where she planned on opening the farm stay were within sight of the main road but set far enough back to ensure privacy. And the silos, paddocks, and sheds housing equipment were situated behind a line of trees that effectively hid the day-to-day operations. Though she loved the silo art in the region and once she had enough capital would love to pay a local artist to paint her silos with local flora and fauna. It could be a drawcard for the farm-stay occupants, something for them to see on the farm other than the day-to-day running.

She loved every aspect of lentil farming: the unique names of the red lentils like Nugget, Digger, Aldinga, and Northfield; the paddock preparation that required adequate weed-control measures before sowing; the rolling to flatten any ridges caused by sowing; how lentils flower profusely in a short period of time. And the satisfaction when she sold a crop at a decent price, a direct result of her hard work... that feeling was priceless.

There was no way she'd lose Hills Homestead without a fight and if she could just get the farm stays up and running, she had a chance. Though starting this project was about more than money and she knew it.

She wanted people to experience the same feelings she got when she opened the front window every morning, inhaled the crisp country air and watched the sun crest the horizon in a blaze of gold and sienna. The uniqueness of a cricket cacophony as dusk streaked the sky in mauves and magentas. The warbling of magpies, the rustle of eucalypts, the hooting of owls.

The vastness of the farm engulfed her and she wanted to share her love of the land with those who spent most of their lives running for trams or trapped in a cubicle in a city high-rise.

As they rounded the corner of the shed, the first cottage came into view and Sawyer wolf-whistled.

'Wow. You did all that?'

'With the help of the odd tradesmen or two. Gramps helped too.'

'How does Jack feel about you changing things around here?'

She shrugged, wishing she could share her struggles with her grandfather, but she didn't want to burden him when he'd left the farming life behind. She'd seen the toll it had taken over the years, though she attributed his stoic sadness to her grandmother leaving as much as the rigours of farming life. He'd always been a quiet man, withdrawn rather than gregarious, and that only intensified after Addy left. But she shared a special bond with her grandfather, and they were happiest when riding quad bikes around the farm or overseeing the sowing of a new crop.

When he'd sold her the farm, she'd been ecstatic. She'd farmed alongside him long enough and it had been time for her to be her own boss. He'd bought a small block of land on the outskirts of town and built an amazing sandstone cottage, leaving her to run the farm on her own.

It's what she wanted, but lentil farming had been in Gramps's blood, and a small part of her thought he might pop around more often.

'Gramps walked away from the farm when he sold it to me. Though he thinks I'm mad pouring more capital into the place when I'm still paying off a mortgage. And as he says, *"All it takes is one bad crop"*' She shook her head. 'The farm is run well but I've had a string of bad years so I need the farm stay to take off so I can pay off my debts.'

Respect glinted in his eyes. 'You have it all figured out.'

'I have plans. There's nothing wrong with that.'

He held up his hands in surrender. 'Didn't say there was. Why so defensive?'

She couldn't tell him the truth—that insomnia had become a constant companion since she undertook the farm-stay project, that she worried about money constantly, that she couldn't fathom what she'd do if she lost the farm—so she settled for, 'So how's the land-broking business treating you?'

'I love it,' he said, pride audible in his smoother-than-caramel tone, the depth of his voice eliciting the same visceral reaction it had when she'd been a teen. 'I work hard, I get recognised for my efforts. It's rewarding.'

'I always knew you'd be amazing at whatever you did.'

A blush stole into his cheeks and he looked away,

unable to meet her eyes. 'You were the only one who believed in me.'

She wanted to ask so much—why he'd hidden his intelligence behind banter in school, why he'd never applied himself, why he'd antagonised teachers—but it wasn't her place. They hadn't seen each other in fifteen years, hadn't spoken once in all that time, and they were more like acquaintances now rather than the friends they'd once been.

'Thanks,' he murmured, staring at the farm-stay cottage ahead of them. 'You were a good mate back then.'

'You're welcome,' she said, surprised by the lump of emotion in her throat. If he only knew how much she'd wanted to be more than a mate, how many nights she'd lain awake fantasising about him kissing her, how hard she struggled with her overwhelming feelings.

'Can I ask you something?'

'Sure,' she said.

'Why did you stay?'

'In town, you mean?'

'In town. Here on the farm.' He paused and shot her a sideways glance. 'You were smarter than Will and could've been anything.'

'Don't let Will hear you say that,' she said. 'He's got a bigger ego than you.'

He chuckled. 'Nice deflection, but you didn't answer the question.'

'It's simple, really. I love this farm. There's no other place I'd rather be.'

Which is why she had to come up with a solution to save it—fast.

CHAPTER EIGHT

Sawyer couldn't believe it. Mila had done all this?

'My vision is to have three cottages, spread out across this acre.' She gestured at the scrub bordering a fence on their left. 'I'd love to rent out this first cottage once it's completed but it's not very relaxing for guests when construction is happening on the other two.'

Her nose crinkled adorably. 'Not to mention that slight problem with funding to get the other two to lock-up stage.'

'You've done a great job so far,' he said, blown away by what she'd managed to build on her own with the help of a few tradies and her grandad. 'What's your vision?'

She eyed him with respect, like he was the first bloke to ask such an enlightened question.

'Ultimately, I'd like to cut back our crops. I know the lentils are my major money-spinner but the instability of the market is stressful. And I'm already in enough debt with paying off the mortgage, so the income from the farm stay when regularly booked will be a nice earner.' She tapped her temple. 'I've done the maths. It's going to work, if I can ever get it off the ground.'

'You've got a business plan?'

She nodded. 'A solid one. There's an accountant in town who crunched all the numbers for me. Freddie's the best.'

A surprising stab of envy made him study her closely. Freddie? The way she said the nerd's name sounded way too familiar. As for Freddie being the best, Sawyer didn't like that. Not one bit.

'Freddie, huh? You two close?'

'Like this.' She intertwined her index and third finger, and that stab came again, more potent this time.

Crazy, because he had no right to be jealous. Mila was a mate. A mate he hadn't seen in fifteen years. If only his libido could get with the mate-ship program.

She'd been cute as a kid, tempting as a teen, but now... Mila had a way of looking at him with those big blue eyes that made him feel like the only man in the world. Those minuscule gold flecks in her eyes glowed when she was angry—he'd borne the brunt of her tirades several times growing up—and now he couldn't help but wonder if they'd glow in the throes of passion too...

'Hey.' She snapped her fingers in front of his face, her guffaw loud in the descending dusk. 'I'm kidding, but for a second there it's nice to think you were jealous.'

'Dream on, Gumnut.'

She rolled her eyes, but they hadn't lost their sparkle. 'If you call me that one more time, I may have to take drastic action.'

'Like?'

He enjoyed sparring with her way too much. They'd always been like this; baiting each other, teasing, in a constant game of one-upmanship. Though their banter had an edge now, an underlying tension he knew had to be sexual awareness. On his part, at least.

'Remember Kaz Mahoney?'

How could he forget? Kaz had trailed after him all through high school, twirling her hair around her fingertip, licking her lips, leaning over his desk with her uniform unbuttoned to her cleavage. He'd been politely indifferent but there was no deterring Kaz. She interpreted a smile as an offer to go steady. She'd been one of the things about Ashe Ridge he definitely didn't miss when he fled.

'Sure,' he said, with a nonchalant shrug. 'How's she doing?'

'Divorced and on the prowl again.' Mila clawed the air and growled like a cougar. 'And if you keep calling me Gumnut, I might accidentally on purpose give her your phone number.'

He bit back a smile. 'You don't have my number. Because if you did, and you haven't used it all these years, I'll be heartbroken.'

'Yeah, right.' Her lips curved into a coy smile. 'Besides, you could've called me.'

'Didn't need to. Will keeps me up to date with your comings and goings.'

Her eyebrow arched. 'Is that so?'

'Of course. I like to keep abreast of how my best girl is doing.' Before she could call his bluff, he captured her in a headlock and gave her a noogie. 'My best gumnut.'

She elbowed him, hard, and he let out a loud *'Oomph'* as she caught him off guard, making him momentarily stagger before he landed on his butt. Not so bad, considering Mila landed on top of him.

The momentum of her falling with him pitched her forward and their foreheads collided. She reeled a little and he slid an arm around her waist to anchor her, ignoring the throbbing of his head, preferring to focus on the feel of her in his lap. Which prompted a throbbing of an entirely different kind.

'Speaking of best girls, are you in a relationship?'

He shook his head. 'I date occasionally, but relationships are more trouble than they're worth.'

'You'll get no argument from me.'

'Says the woman who was getting married today.'

'A financially beneficial marriage.'

'In that case, you should marry me for money. I'm loaded.'

Their gazes locked and they exhaled at the same time, their soft breath sounding suspiciously like a wistful sigh.

'I'd never marry anyone who calls me Gumnut.' She leaped to her feet, dusting herself off, and for one crazy moment, Sawyer wished she'd taken him seriously.

Not that he'd meant it. It had been a throwaway comment, part of their sparring, but did she have to react like she'd rather marry anyone but him? Could she have got off him any quicker?

'Do you want to see the rest of the place?'

She didn't wait for his answer, her strides long as she walked away from him, shoulders squared, her ponytail bouncing with every step.

Sawyer had no intention of marrying anyone, but her quick refusal stuck like a burr and resurrected insecurities he'd long buried. According to everyone in this godforsaken town when he'd been growing up, he wasn't good enough. His family hadn't believed in him, his teachers hadn't either. He'd shown them. He wasn't kidding about being loaded and he knew one thing for certain.

He'd help Mila out financially whether she liked it or not.

CHAPTER NINE

Adelaide had been grateful when Jack said he needed to fix a broken fence an hour ago and absconded. It had given her time to gather her wits following the shock of seeing him after all this time. She hadn't moved from the sofa, despite her curiosity about the rest of his place, for the simple fact it was wrong to poke around in his new life. And going by the beauty of this living room, a new life he was thriving in.

She could've called a tow truck or mechanic in his absence, but it would've been rude to leave while he'd been out, so she'd waited, demolishing the crackers and brie, sipping at her drink. Now, with Jack stomping as he came through the back door, her reprieve was over.

Grateful for the crackers and cheese in her stomach, Adelaide knocked back the rest of her manhattan, steeling her nerve for 'the talk' she needed to have with Jack. He entered the living room as she placed the empty glass on the coffee table, his lips compressed into a grim line.

'Is it true you ended up here by sheer chance because your car broke down or is this another of your lies?'

Shocked by his change from solicitous host when she'd first arrived to accusing ex, she said, 'I never lied to you.'

'Yeah?' His eyebrows rose. 'Then what was that whole *"till death do us part"* vow?'

Annoyed he had her on the back foot already, she kept her tone steady, with effort. 'My car has broken down, so I'll need to use your phone to contact a tow truck, please. As for you opening the door to this place...'

She cast an envious eye over the interior again. 'Trust me, this is the last place I expected you to be.'

'Why's that?'

'Your feet are rooted to the farm. You'd never leave it, as you told me many times. So I'm assuming this belongs to a *friend*?'

If he caught her implication, he didn't acknowledge it. 'Mila didn't tell you?'

'Tell me what?'

'I moved out of the farm when I built this place about five years ago. She bought the farm.' A frown dented his brow. 'I didn't want her going into that much debt, but you know Mila, headstrong to a fault. I actually wondered if that's why she was marrying Phil, for financial assistance, but she denied it.'

Adelaide heard what Jack said but she couldn't compute it. He'd sold the farm.

He'd built this cottage. Her dream home.

And he'd lived here for five years. What the hell?

Why couldn't he have been so flexible when they'd been living together? Why hadn't he acknowledged what she'd wanted, rather than shooting down every suggestion she made for them to have a better life away from the farm? Why hadn't he seen how unhappy she was and done something, anything, as an incentive for her to stay?

Adelaide didn't regret a single moment of the last fourteen years, when she'd found happiness and reawakened parts of herself she'd thought lost forever during the fraught years of her marriage. But the realisation that Jack had followed through on a part of *her* dream rankled. A hell of a lot.

Unless he didn't remember and had built this by pure chance?

Only one way to find out.

'Why did you build my dream house?'

The telltale flush staining his cheeks gave her an answer before he spoke. 'I like sandstone too.'

A lame response and he knew it.

'I'm glad your new partner has more influence over you than I ever had,' she muttered, bitterness lending bite to her words.

Not that she had a right to give him grief. She'd walked away from him without looking back. She shouldn't begrudge him happiness. Especially considering she hadn't been celibate in the years since she'd left. But seeing concrete evidence of what she'd once wanted from him, and he'd never been invested enough to give it to her, infuriated her.

Confusion creased his brow. 'I don't have a partner.'

She snorted. 'It's okay, Jack, my feelings won't be hurt if you've moved on.'

She hesitated, realising he'd given her the perfect segue to start the discussion they needed to have. 'In fact, why don't we put the past behind us once and for all?'

A gentle way of leading into the divorce conversation they needed to have.

He blanched, his pain-filled eyes stark in his face. 'If that's what you want.'

'It's been long enough. Isn't it what you want too?'

'You've never been particularly interested in what I want,' he mumbled, shooting to his feet and stalking towards the window so she had no hope of reading the expression on his face.

'We could talk while I'm in town.'

He thrust his hands into his pockets, stretching the flannel across his shoulders. He'd worn nothing but flannies when they'd been married, reluctant to change his fashion—and every other aspect of his life. Jack had been a quiet, stubborn, old-fashioned, stick-in-the-mud in his early twenties and she'd never expected the fun-loving charmer she'd fallen for at that B & S ball to morph into a non-communicative grump so quickly.

She knew he'd taken his farming responsibilities seriously and had done her utmost to support him. But the more Jack retreated inward, the greater the emotional distance between them, until she'd had no option but to leave.

Simply, she'd woken up one day and given up trying.

'Fine. We'll talk.' Jack's soulless monotone made her wish she could go to him, wrap her arms around him from behind, and rest her cheek against his back like she used to. But she'd given up the right to comfort or do anything else with this man a long time ago and she needed to harden up for what was to come. 'Is your number the same?'

'It's the same,' she said. Of course it would be, considering a small part of her had never given up hope in those first few years after she left that he'd come to his senses and call. 'Speaking of phones, can I call Mila please?'

He swung back to face her, his expression carefully blanked. 'Probably best to give her a bit of space today.'

Adelaide had never liked being told what to do, especially by this man, but Jack was probably right. Though she'd been hoping to stay on the farm with her grand-daughter. A farm Mila apparently owned but had never told her. It hurt that her granddaughter, who she thought she had a close bond with, had kept something so monumental from her.

Then again, if Mila had told her about buying the farm, her granddaughter would've had to field questions about where Jack had gone and maybe she didn't want to get caught in the middle.

'Okay, I'll call her tomorrow. But can I use your phone to call a tow, then the motel?'

She assumed Shazza still ran the motel. It had been her pride and joy back in the day and Shazza treated every guest like they were staying at a five-star hotel rather than an ageing motel.

Jack's frown returned. 'Want me to take a look at the car?'

She wanted nothing from him—discounting a divorce —but if something simple had caused the breakdown, maybe Jack could fix it and she could be on her way sooner rather than later. He'd always been tinkering with the tractor or some other piece of equipment on the farm and had been adept at fixing them.

'That'd be good, thanks.'

'Let's go.' He picked up his keys from the coffee table and pressed a button on a small rectangular remote control, to open the garage presumably. 'I'll call a tow from the car if I can't fix it.'

'And the motel?'

The strangest expression crossed his face, one she had no hope of interpreting. 'I'll drop you there.'

He'd crossed the living room before he paused, shooting

her a glare that made her heart sink. 'Though if you ever gave half a shit about me, you'd realise that staying at the motel will make me the talk of the town and you'd reconsider where you'll shack up while you're here.'

His low tone barely above a growl held a tonne of hurt and made her feel lower than she already did.

'I'll talk to Mila.'

But that meant bothering her granddaughter at the worst possible time, when she'd been dumped on her wedding day—though what other option did she have?

'She needs her space,' he muttered, his lips compressing into a thin, unimpressed line. 'There's a room out the back you can use for tonight if you want.'

Her jaw must've dropped a little because Jack barked out a laugh. 'Don't worry, it's a good distance from the house and is self-contained so you won't encounter me.'

An enormous gratitude welled in her chest, and she couldn't speak for a moment. She'd treated Jack badly when she'd walked out on him, testing him, expecting him to come after her. When he didn't, it had vindicated her choice to walk away. She must've hurt him badly yet here he was, offering her a place to stay when she didn't deserve it. It made her want to bawl.

She blinked away the tears stinging her eyes and cleared her throat. 'Thanks, Jack.'

'You're welcome,' he muttered, gruff and surly as he turned away and headed for the internal access door leading to the garage. 'Follow me.'

She had once, all the way to a rundown farm in Ashe Ridge. And look where that had got her.

A broken heart, broken dreams, and a broken marriage about to end in divorce fourteen years too late.

CHAPTER TEN

Mila had walked Sawyer to his car—not a moment too soon, considering their old camaraderie had taken little to flare to life— when Phil pulled up in his ute.

Great, just what she needed: a reminder of how this all-round shitty day had gone awry.

Sawyer stiffened and slammed his car door shut without getting in. 'What's he doing here?'

'No idea.'

'I'll gladly kick his arse if you want me too,' Sawyer muttered, drawing his shoulders back and leaving Mila in little doubt he'd make good on his offer if she wanted.

Not that she'd take him up on it, but it was nice to see Sawyer in defensive mode, ready to protect her honour if she asked. A bonus, seeing his shirt stretch across his chest, hinting at muscles she had no right ogling. Those few illicit moments in his lap had addled her brain, along with his joking proposal. Because while thrown out in jest, for a second she'd envisaged being married to Sawyer and known it would've been far from platonic.

'I can take care of Phil,' she said, raising a hand in a half-hearted wave at her runaway groom.

'That's what the lech is counting on,' Sawyer muttered. A deep frown grooved his brow as Phil strode towards them.

'Be nice,' she murmured, seeing Phil's steps falter the exact second he recognised Sawyer.

'Sawyer Mann. Long time no see.' Phil held out his hand. 'What brings you to town?'

'A wedding that's not happening because of you, apparently.' Sawyer ignored Phil's hand and the older guy lowered it, his expression sheepish.

'That's between me and Mila—'

'Cut the bullshit, Phil. I know all about your fake marriage.' Sawyer's glower made Phil take a backward step and Mila stifled a grin.

Not that she needed Sawyer to protect her but having him bristle at Phil like a guard dog felt kind of nice. She'd been taking care of herself for a long time and wore her independence like a gold medal. But Phil had ruined her plans for saving the farm so having Sawyer give him a hard time made her want to hug him.

'Actually, that's what I wanted to talk to you about,' Phil said, his lopsided smile not earning any brownie points with her. 'I've contacted everyone and told them I've met someone and I called off the wedding because of the other woman, so you don't look bad.'

Animosity radiated off Sawyer and she laid a hand on his arm. 'Actually, Phil, that doesn't make me look bad, but it does make me look like a loser.'

Phil's confused gaze swung between her and Sawyer. 'But I thought I was doing the right thing, taking the blame for the wedding not going ahead.'

She should be more magnanimous, but it wasn't until this moment that Mila realised she'd be the talk of Ashe Ridge for months to come. She'd done such a good job of fooling herself and the rest of the town into believing this marriage was real—dinners at the pub with Phil, shopping at the farmers market together, baking for the school's fundraising stall—that she'd probably have to fend off countless questions and pitying hugs for ages.

'I'm sorry, Mila.' Phil held out his hands, palms up, like he had nothing to hide. 'I wish things could be different.'

'I don't.' Sawyer glared at Phil with such ferocity that fear glinted in Phil's eyes. 'Now why don't you piss off and leave Mila alone.'

'We're neighbours and friends, so why don't you head back to where you came from?'

Phil reiterating they were neighbours and she'd be stuck with him for the foreseeable future—unless the unthinkable happened and she lost the farm—must've hit home for Sawyer. Some of the tension drained from his shoulders and he managed a brief nod.

'See you round, Phil.'

She almost felt sorry for her friend as his gaze swung between her and Sawyer, wondering if she was okay.

'Thanks, Phil,' she said, effectively turning her back on him when he looked like he'd stick around.

Hearing his footsteps crunch on the gravel as he walked away, she finally relaxed, surprised by the emotion clogging her throat again. She'd always hated being the centre of attention and to have people staring at her over the next few weeks, ugh.

'Are you okay?' Sawyer tipped her chin up. 'It's not too late for me to whip his arse.'

'I'm fine,' she said, but it came out shakier than she intended.

'Hey, let me take you out to lunch. You'll be doing me a favour. I hate eating alone.'

The last thing Mila felt like doing was parading herself through town on what should've been her wedding day. Then again, showing everyone how completely unaffected she was by Phil dumping her would stave off the inevitable pity and quash the gossip.

'Sounds like a plan.'

He walked around the car and opened the passenger door. 'Hop in.'

'But then you'll have to drive me back to the farm afterwards and head back into town.'

'So?'

He wiggled his eyebrows suggestively and she laughed, just as he must've intended. He'd always had the knack to make her feel better and she appreciated his offer—and his presence—more than he knew.

'Just because I had a crush on you in my delusional teens doesn't mean I'll fall for your charms this time around.'

Oops. Mila mentally clapped a hand over her mouth as Sawyer studied her. Where had that come from?

Thankfully, he recovered from her verbal diarrhoea first. 'You liked me, huh?'

Okay, so they were doing this. Having a discussion about how smitten she'd been. Maybe it was a good thing? Clear the air so there were no misconceptions, so he wouldn't think seeing him again after all this time had awoken her old crush and made her yearn for things she had no right yearning for. Like Sawyer Mann in her bed.

'You didn't know?'

'I thought we were mates,' he said, his deep voice sending a shiver of longing through her that they could be more.

'We were. We are,' she clarified. 'Now that I've embarrassed myself enough by taking a stroll down memory lane, why don't I meet you at the pub in thirty minutes?'

'You sure you don't want a lift? I'm happy to drop you back afterwards then head back into town.'

'I'm sure.'

The last thing she needed was to be confined in his car, with his potent presence overwhelming her more than he already had.

'Suit yourself.' He nodded and opened the car door. But he paused as he slid behind the wheel and started the engine. 'For what it's worth, I'm glad you didn't marry that prick.'

With a cheeky smile that made her heart leap, he revved the engine, gave her a half salute, and gunned it, leaving gravel spraying in his wake.

But twenty minutes later, Mila couldn't stop second-guessing the wisdom of having lunch with Sawyer at the pub. All those prying eyes, judging her, wondering what happened in her relationship with Phil for him to call off the wedding.

Then again, she could do with the distraction, so she grabbed her bag and keys, then shut the door. But she hadn't made it two steps along the verandah before her phone vibrated in her pocket, and as she slid it out and glanced at the screen, her gut tightened.

Any time Christopher Maddox called, it wasn't good. She contemplated ignoring his call, diverting it to her messages, but she'd already tried every tactic to stall the bank manager and the last thing she needed was for his patience with her to run out.

Taking a deep breath and exhaling, she tapped the answer icon. 'Hey, Chris, how are you? Shouldn't you be taking a lunch break?'

'I'm on my way out shortly, but had to give you a call now, Mila.'

'It couldn't wait until later?' She forced a laugh, surprised any sound came out considering the lump of foreboding in her throat.

'No.' He paused and she gripped the phone tight. 'I'm afraid the bank has given you all the leeway we can, Mila. I know times are tough and the farming community in general is suffering, but I've held off foreclosing as long as I can.'

He cleared his throat. 'If you don't make a loan repayment by the end of the month, you'll lose the farm.'

Her heart stalled and she gritted her teeth to stop a sob from escaping. She knew her situation was dire and had hoped that the cash injection marrying Phil would've provided could've bought her a few months, so she could get the farm stay operational.

Now, with Chris giving her a three-week deadline, she was out of time.

'Mila? You still there?'

'Yeah, Chris. Just processing.'

'I know this isn't the best time, especially today. I'm sorry.'

Wow, news certainly travelled fast in this town. Even her bank manager had heard about her aborted wedding.

But she didn't need his pity. She needed a solution to her financial problems. Fast.

'Thanks for calling, Chris. I'll sort something out and get back to you.'

'Make sure you do, because I'd hate for you to lose Hills Homestead, especially when it's been in your family for generations.'

That made two of them.

'Thanks, I'll be in touch.' Mila disconnected before she did something crazy, like release the scream building in her chest.

She had to come up with the money. But damned if she knew how.

CHAPTER ELEVEN

Sawyer had no idea what possessed him to drive off like a hoon.

Actually, he did, and it had little to do with showing what his prized V8 engine could do, and everything to do with Mila's honesty.

She'd had a crush on him.

And by the sly glances she'd cast him today when she thought he wasn't looking, not much had changed.

So where did that leave him, considering the feeling was mutual? It had been an unspoken rule between him and Will that his best mate's little sister was off limits. Hell, it was an unspoken rule between most blokes.

But Will was a million miles away in London and Mila was all alone on the farm, doing whatever it took—including marrying Phil bloody Baxter—to save it.

Surely Will wouldn't begrudge him sticking around to help Mila do that?

As he reached the outskirts of Ashe Ridge, Sawyer swiped a hand over his face. There was a big difference between staying in town longer than anticipated to help

Mila come up with a solution to save Hills Homestead and sticking around because in one day she'd got under his skin all over again.

It had shaken him to his core, how much he'd wanted to pummel Phil. Maybe Mila couldn't see how smarmy the prick was because she'd always seen the best in people, or maybe she'd wanted to save the farm that badly, but whatever her rationale, a huge part of Sawyer was nothing but relieved that one of them had come to their senses and called off the wedding.

At least Phil had done the right thing and shouldered the blame. But if Sawyer remembered correctly, nobody could look sideways in this town without someone pointing a finger and asking why, and that meant Mila would be gossip fodder no matter how chivalrous her neighbour had been.

Sawyer hadn't driven through town earlier, taking the backroad to Hills Homestead instead, so entering Ashe Ridge now catapulted him back in time.

Nothing had changed.

The two-storey red-brick Main Hotel stood sentinel on one corner after he passed the Ashe Ridge sign, the supermarket on the other. The op shop and Chinese restaurant hadn't been painted in fifteen years, the post office looked the same, and the three clothing boutiques hadn't changed bar the fashions in the windows. Two small cafés on opposite corners bookended the other side of town, before he caught sight of the landmarks he hated the most.

Ashe Ridge Primary and Ashe Ridge High School.

His life had been a misery inside the walls of those institutions and even now he broke into a cold sweat remembering how utterly inadequate, how stupid, he'd felt every time he entered a classroom.

The only person who hadn't made him feel dumb back then was Mila. She saw through his clowning around to the embarrassed kid beneath, a kid so terrified of being labelled a loser by everyone that distraction became his thing.

Even Will hadn't seen beneath his joker exterior. His friend had stood up for him when kids teased him for being a dummy in primary school, and later Sawyer had fought his own battles in high school as he filled out and played centre half-back for the footy team. Turns out, the girls didn't mind if he was all brawn and no brains, so he'd gone along with it, but it irked that most treated him like a shallow pretty boy.

He wondered if any of the old teachers were still around and what they'd think of him now. How he'd accumulated wealth through wise investing. How he brokered land deals that benefited all involved. He was damn good at his job and proud of how far he'd come from the laugh-a-minute kid who they thought would never amount to anything.

Thinking about land broking made him ponder Mila's quandary. He had a few ideas, but he wouldn't tell her until he had a solid plan in place. Even then, he'd need to couch it in favourable terms because her stubborn streak meant she wouldn't accept his help.

Hell, he'd virtually offered to marry her himself but she'd shied away from that quick smart. Not that he'd meant it. Not really.

The Ashe Ridge Motel was another mile out of town past the schools, but he'd wait until after lunch to check in. He made a U-turn just past the high school and headed back to the pub, looking forward to dining with Mila way too much.

He hadn't lied when he told her he'd kept up to date with her via Will. But there was a vast difference between asking his best mate an offhand question occasionally and sparring with Mila face-to-face.

She intrigued him like no other woman.

Not that he'd do anything about it. The last thing she needed while dealing with the fallout from being ditched at the altar was a fling with the town dunce, as the locals would see it. He respected her too much to toy with her, no matter how badly his libido insisted otherwise.

As he parallel parked outside the pub and got out of his car, he remembered the last time he'd entered the Main Hotel. It had been the last day of school and Will had insisted they meet a bunch of kids here for a celebratory beer before their exams kicked off in a week. He'd arrived before Will and sauntered inside, full of swagger and false bravado, because he knew everyone would be talking about the upcoming exams and the thought alone made him want to puke.

Not that he hadn't worked in his final year of school. He'd tried, hard, but the more he tried to cram facts into his head, the more distracted he'd become. He was destined to fail and it gutted him, because he wasn't stupid, no matter what his teachers and classmates thought.

That night had been the pits. Sure, he'd laughed and joked with his classmates, he'd won a few drinking contests, but he'd tolerated endless smart-arse barbs about what he'd do when his ATAR came back lower than his IQ. Everyone expected him to fail. Which is why he left town the day after the final exam and never came back. His results were nobody's business but his and it had taken a chance encounter with a part-time tutor in Melbourne who ended up being his girlfriend to set him on a path to success.

He owed Cheraline, big time.

Not that she wanted much to do with him these days, considering he broke her heart.

Taking a deep breath, Sawyer slammed his palm against the pitted wooden door and pushed it open, the pungent aromas of yeast, fried chicken, and onions assaulting him. The pub smelled the same, though the flatscreen TV over the bar was a new addition, as were the five pennants for a regional darts competition.

He bypassed the sports bar on the right and headed for the bistro on the left. A few families were tucked into a corner by the ancient play equipment, and an older couple sat near the counter, giving him the pick of tables when a young waitress he didn't recognise approached. 'Table for one?' she asked, appearing bored and exhausted simultaneously.

'For two, please.' He pointed to a quiet spot away from the families. 'Over there, preferably.'

'No worries.' She grabbed two menus. 'Follow me.'

When they reached the table, she said, 'Order at the counter, drinks at the bar.'

'Thanks,' he said. But she'd already headed back to the kitchen, sliding her phone out of her pocket on the way.

Unlike the main bar, the bistro had been revamped. Polished floorboards, pale green walls, forest green padded chairs, ivory cast iron tables. It gave the pub a fresh vibe and he imagined the place would be packed on the weekends.

He'd barely glanced at the menu when Mila strolled in and his heart gave an annoying thump. She spotted him straight away and as she walked towards him, he wished he hadn't stayed away so long.

However, before she reached the table, the older couple he'd spied as he entered stood and made a beeline for her.

'Mila, sweetheart, are you okay?' The older woman clasped her arm in a vice-like grip. 'We heard the news and we're terribly sorry, aren't we, Barry?'

Barry nodded in agreement, but the guy looked so downtrodden he probably agreed to everything his wife said.

'Is there anything we can do?' The woman leaned in close. 'You know, the best way to get over one man is to get under another.'

The woman cackled loudly and both Barry and Mila flinched, as her beady gaze zeroed in on him. 'Speaking of which, who's this?'

That's the moment Sawyer recognised the woman. Anne Curruthers. The school librarian. She'd made snide remarks any time he'd borrowed a book from the library. Obviously, news spread in school about the kids who were brainiacs and those who weren't. He'd avoided the place in his final years, preferring to use the prescribed texts online.

Mila fixed a polite smile on her face that came out a grimace. 'Anne, this is—'

'Sawyer Mann.' Anne snapped her fingers. 'Didn't recognise you at first.'

Sawyer stood to greet the couple and Anne's gaze roved over him from head to toe.

'Well, well, you filled out rather nicely, young man.' Anne cackled again and Sawyer shared a sympathetic glance with her husband. 'What are you doing back in town?'

Before he could answer, Anne's eyes narrowed. 'Ah, you must've come for the wedding. You, Will, and Mila were always thick as thieves. Too bad there's not going to be a wedding, but I guess it's gallant of you to squire Mila around.' Anne winked. 'Can't have her back on the shelf for too long, am I right?'

Sawyer clamped down on a surge of anger with effort, and sensing his wrath, Mila laid a hand on his shoulder.

'Sawyer's always been the one that got away, Anne. Now he's back and I'm single again, who knows?'

Anne's eyes bulged and Sawyer suppressed a chuckle as Mila deliberately schooled her expression into faux nonchalance.

'Now, if you'll excuse us, Anne, Sawyer and I have some catching up to do.' Mila's hand slid from his shoulder to his cheek, which she patted with affection. 'Be a love and grab me a chardonnay.'

'Coming right up,' Sawyer said, glaring at Anne so she'd get the message to leave them the hell alone. He should be grateful the old bag hadn't grilled him on what he'd been doing since school.

'Before we leave you young ones to get reacquainted,' Anne winked, 'what are you doing with yourself these days, Sawyer? You were never one for the books.'

His relief had been short-lived, and he gritted his teeth against the urge to tell Anne where she could stick her nosiness.

'Sawyer's made a squillion in land broking,' Mila said before he could respond. 'And he better be careful, otherwise I might drag him to the altar.'

Once again, Anne was speechless, and thankfully Barry murmured something in her ear before leading her away.

'Why did you encourage her like that?' Sawyer asked, equal parts chuffed and annoyed that Mila had leaped to his defence.

'Because she's an incorrigible gossip and I didn't like what she said about you.' Mila touched his hand, sending a little spark of electricity up his arm. 'I love Hills Homestead and Ashe Ridge, but the small-town mentality I can do without.'

'One of the many reasons I left and didn't look back,' he said, hoping she didn't hear the bitterness in his voice.

When her head tilted to one side like she was about to quiz him, he forced a smile. 'One chardonnay coming up.'

He felt Mila's inquisitive stare boring into his back the entire way to the bar.

CHAPTER TWELVE

Unfortunately, Jack hadn't been able to fix Adelaide's busted radiator, so he'd called a tow truck and made himself scarce while she'd waited over an hour for it to arrive. She'd been glad, because they would've been forced into making small talk and she didn't want to blurt that she wanted a divorce, not after the way he'd reacted to her leading into it.

She'd said it would be good to lay the past to rest and he'd looked like she'd stabbed him. Right then, she'd decided to be friendly towards him, get them to a better place, before springing the news on him. Though she doubted it would be easy whenever she brought up the D-word.

After her car had been towed to the mechanic in town —a newbie she hadn't heard of, because what had she expected, for Ashe Ridge and its inhabitants to be unchanged after fourteen years?—she headed back to the cottage. When she knocked on the door, Jack opened it and frowned. So much for hospitality.

'I'll show you where you'll be spending the night,' he said, his frown deepening.

She should be grateful he had a detached bungalow on his property.

It could be worse.

He could've offered her a spare room in his house.

Seeing him again had affected her way more than anticipated and knowing he was a short stroll across the backyard... Definitely too close for comfort.

An awkward silence yawned between them as he led her to her lodgings, so she said the first thing that popped into her head. 'Did you build the bungalow for guests?'

He grunted in response and slid a key into the lock. 'Something like that.'

She didn't believe him. Jack had a tell when he was being evasive and as he rubbed the top of his boot against the back of his jeans on his opposite leg, she knew he wasn't telling the truth.

It irked that he didn't trust her enough to answer a simple question. Then again, considering she'd been the one to walk away, he didn't owe her anything. Not anymore.

'It's beautiful,' she said, meaning it.

Like the house, the bungalow had been built with sandstone bricks, and she trailed her fingertips across their rough surface, surprised by a swift stab of envy.

She liked the studio she rented in Tally Bay, mainly because it was all hers. She'd never lived alone, moving from her parents' mansion in outer Melbourne direct to Jack's farm, so having a place of her own to call home soothed her at the end of a long day at the juice bar. If the young tourists and hippies were surprised to find a seventy-something woman serving their customised juices, they didn't show it, but she caught the occasional judgemental glance from older customers, like they pitied someone her age working such a menial job.

They had no idea that Raven, the guy who owned the juice bar, had given her a job when nobody else would, that the minimum wage supplemented the income she earned from her paintings and paid her rent, that she lived frugally by choice and didn't care that she couldn't afford luxuries because everything she had was hers and she'd acquired it the hard way.

But she knew where her jealousy for Jack's new place stemmed from. She would love to live in a place like this, a place she'd once dreamed about. A dream he'd torn down with his scoffing. A dream she'd left behind when she'd abandoned their marriage.

She'd never been happier, so why was the touch of cool sandstone beneath her fingertips making her feel maudlin?

'It's sparse but comfortable.' Jack opened the door and dumped her duffle. 'The sofa folds out into a bed. The kitchenette is stocked with basics. The plumbing works.'

'Great,' she said, following him into the bungalow, annoyed by the sting of tears yet again.

The place was perfect. From its exposed sandstone walls to its ash floorboards, from the low-slung pale green and white striped sofa to the cutest kitchenette she'd ever seen, the bungalow beckoned a weary traveller. Oddly, it felt like home.

'This is gorgeous, Jack.' She smiled. 'Thank you.'

'You're welcome,' he mumbled, a faint blush staining his cheeks. 'Help yourself to everything. Call me if you need anything.'

The last thing she needed was Jack in his sleep attire—nothing but jocks—coming to her aid in the middle of the night. But she forced another smile, her gaze landing on a door next to the bathroom.

'Where does that lead?'

His expression morphed from reluctant to downright hostile in a second. 'It's locked for a reason, so stop sticking your nose where it doesn't belong.'

She must've gaped a little at his swift change of mood because he swiped a hand over his face and when he lowered it, his anger had faded.

'Sorry. Long day. And the shock of... this... us...'—he waved a hand between them—'has taken a toll.'

'I get it,' she said, wishing for the second time today she could comfort him, aware she'd given up that right a long time ago. 'I feel the same way. It's overwhelming.'

'Yeah.' With one hand on the doorknob, he eyeballed her. 'It's good to see you, Ads.'

Her heart turned over at the use of the nickname only he'd ever called her, but before she could say anything, Jack slammed the door.

CHAPTER THIRTEEN

Mila had a theory. There was nothing a good parma at the pub couldn't fix.

But when she'd forked the last morsel of perfectly fried chicken schnitzel smothered in tomato and cheese into her mouth and emptied her glass of Barossa Valley chardonnay, she still couldn't shrug the sadness that dogged her.

As if that phone call from Chris hadn't been bad enough, she should've been celebrating her wedding today.

After the ceremony and brief celebration, she'd envisaged sharing a bottle of shiraz with Phil as they did regularly, joking about their nuptials, relaxed in each other's company. Then later, poring over plans for the third cottage, securing vendors, being able to afford the finishing touches and an online PR company to promote the farm stay because Phil said he'd transfer the money once they were married.

With Phil's cash injection removed from the equation, she was screwed.

And she wished she hadn't sold last year's harvest of lentils to pay the mortgage sixteen weeks ago, effectively removing her safety net. How many times growing up had Gramps stressed the importance of a safety net? Countless, and she could hear his voice in her head now. *'Lentils won't go mouldy, so we can store them for years and wait for the best price. And that price is paramount to a small farm like ours. In our good years, we yield about 2.5 tonnes per hectare, and with the long-term average price around seven hundred dollars, it pays to hold out for that higher range when it gets up to around a thousand bucks per tonne. Never forget that, Mila. Always keep some in storage.'*

Now, she had nothing for a rainy day, leaving her in deep trouble. Even if the next crop yielded, it would be too late.

'I got us lemonades as we're both driving,' Sawyer said, placing a jug and two glasses on the table before resuming his seat opposite. 'You looked deep in thought. Not still lamenting the loss of your groom, are you?'

'No.' Though not marrying Phil was part of her problems. 'Thanks for lunch. A parma is just what I needed.'

'What about the company?'

'You've been alright.'

He saw through her flippancy. She could see it in the astute gleam in those beautiful bluey-green eyes.

'If you don't want to be alone, I'm happy to come back to the farm.'

She quirked an eyebrow. 'Are you propositioning me?'

The corners of his mouth kicked up. 'No. I'd never take advantage of a vulnerable woman.'

'Who said I'm vulnerable?'

She couldn't afford to be, not when she had a massive mortgage and a dream to fulfil.

'This is me you're talking to.' He leaned forward a little

and rested his forearms on the table. 'You forget, I've seen you at your best and your worst.'

Therein lay the problem, because the way she was feeling— wrung out and a little unsteady—having an old friend, someone who knew her almost as well as she knew herself, be supportive and kind, might undo her completely.

The thought of Sawyer coming back to the farm with her, comforting her, beckoned like the Southern Cross guiding a weary traveller home, but she had to resist.

Because if Sawyer held her in the way she yearned to be held, she'd end up making a mistake she'd regret tomorrow. She had enough to worry about without adding 'sleeping with my brother's best friend' to the list.

'Thanks, but I'll be fine,' she said, injecting confidence into her tone. 'You've done enough by meeting me here.'

'My pleasure.'

They glanced around the bistro that had emptied in the last half hour. But Mila had seen the sideways glances of a few couples who came in after them, and the odd pitying expression—thankfully, no one approached like that busybody Anne had. No matter what Phil had told people, she still came out the loser in this scenario. A jilted bride in a small town provided enough gossip fodder to last a few weeks yet.

'Actually, do you mind if we call it a day?' She faked a yawn. 'I'm beat.'

'I bet.' He topped up two glasses with lemonade and held one out to her. 'But not before we make a toast.'

'To?' She accepted the glass with a smile, remembering the time they'd tried to make homemade lemonade and ended up putting so much sugar in it their teeth ached.

He paused for a moment, screwing his eyes up like he

was thinking, before a grin crept over his face. 'To you having better taste in grooms next time.'

'There won't be a next time,' she muttered, before clinking glasses with him. 'To old friends, who should know when to shut up.'

He laughed and raised the glass to his mouth. 'I'll drink to that.'

They finished their lemonade quickly and as Sawyer walked her to her car, his hand in the small of her back, she willed herself not to do something insane, like grab the lapels of his jacket, tug him close, and kiss him senseless.

'You sure you'll be okay?' he asked when they reached her car.

'I'm sure,' she murmured, not sure in the slightest.

He leaned forward and Mila could've sworn the air between them crackled with electricity. Heck, was he thinking along the same lines she was and wanted to kiss her? Maybe she should've popped a mint after her parma or had that choc-mint parfait for dessert.

'Take care, Gumnut,' he said, pressing a soft kiss to her cheek before straightening, leaving Mila practically swooning. 'It's been really good to see you again.'

Mila managed to mumble, 'You too,' before Sawyer ambled away, taking a little piece of her teenage heart with him.

CHAPTER FOURTEEN

Sawyer gripped the steering wheel hard and counted to ten, using every ounce of his meagre self-control not to get out of his car, jog back to Mila, and insist on taking her home.

When they'd parted, he'd never seen her like that: lost, bereft, vulnerable.

He'd wanted to insist he accompany her but knew she'd never agree. Mila was too proud for that. Hell, the fact she'd agreed to lunch had been a big deal. They'd made small talk all through the meal, skirting the big issues—namely, what she'd do now to ensure financial security for the farm—and it had been surprisingly easy.

Reminiscing about funny times during their youth had been a blast, but he'd seen the glimmer of anxiety in her eyes despite the levity, and it made him want to slay whatever demons haunted her.

Thanks to Will, he knew she'd done an accelerated marketing degree online after she'd finished school and had worked alongside her grandfather on the farm the entire time. Farming was tough for the most hardened and he couldn't imagine Mila assuming ownership of Hills Homestead on her own.

An average lentil farm in the Wimmera had between three to five thousand hectares, making Hills Homestead barely viable at a thousand. Jack had done a lot of niche marketing to turn a profit. Sawyer assumed Mila had continued that trend, but she must've gone into a lot of debt with the bank to keep the farm afloat, and now hoped expanding into the farm-stay market would do the same.

She'd been a homebody growing up, but he'd always assumed she'd follow in her parents' wanderlust footsteps and leave Ashe Ridge after she finished school. He'd been shocked to learn she'd bought the farm and had hated the thought of her settling down with one of the bozos he'd gone to school with. She deserved so much better.

When Will couldn't make the wedding and asked him to attend instead, the thought of watching Mila get married had gutted him a little, swiftly followed by disgust when he learned the groom was Phil Baxter. Will had been unfazed, saying he trusted Mila's judgement and wanted his sister to be happy, and Sawyer had bitten his tongue.

He hadn't wanted to attend in Will's stead, not trusting himself when it came to Phil having his hands anywhere near Mila, but he'd been fuelled by curiosity and masochism, so he'd come.

Thank goodness he had because Mila needed him despite her bravado. He would've happily joined her in demolishing that arbour, then taken the mallet to Phil too if she'd asked. She may not have a broken heart, but Mila's financial worries were weighing heavily, and he'd do whatever it took to help.

He waited until her tail-lights faded into the distance before heading to the motel. He hadn't made a booking, expecting to attend the wedding then hit the road back to Melbourne late afternoon. It didn't matter. The place was rarely booked out—not many tourists stopped in Ashe Ridge, preferring Nhill or Kaniva— but disappointment filtered through him when he saw the 'Vacancy' sign, because a full motel would've meant Mila had to offer him a bed for the night.

'Idiot,' he muttered, grabbing the gym bag with toiletries and clothes he always kept in the boot, and heading up the cracked concrete path to reception.

The motel had been painted, the olive-green exterior now a gleaming ecru and the window trims a shiny ebony, but the neon still had a flashing R in the *Ashe Ridge Motel* sign.

He pushed through the glass doors and approached a tidy front desk lined with maps of the region. The place appeared abandoned, so he tapped a bell, not having to wait long before a woman a few years younger than him popped her head out from a room at the back.

'Be there in a sec,' she called, and he waited, remembering the last time he'd been in here.

He'd been caught with Simone in one of the rooms at the end of Year 11. Simone's mum Shazza had run the motel so she had easy access. Unfortunately, someone tattled on them and Shazza had barged into the room—thankfully before there'd been any frantic teen undressing—and dragged them out. Simone had been banished home and Sawyer had to wait in reception for his mother, who'd appeared resigned rather than disapproving when she'd finally shown to pick him up.

He'd steered clear of Simone all through Year 12, even when she made it blatantly clear they wouldn't need a motel room to have fun. Seeing his mother look at him like she expected him to disappoint had hit hard and he'd made sure during his final year at home that she wouldn't have any reason to look at him like that again.

'Are you wanting a room?'

He turned back to the desk and smiled at the woman who looked vaguely familiar. 'Yes please. Not sure for how long, but let's say three nights for a start.'

'No problems.' She tapped at a keyboard and scrutinised a computer screen. 'We've got our best suite available at the moment, two hundred a night.'

'That'll be fine.'

She continued typing, not asking his name, which he thought odd, until she glanced up, a cheeky glint in her eyes. 'Pity Simone isn't around. Or Mum for that matter. Could've made your stay interesting.'

Startled for a moment, Sawyer tried to place her and she laughed. 'I'm Maggie, Simone's younger sister. I was in Year 7 when you were caught here by Mum. I laughed my head off.'

He didn't remember Maggie. Then again, he barely interacted with the kids in his own year, let alone kids four years younger.

'Glad I could amuse you,' he said, with a smile. 'How is Simone? Your mum?'

'Mum does the day shift here, I do nights. Works well, because it's quiet and I'm doing some part-time study online. Though I had to cover Mum's afternoon shift today.'

Thank goodness Sawyer hadn't checked in earlier.

As if reading his mind, Maggie smirked. 'I'm sure Mum will be pleased to see you tomorrow.'

'I'll make sure I'm gone by dawn,' he deadpanned, and they laughed.

'I'll just need a credit card and you're all set,' she said.

'No worries.'

He handed over his card and she swiped it through a terminal before handing it back to him, along with a key card for the room.

'You've gone high-tech, I see?'

She smiled. 'I reckon Mum updated when she realised it was easy for us girls to swipe keys to access the rooms, but not so easy to program the computer for cards.' She winked. 'I guess I have you to thank for that.'

He chuckled and pocketed the card. 'It's been fifteen years since I left town, and sixteen since your mum caught me with Simone. Do you think there's a hope she's forgotten?'

'Not a chance,' Maggie said, her eyes alive with amusement. 'Do me a favour? Make sure I'm here to witness your reunion with Mum.'

He mock-shuddered. 'Thanks. I'll see you round.'

'Not if Mum gets her hands on you.' Maggie waved. 'Enjoy your stay, Sawyer.'

He intended to.

As long as Mila was amenable to the ideas he had buzzing through his head.

The sooner he solidified his plans for her, the better.

CHAPTER FIFTEEN

Adelaide's left hip gave its usual morning twang as she rolled over in bed. Hours on her feet at an easel or serving juices weren't conducive to limber joints but she'd got used to her bung hip over the years. Her very own personal alarm clock that woke her when she'd spent too long in bed.

She sat up slowly, stretched, and opened her eyes, momentarily disoriented.

Sandstone wall.

White trimmed window.

Sunlight peeking around the frame.

And an odd scratching at the front door that sounded suspiciously like a key being inserted.

As the door creaked open, it all came flooding back. Her car breaking down, trudging to the cottage, discovering Jack lived here, him offering her a bed for the night.

She pressed her hands to her cheeks as the door swung open and the man in question tried to slink in, carefully balancing a tray in his hands.

When he caught sight of her, he stumbled, his eyes wide as his gaze raked over her, and for a horrifying second she thought she'd slept naked. Her cheeks flushed as she glanced down, grateful she wore her favourite cotton nightie covered in tiny paintbrushes slashing at rainbows.

'Sorry, I thought you'd be asleep,' he mumbled, placing the tray at a small dining table. 'I didn't want to wake you. Just wanted to leave this.'

'Thanks,' she said, standing and padding over to the table, unsure what shocked her more. Jack's thoughtfulness or the cooked breakfast—scrambled eggs, bacon, fried tomato, and toast—with orange juice on the side.

When they'd been married, he'd barely set foot in the kitchen other than to grab a quick sandwich at lunch or a snack in the middle of the night. She'd done all the cooking, her resentment growing with every dinner dished, especially when he barely spoke as they ate and left the table as soon as he'd eaten the last morsel off his plate.

'You're welcome,' he said, his voice gruff. 'How did you sleep?'

'Surprisingly well, considering I rarely get more than six hours a night.'

When his expression tightened in anger because he wrongly assumed she wasn't getting much sleep because of possible nocturnal activities, she rushed on, 'I paint at night. I find it's when I'm at my most creative, and I often lose track of time so often stumble into bed in the wee small hours.'

'What do you paint these days?'

'Beach scenes mostly. Boats. Wharves. Lighthouses.'

Anything that encapsulated her new life, symbols of her freedom.

'I'm sensing a theme,' he said, his voice devoid of judgement, and she made an impulsive decision.

'Why don't you join me for breakfast?' She gestured at the tray. 'This is a lot and I can make us coffee.'

He hesitated, glancing at the door like he couldn't wait to escape, and she second-guessed her invitation. What did she expect, for his kindness in cooking her breakfast to extend to forgiveness for her abandoning him years earlier?

'I won't say no to a coffee,' he said, after what seemed like an eternity. 'I'll make it while you get dressed.'

Heat scorched her cheeks for the second time in as many minutes as she realised she'd been so surprised by his presenting her with breakfast that she'd forgotten she wore nothing but thin cotton that ended at her knees.

'Thanks, I won't be long,' she said, grabbing her duffel and dashing for the bathroom, grateful when she closed the door so she could sag against it.

She should be mortified, but knew the blush staining her cheeks had less to do with embarrassment and more to do with the appreciation she'd glimpsed in Jack's eyes.

At seventy-three, she rarely felt attractive. She didn't look bad for her age—she took care of her skin with organic moisturisers and serums, her brown hair streaked with grey hadn't yet turned white, she ate predominantly vegetarian, and she exercised daily with long walks on the beach.

But it had been a long time since a man had stared at her with such hunger, and her body tingled in places that hadn't tingled in a long time.

What the hell had gotten into her?

She splashed water on her face, twice for good measure, and snagged her shoulder length hair into a messy bun at her nape before slipping into wide-leg khaki pants and an ivory sleeveless top with bright crimson hibiscus all over it. She'd hand-painted them, proud of the result whenever she wore it and got compliments. Not that she was dressing up for Jack, but she needed a confident front to hide the tumultuous nerves making her stomach tumble.

Could she possibly be attracted to Jack after all this time?

Before she could mull that alarming question, she wrenched open the door and marched back into the bungalow, the aroma of coffee a comfort. She could do this. Have breakfast with the man she'd been married too. Was still married to, technically, but not for much longer. If spending a few minutes in his company made her feel this out of control, she needed to wrest it back, starting with instigating divorce proceedings.

'Here you go.' He placed a steaming mug of coffee next to the breakfast tray and took a seat opposite. But considering the size of the round table, he may as well have been sitting next to her, as their knees still brushed when she sat.

Awareness zapped her and she reached for the orange juice, gulping it to soothe her dry throat. When she'd finished it and Jack hadn't said anything, she picked up a fork and stabbed at the scrambled egg.

'Are you sure I can't tempt you?'

Jack lowered his coffee mug, not breaking eye contact. 'You can and you do.'

Her fingers trembled a little as she lowered the fork before the egg dropped into her lap.

Was Jack flirting with her?

Or was her bizarre attraction to her ex flaring to life and confusing the hell out of her?

'But I'm not really hungry,' he added, leaving her more confounded than ever.

Did that mean he was tempted by her and not by the food?

Before she could think of something to say, he snaffled a

triangle of buttered toast from her plate. 'Though I better eat in case you nag me like you used to.'

The twinkle in his eyes indicated he hadn't meant it as a barb but she bristled nonetheless. She'd hated when he implied she nagged him, when all she'd been doing was asking for the simplest things, like help with giving toddler Cam a bath, or reading their son a bedtime story. But Jack had always been too tired at the end of a long day and cited the farm work as an excuse on countless occasions. The lentil crops came first, always.

Little surprise she hadn't been able to stomach lentils once she'd fled Hills Homestead.

'I was joking,' he said, his gaze wary as he held hers for a moment longer before dipping to his coffee.

She remembered that too, his inability to look her in the eye when things got uncomfortable between them, and she'd raise her voice to make him take notice of her.

'It's okay, I'm not a morning person,' she said, keeping her tone light to defuse the situation. 'Even when I've had the first good sleep I've had in ages, apparently.'

'Sofa bed comfortable?'

'Very.'

They lapsed into silence again and she busied herself with eating, even though the feel of Jack's gaze on her curdled her appetite. When she'd cleaned half her plate, she laid the fork and a half-nibbled piece of toast down.

'I can drop you at Mila's if you like.' He glanced at his watch. 'I called her earlier, said you'd be over.'

'Thanks. And do you have a spare charger? In all the excitement last night, I forgot to charge my phone.'

Jack's brow arched. 'Excitement?'

Damn, another blush hovered, and she rushed on. 'My

car breaking down. Discovering you lived here. You kindly letting me stay.'

'Glad you clarified,' he said, a surprising smirk curving his lips. 'I'll meet you out the front in fifteen minutes?'

'Sure.'

As she watched Jack pick up the breakfast tray and perch it on his hip as he opened the door, an overwhelming rush of regret swamped her.

Why couldn't he have made her breakfast even once when they'd been together?

Why couldn't he have tried harder in their marriage? Why couldn't she?

But this wasn't the time for regrets and as Jack gave her a lopsided smile before closing the door behind him, Adelaide knew she had to make a call once her phone charged.

To the town's lawyer.

CHAPTER SIXTEEN

Mila had barely slept a wink last night and had woken grumpy, with grit in her eyes and worry in her heart.

Now this.

Gramps had called half an hour ago, saying he'd be dropping her grandmother at the farm shortly. After Mila had picked her jaw up off the floor, she'd asked what had happened—namely, why Adelaide had popped in to see Jack rather than coming straight to the homestead. But her grandfather had been his usual brusque self and told her to ask her grandmother.

Which Mila fully intended on doing, once she got her head around seeing Adelaide smile at Jack and raise her hand in farewell when he drove away.

Since when were her grandparents on speaking terms?

Gramps never mentioned Gran. Ever. Mila had tried broaching the subject when she'd started catching up with Gran in Sydney for an annual girls' weekend, but Gramps would always shut her down and she soon gave up.

Gran did the same whenever Mila mentioned Jack, so she never did after the first year or so. Gran didn't even know Gramps had moved out of the homestead and sold the farm to her. It always pained her to think how far apart they'd drifted, that the mere mention of the other person caused a catatonic reaction.

From her childhood memories, she remembered Adelaide—or Addy as she'd always thought of her grandmother—and Jack having a cohesive marriage. Gramps worked hard on the farm, didn't say much in the evenings, and went to bed early to read agriculture books, while Addy kept the rest of his life running like clockwork. They weren't romantic and there were no PDAs but she'd assumed their lack of affection stemmed from their age.

Then, the morning after her final exam, before she'd gone out celebrating with her friends, her grandmother had sat her down, held her hand, and said she was leaving. Mila had said, 'Good for you, Gran, you deserve a holiday'— which was when her grandmother started crying and Mila had the first inkling that her life was about to change.

Addy said she needed a break and didn't know when she'd be back, that she loved her, and would be a phone call away whenever Mila needed her. Mila assumed her grandparents must've had a massive fight and Addy was trying to teach Jack a lesson. Even when Addy hoisted two bulging suitcases and a duffel into the boot of her car and drove off, Mila thought it wouldn't be for long. Jack would go after her, apologise, and Addy would be back in the kitchen baking up a storm.

But Gramps didn't go after Addy, and her gran never returned. Until now.

Mila jogged down the verandah steps and ran towards her grandmother. She'd never been so glad to see someone in her life.

Addy opened her arms and Mila flew into them. When

her grandmother hugged her tight and murmured, 'My precious girl.'

Mila lost it and burst into tears, all the pent-up emotion of the last twenty-four hours taking its toll.

Addy's arms tightened around her and Mila squeezed her back, knowing her grandmother's presence here would be temporary but intent on making the most of it.

When her sobs petered out, she released Addy and stepped back. 'I'm sorry you came all this way for a wedding that didn't happen.'

'I came all this way for you, dear girl.' Addy cupped her cheek, blinking away the sheen in her eyes. 'How are you? Really?'

'What, the tears weren't a dead giveaway?'

'You've been through a lot.' Addy slipped an arm through her elbow. 'Come inside and tell me all about it.'

'Not much to tell.'

Addy's eyebrows rose. 'When my granddaughter's about to marry our neighbour, then he ditches you at the altar, there's a story there.'

Mila smirked. 'Maybe a little tale.'

They laughed and Mila tugged her grandmother closer through their linked elbows. 'I'm glad you're here, Gran.'

'Me too, sweetheart.'

As they fell into step and headed for the homestead Mila wondered how she could broach the touchy subject of her gran's ride to the farm without the mention of Jack causing her to clam up.

'You're wondering why your grandfather dropped me off.'

'You've always been able to read my mind.'

Except that time Addy left Hills Homestead behind and never returned, leaving Mila bereft. Bad enough her parents abandoned her when she was ten, her beloved Gran followed suit. For a long time, it made her wonder what was so unlovable about her that the most important people in her life walked away.

'To cut a long story short, my car broke down yesterday on the way to your wedding. I walked to the nearest place, a sandstone cottage on the outskirts of town—'

'You broke down near Gramps?' Mila whistled. 'How's that for serendipity? Or the best meet-cute ever?'

Addy blushed and that's when Mila realised her gran had said she broke down yesterday. Meaning she'd spent the night somewhere. Probably at the motel and Gramps had picked her up this morning, but what if...

'Did Gramps drive you into town?'

'Uh... my car got towed and Jack was kind enough to offer me a place to stay.'

Shocked to her core, Mila muttered, 'Way to go, Gramps.'

'It's not like that,' Addy said, her blush intensifying. 'He has a small bungalow out the back of his cottage and I was there for the night.'

Mila held up her hands. 'Hey, you two are still married so it's got nothing to do with me if you waltz back into town after fourteen years for a booty call.'

'You are incorrigible,' Addy said, slipping her arm out from Mila's elbow and rushing up the stairs and into the house. 'Just for that, I'm not going to bake your favourite brownies.'

'Harsh,' Mila said, her smile teasing. 'Seriously, Gran, I can't mention Gramps to you usually and vice versa, which is why I never told you I bought the farm, so excuse me for being shocked when I see him drop you off. I mean, the fact you were in the same car for more than a few minutes is a big deal, right?'

'I can't believe you never told me you bought the farm.' The oddest expression flickered across her grandmother's face—regret tinged with hope—as she nodded. 'But yes, Jack has been surprisingly magnanimous since I fronted up at his door yesterday. His generosity has been more than I deserve.'

Addy blinked rapidly again, staving off tears, and Mila slipped an arm around her waist and guided her into the house. 'I think it's great you're on speaking terms. I had wondered how I'd keep you apart at the wedding.'

'Speaking of the wedding, tell me everything while I make tea. Peppermint?'

'Sure.' Mila allowed her gran's diversion for now, choking up as she remembered that was the tea they'd always shared in the evenings while sitting around the fire.

Addy entered the kitchen and Mila followed, watching her gran move around with ease. Mila hadn't changed much when she'd bought the farm, deriving comfort from the familiarity when everything—or everyone—in her life seemed to be in flux.

She'd never expected her grandfather to move away from Hills Homestead. Even after he sold it to her, she thought he'd live in the main house. Or at worst, move into the small self-contained barn where temporary workers occasionally stayed.

But he'd been determined to leave, and she couldn't begrudge him his freedom, not after he'd been tied to this place for so long. Taking on a family legacy was a big deal— she felt the burden every day. How much harder must it have been for him when his parents died and he was forced to take over at twenty?

She'd chosen this life, knowing it would be hard, but also aware she wouldn't have it any other way. Not that Gramps had abandoned her completely. He imparted wisdom on lentil farming in this region whenever she asked for his advice. It had been extremely tough to hide her financial predicament from him, but she didn't need to hear '*I told you so*'—which is why she hadn't approached him for help. She had to do this on her own.

As the water boiled, Gran opened the cupboard where tea and coffee were stored, grabbed a tin, and spooned peppermint leaves into a teapot. Mila savoured the moment, watching her grandmother move around this kitchen as she once had.

'You're staring,' Addy said, folding her arms and resting against the benchtop.

'I'm just glad to have you here,' Mila said, clearing her throat when it tightened with emotion.

She hoped Addy would say, 'It's good to be back,' but her grandmother forced a tight smile and spun around when the kettle whistled.

For someone who didn't have a romantic bone in her body, and who'd viewed marriage as a financial means to an end, a small part of her hoped her grandmother's presence here meant she might be ready to return home. But Mila had given up believing in fairytales around the time her folks had dumped her here and taken off without looking back, so she knew it was wishful thinking.

Addy poured boiling water into the teapot and brought it across to the table along with two mugs. She sat opposite Mila and fixed her with a stare that Mila knew well: she'd have to 'fess up or else.

'Tell me about the wedding and why it didn't happen.'

'Not much to tell. Phil arrived here yesterday morning,

told me he'd met someone online, and didn't want to marry me. End of story.'

Incredulous, Addy snorted. 'You've just told me your future husband abandoned you with as much emotion as if you were reciting new silo prices. What's going on?'

Mila didn't want Gramps knowing the truth of why she'd been about to marry her neighbour, because the last thing she needed was him reiterating the burdens of taking on a big loan or swooping in to try and fix everything. Not that he could. If Gramps could offer financial aid she would've already approached him. But he'd invested the proceeds of the farm's sale in a long-term deposit that paid him annual interest, enough to live on but not enough to bail her out.

But confiding in Gran would be okay, assuming Addy wouldn't run to Gramps and tell him everything. Unlikely, considering they hadn't spoken in years.

'You can't tell Gramps this.'

Addy rolled her eyes and made a zipping motion over her lips. 'Jack may have been chivalrous last night in letting me stay and dropping me here this morning, but that doesn't make us besties. We haven't spoken in fourteen years so I'm not about to go telling him anything you divulge in confidence.'

Mila smiled. 'In that case, do you remember those romance books you used to read which occasionally had a marriage of convenience?'

Addy's eyes widened. 'You're telling me you were going to marry Phil but didn't love him?'

'Yes.' Mila sighed. 'Phil and I are mates, and he's good company. It gets lonely out at the farm, and we've spent a fair bit of time together, so it made sense that our marriage would be based on friendship while being a business arrangement. He'd get some of my land and I'd get some of his cash to fund my farm-stay project, which I'll show you later.'

Her grandmother's eyebrows rose. 'So your marriage would've been a mutually beneficial financial agreement and that's it?'

Mila nodded. 'We had a frank conversation. There were no romantic expectations.' She shrugged. 'As you know all too well, farming life can be isolating and it's nice to have someone who understands. Someone to offload to at the end of a hard day. Phil and I were already doing that some nights, so making a more permanent arrangement would've given us both comfort.'

Addy touched her arm. 'Sweetheart, it sounds like you were settling.'

'Not settling as much as making the most of our situation. Anyway, it's irrelevant now.'

Addy frowned. 'Well, I for one am glad you didn't marry Phil. He's not the right man for you.'

'Then why didn't you say anything when I let you know I was marrying him?'

Guilt shadowed Addy's face and she glanced away. 'Because I hadn't been here in years and I had no right to judge. For all I knew, you'd discovered Phil was the love of your life.' She shook her head. 'I had no right to interfere in your happiness, so I kept my opinions to myself.'

'Fair enough,' Mila said, knowing she wouldn't have taken her gran's advice even if Addy had offered it. Saving the farm was too important to her.

'For what it's worth, Jack mentioned he thought you might be marrying Phil for his money.' Addy tapped her temple. 'Your grandfather may be the strong, silent type, but he's astute.'

So much for keeping Gramps out of the loop. 'Don't confirm his suspicions, okay?'

'So you are in financial trouble?' Addy sighed and reached across the table to grab her hand. 'This is serious, sweetheart, and I'm sure Jack can help if you need—'

'I need to do this on my own,' Mila said, her tone resolute. 'Surely you of all people can understand?'

Confusion creased Addy's brow and Mila continued. 'You're strong and independent and left your family behind to make it on your own. You're self-sufficient, and that's what I want. To make my mark.'

Sombre, Addy nodded. 'I understand, but there's a big difference between painting and working in a juice bar to earn a living and farming in the Wimmera. You've got droughts to contend with, and fluctuating legume prices, not to mention the hardship of being out here on your own and trying to make this place viable.'

'Is that why you left? It got too hard for you?'

Mila hadn't meant to sound accusatory, but Addy paled and released Mila's hand, leaving her wishing she could take back the question. Though she'd always wondered what had driven her grandmother away to the point she never came back.

'Everything got too hard for me,' Addy murmured, pain clouding her eyes as she blinked and reached for the teapot.

An awkward silence descended as Addy poured the tea, but her grandmother being here was an opportunity too good to pass up to grill her some more. Their annual catch-ups in Sydney were a time when they drank champagne out the front of the Opera House, indulged in a high tea at a five-star hotel, strolled between Bondi and Coogee, and chatted about their lives, but on a superficial level. They avoided the tough stuff because they loved each other and didn't want to mar their brief catch-up.

But having Addy home after fourteen years, Mila wanted to know why her grandmother had left her.

'I know it's not my place to grill you about your marriage, Gran, but to stay away so long...' Mila sighed and took a sip of tea to ease the tightness in her throat. 'You might've been punishing Gramps, but I got hurt too.'

'Oh, my dear sweet girl.' Addy stood and moved around the table to kneel and wrap her arms around Mila. 'It was never about you. I know that sounds selfish, but after so many years of unhappiness I'd had enough, and I had to get out or lose myself completely.'

Mila sat rigid, not wanting to give in to the tears burning her eyes because she knew if she started crying again she'd never stop. Not just because of this conversation with her gran, but from the building pressure of her financial predicament.

'But to stay away so long, to never come back...' Mila shook her head and Addy tightened her hug until she could barely breathe. 'I've missed you so much.'

'I've missed you too.' Addy clung to her and rested her head against her arm.

Mila had no idea how long they sat like that. While Addy hadn't divulged much, for now her grandmother's hug would have to do.

CHAPTER SEVENTEEN

Sawyer opened the door to his room and snuck a glance left and right to see if Shazza might be strolling the motel car park, because he remembered the last time he'd been in a room here.

Back then, Shazza had flung open the door so hard it cracked the plaster of the wall behind it and Sawyer had almost crapped himself. Simone had been ballsy, standing up to her mother, but he'd been a wreck, knowing the ridicule he'd face. He didn't mind the laughs when he deliberately solicited them but being teased... he hated it.

He wouldn't have been surprised if Shazza had grabbed his ear and twisted it as she dragged him out of the motel room. Instead, she'd settled for yelling so loud he had tinnitus for a week and pinning him with the evil eye until his mum had come and picked him up.

It had been the most embarrassing moment of his life and he'd never expected to find himself back here.

Mila better appreciate the hardship he was going through for her. With the coast clear, he pulled the door shut and headed for his car. He'd nearly made it when an ear-splitting whistle shattered the early morning silence.

'Well, well, well. If it isn't Sawyer Mann himself, still sneaking around my motel.'

Feeling like a recalcitrant seventeen-year-old all over again, he fixed his best smile and turned to see Shazza glaring at him, arms folded, her frizzy brown hair now streaked grey, and sporting a lot more wrinkles.

'Hey, Mrs Knowles. Long time no see.'

She waggled her fingers at him. 'Don't you Mrs Knowles me, young man. I haven't forgotten what you did, corrupting my poor Simone.'

Sawyer stifled a laugh. If anyone did the corrupting back then, it was Simone. She'd targeted him relentlessly— texting him, slipping notes into his backpack, staring at him in class—but he'd keep that to himself. The last thing he needed was Shazza booting him out of the motel before he'd solidified plans to help Mila.

Not that she'd be foolish enough to evict a paying customer, considering how empty the car park was, but he knew this woman was tough and had a memory like an elephant.

'How is Simone?'

'Better off without you,' she muttered, fixing him with a baleful stare. 'What are you doing back in town anyway? Thought we'd seen the back of you.'

'Thought I'd revisit my youth and your wonderful establishment.' His droll response earned a bark of laughter.

'Still a cheeky one, huh?'

'I try.'

Her expression softened and she jerked a thumb over

her shoulder. 'Fancy a cuppa? I've got a brilliant new espresso machine in the back office.'

The last thing he needed was to spend time with Shazza, being grilled about every aspect of his life since he left town, so he shook his head.

'Thanks for the offer, but I'm lining up some meetings while I'm in town.'

When her eyes narrowed like she thought he was bullshitting, he added, 'I'm a land broker.'

The grudging respect in her eyes made him want to stand a little taller. 'Looks like you made something of yourself after all. Good lad.'

He didn't need her approval, but it went some way to easing his defensiveness. He knew he should be over his feelings of inadequacy by now, that he'd proved to himself rather than the narrow-minded judgemental fools in this town that he was better than what they thought, but perhaps old habits die hard.

The thing was, if one brief encounter with Shazza raised his hackles, imagine how he'd feel if he ran into any other old 'acquaintances' while in town?

Stupid, to be bothered by opinions after all this time, but this town and its inhabitants had made his life hell—even if he'd never let them know it—and he'd be damn sure to stride down Main Street without a care in the world shortly.

'I better get going,' he said. 'Nice seeing you again.'

'Yeah, right.' Shazza winked. 'So you're staying a few nights?'

'At this stage, yes.'

'Don't hesitate to holler if you need anything.'

'Thanks.'

He'd almost made it to his car when Shazza called out,

'From the view back here, I can see why Simone risked getting grounded for a month.'

Embarrassed that she'd been checking out his arse, he raised his hand in a wave without looking back and slammed the door on her loud cackling.

He made it to the bakery in under two minutes and, thankfully, didn't recognise the young women working behind the counter. After ordering a latte and the Big Breakfast, he took a seat at the table furthest from the window and got out his phone to peruse the pesky subdivision clause on Mila's land. Having access to records was a major perk in his job and was coming in mighty handy today.

However, after demolishing his fried eggs on sourdough, bacon, hash-browns, mushrooms, and spinach, he realised coming up with a workaround to the clause would take more time, and he wouldn't be able to present Mila with a solution today.

Meaning he was back to square one.

Though all wasn't lost, and as he contemplated a last-resort solution to Mila's problem, he knew that following through with this plan might cost him her friendship.

CHAPTER EIGHTEEN

After finishing her peppermint tea, Adelaide told Mila she needed to take a walk, the first excuse she came up with to escape her granddaughter's all-seeing stare.

Hearing the hurt in Mila's voice, seeing the pain in her eyes when she'd asked why Adelaide had stayed away so long... it broke her heart. She had to get out of that kitchen before she blurted the truth. Because even though many years had passed and her granddaughter was now a capable thirty-two-year-old, Mila didn't deserve to bear the burden of Adelaide's secrets.

Besides, her granddaughter had enough to contend with. The thought of how much stress Mila must be under to consider marrying Phil Baxter for his money... For the first time since she'd left, Adelaide wished she hadn't been so carefree and had saved more than a small rainy-day nest egg, because she'd gift the lot to Mila in a heartbeat if she could.

She wanted to tell Jack but couldn't betray Mila's confidence when she'd specifically asked her not to, especially after discovering the depth of her granddaughter's hurt by her abandonment. She'd give it a couple of days and try discussing it with Mila again. Hopefully, with her granddaughter's permission, she could tell Jack and he'd save the day.

Considering he'd sold the farm and built a moderately sized cottage he'd have a lot of cash stashed away and Adelaide had little doubt he'd help Mila if her granddaughter asked. It would be convincing Mila to ask that would be the problem.

She strolled along a rough-hewn path, trying to ignore the many times she'd followed this same route decades ago. Jack had been an early riser and his clomping around usually woke her too. She was a night owl and liked to read or sketch until midnight—the only time she had any peace was after Mila, Will, and Jack went to bed—so being woken before dawn never sat well with her. Functioning on five hours sleep made her grumpy but she sucked it up, like many other aspects of her life that had made her unhappy.

The only bright side to waking earlier than she'd like had been walking this path as dawn broke, after she'd shared a cup of coffee with Jack—albeit in silence—and he'd headed off to tend the crops. She'd loved watching the sky lighten, streaked with gold and honey and mauve, listening to the magpies waking up, savouring the cool that came before another scorcher.

Now, like then, she inhaled and exhaled slowly, filling her lungs with pure country air, allowing calmness to infuse her. She'd been practising meditation for thirteen years, taking it up about a year after she settled in Tally Bay. For the first twelve months after she'd left Ashe Ridge, she'd been untethered, reluctant to start anything because a small part of her expected Jack to show up on her doorstep and persuade her to come back.

When that didn't happen, she finally put down roots and immersed herself in all Tally Bay had to offer. Dawn power walks on the beach with a club, meditation, yoga, even moonlight dancing on the beach with a women's empowerment group. That's when she'd applied for a job at the juice bar after she became friends with Raven through the walking club and when she'd signed a long-term lease on her tiny studio. In her mind, once she'd hit that twelve-month milestone in Tally Bay with no sign of Jack, she allowed herself the luxury of feeling like she'd finally come home.

But here, now, with the familiar sights and smells and terrain, she knew deep down she'd always consider this place home.

Her parents hadn't spoken to her since she left their mansion for the farm, and she wouldn't be surprised if they'd disowned her. Both in their late nineties now, she assumed they'd leave their fortune to the local dog shelter when they died. She'd tried reaching out to them once, a few years after she'd settled in Tally Bay, but it had been a waste of time. Her father had hung up on her and when she'd called the next day, her mother had done the same. It saddened her to think Cam, Mila, and Will were her only family these days, and she rarely spoke to or saw any of them.

As she rounded a bend and caught sight of a new cottage and two others being built, with a yawning vista behind them, she knew why this place had the power to make her feel insignificant. Something about the sheer size of Hills Homestead, the strangeness of farming the land, the uncertainty of it, intimidated her. It always had, from the first time an excited Jack brought her here for a grand tour.

She'd been terrified by the magnitude of the place but hadn't wanted to burst his bubble as he outlined the grand plans he had for the farm. Expanding legume crops. Building a bigger storage facility. Adding more silos. Besides, she'd been so smitten, so head over heels in love, he could've told her he was building a rocket to the moon and she would've stuck by his side.

Only later, when Cam had been born and she grew increasingly isolated on the farm from friends in town and her husband, who continued to withdraw with every passing day, did she resent being stuck here. That's when she'd suggested Jack build her dream cottage and he'd practically laughed at her. He was barely making ends meet and she wanted him to invest in expensive sandstone? She could tolerate many things but being laughed at like she was an idiot for even suggesting it didn't sit well with her.

That's the first day the insidious doubt crept in and took root. Had she made a mistake marrying Jack and following his dream at the expense of hers?

She'd given up travelling to Europe to paint followed by an arts degree in Melbourne to be with him, convincing herself that she'd have plenty of time later to re-enrol. But that never eventuated, considering the time suck of raising a child and helping run a farm. Instead, she did a part-time small-business accounting course so she could take over that side of things, leaving Jack to shoulder the onerous task of agriculture and its constant fluctuations.

She'd admired him for pursuing a degree in ag despite hating studying. He'd spend all day in the field, then be stuck reading books half the night, while attending a TAFE an hour away on weekends. She hadn't minded at the time because he said he was doing it for them, for their family, and in the long run it would mean they'd get to spend more time together when the farm flourished and he could hire more employees.

It never happened.

Farming life wasn't for the faint-hearted and in the end, it wasn't for her.

Tears stung her eyes at the recollection of the day she confronted him. She'd waited until Mila finished her last Year 12 exam and told her she was leaving the next day. Mila had been about to spend the day celebrating with friends and Adelaide had hoped that would distract her after she delivered the bad news. Mila had been stoic—she got that from Jack—and hadn't begged her to stay. Her granddaughter assumed her grandparents had a fight and it would resolve soon. Adelaide hadn't corrected her.

Instead, she'd packed her bags and left them at the back door so Jack would see them as he entered. He had, but his reaction hadn't been what she'd expected. She'd thought he'd take one look at the evidence of her intent to leave and talk to her. That they'd finally converse on a deeper level than they had for years. That they'd confront their lack of communication and intimacy issues, he'd beg her to stay, and she would.

Jack had barely glanced at the suitcases before shrugging and heading to the sink to scrub his hands like he did at the end of every day. She'd asked him if he had anything to say and he shook his head, his jaw set, unable to meet her eyes as he trudged into the bedroom.

She yelled out, 'Aren't you going to say something, Jack? Do you care that I'm leaving? Don't you want to salvage this marriage?'

His silence was all the confirmation she needed that her husband didn't give a crap about her, and she'd left. Even as she stored her cases in the boot of her car, she'd half expected he'd come after her and talk her out of leaving. Even when she started the engine she waited, letting it idle for a few minutes, hoping he'd come out of the homestead and run towards her. Even as she drove away as slow as she possibly could, she couldn't tear her gaze from the rear-vision mirror in case he ran after the car.

It didn't happen and she drove away with tears streaming down her face. A glutton for punishment, she spent the night in that motel in Kaniva and sent Mila a text, knowing her granddaughter would tell Jack where she was. He still didn't come for her, yet she waited, and when she drove away a few mornings later, leaving the Wimmera and Western Victoria behind her, she vowed to never look back.

So why was she so heartsore now?

Being back at Hills Homestead should be a stroll down a nostalgic lane; it shouldn't leave her guilt-ridden. Her conversation with Mila precipitated it, but if she was being completely honest with herself, it was Jack being so civil— getting her car towed, offering her a place to stay, driving her around—that made her wish she'd come back sooner for closure.

Once she got divorce proceedings rolling, hopefully she'd feel better, putting a full stop on her past once and for all. To do that, perhaps she should stick around longer than anticipated? Getting the divorce finalised in person would go a long way to emphasising the finality of it. Her past behind her, her future to be lived.

But she couldn't stay at Jack's any longer. How awkward would it be, living in a bungalow on her husband's land when he'd legally be her ex soon?

That's when her gaze landed on Mila's farm-stay project again, the first cottage almost completed, and the idea came to her. She could stay here, spend some quality

time with her granddaughter, and go through the uncomfortable process of formalising her divorce without living in
Jack's pocket.

The perfect solution.

She hoped all parties agreed.

CHAPTER NINETEEN

While Addy took a stroll, Mila called her grandfather.

He picked up on the sixth ring, like he had no intention of answering her call. 'Mila. How are you?'

His standard greeting made her smile. 'Good, Gramps. You?'

'Not bad. I'm getting a coffee in town.'

For someone who'd once told her he couldn't understand why young people wasted money on buying barista-made coffee from a café when they could just as easily make it themselves at home, this was almost as shocking as learning Addy had spent the night in his bungalow.

'You're getting a coffee in town?' Her scepticism made it sound like he was running up Main Street naked, and she heard a subdued chuckle.

'I haven't been in town for a while, thought I'd take a walk. Get something to drink.'

'Clearing your head, huh?'

He'd have a lot to think about, with Addy landing on his doorstep after so many years.

'I've always taught you to be blunt, young lady, so if

you've got something on your mind, say it, and stop implying you know what I'm thinking.'

She chuckled. 'Okay. Let's just say it was a shock to see Gran get out of your car earlier, then to learn she'd spent the night.'

'It's not like that,' he muttered, sounding gruff and adorable at the same time. 'It must've been an ordeal for her, dealing with a broken-down car, then discovering the first door she knocked on was mine.'

'Wow,' Mila mouthed silently. Not only had Gramps been chivalrous in offering Gran a place to stay, when he had every right to slam the door in her face considering how she walked out on him, but he was thinking of how she must've been feeling. Incredibly sweet. 'You're right, Gramps, she seems a bit discombobulated. It must've been tough on her.'

And you—but she wisely kept that to herself. Her grandfather couldn't abide pity.

'You two are okay?'

After a long pause, Gramps cleared his throat. 'Yeah. Though your grandmother wasn't the only one who got a shock when I opened that door, but it was nice to see Addy after all these years.'

Better than nice, considering the nostalgia in his tone. Where she'd expected animosity if the two of them crossed paths at her wedding, she heard nothing but cautious optimism in Gramps's voice and it gave her hope.

Not that she was under any illusions they'd reconcile— not after all this time—but it would be nice for some of her family to be civil enough to have regular catch-ups. Her parents were a lost cause— she was closer to the town butcher than to her folks. But Addy and Jack had been her world growing up and it pained her to see them separated by years of unresolved issues.

'Do you know how long she's staying?'

'Not a clue,' Gramps said, sounding annoyed. 'I'm not her keeper.'

'Just asking,' Mila said. 'Are you picking her up later?'

'No. I thought you could drop her wherever she needs to go.'

'At your place, you mean, considering that's where her stuff is?' She didn't understand her grandfather's abrupt change in mood.

'You two sort it out,' he said, muttering something unintelligible under his breath. 'I've got to go.'

Jack hung up, leaving her staring at the phone in consternation a moment before she caught sight of Addy striding towards her with purpose in her step.

'My darling girl, I've had an idea,' Addy said, her smile wide. 'We rarely get to spend time together and as I've come all this way, why don't I stay a while?' She pointed over her shoulder. 'That farm-stay cottage looks charming from the outside so why don't I be your first guest? What do you think?'

Mila would like nothing better than to spend quality time with her grandmother. But Jack was lonely and had been for a long time, and from the sound of his voice earlier —and what he'd said about Addy going through an ordeal —he obviously still cared for her.

What would happen if Gran spent longer at Gramps's bungalow rather than being stuck all the way out here?

Mila didn't expect them to rekindle their marriage, but it would be good for them to have a chance to resolve their differences and part more amicably this time around.

Besides, it would be nice if the two people she was closest to in the world could visit her and coexist harmoniously.

'I'd love to spend more time with you, Gran, and I will, but I'm sorry, you can't stay at the cottage.'

Addy's shoulders slumped. 'That's a shame.'

'Yes, it is. The wiring's not sound yet and the plumbing isn't done, plus it needs to pass a building inspection before it's habitable. I can't run the risk of anyone staying there, even you, if it could jeopardise the farm-stay project in the future.'

She made it sound convincing, even the part about the inspection, because she knew her gran would probably suggest she live in the unfinished cottage and shower in the main homestead.

'I understand,' Addy said, disappointment lacing her tone. 'Not to worry.'

Mustering her best cajoling tone, Mila said, 'I would love to spend more time with you though, especially when I'm under all this stress from the aborted wedding.' She laid it on thick. 'So why don't you stay longer at Gramps's place? I'm sure he won't mind, what with the bungalow being empty all the time anyway.'

She'd always wondered why her grandfather, a confirmed recluse since Addy left him fourteen years ago, would build a bungalow on his land. He never had anyone come to stay and if her parents ever returned from their travels, he had two spare rooms in his cottage. Not to mention the fact her parents would probably stay with her at Hills Homestead if they ever stopped travelling long enough. They hadn't been home once since she'd bought the farm so the likelihood of them dropping by was minuscule.

Addy's eyes narrowed slightly. 'He never has anyone to stay?'

'Not that I know of, and I'd hear, considering the grapevine in this town.'

'Hmm...' Addy murmured, absentmindedly, and for a second Mila could've sworn her gran had asked out of jealousy. 'I'll ask him if it's okay.'

'Great idea.' Mila enveloped Addy in a quick hug so her grandmother couldn't see her triumphant expression. 'I can't wait to see more of you.'

Mila hoped Jack shared the same sentiment.

Fate gave Mila a helping hand in playing matchmaker for her estranged grandparents. As luck would have it, she couldn't give Addy a lift to Jack's courtesy of an emergency meeting with her farm manager.

As Dazza approached, she didn't like his sombre expression. He'd already given her a heads-up about a potential problem with one of the paddocks when he'd texted her to meet a few minutes ago, and by the looks of it, the news wasn't good.

'How bad is it, Dazza?'

The sixty-year-old who'd been Jack's right-hand man for a decade wrinkled his nose. 'Even though we undertook adequate paddock preparation last spring before sowing, somehow the weed is spreading.'

Mila's heart sank. Because lentils grew slowly and couldn't compete with a variety of weeds, maintaining good weed control was essential for a healthy crop. If her current crop had been damaged... she couldn't contemplate the additional financial strain that would place on her.

'Can we control the spread?'

Dazza paused before nodding. But his hesitation, combined with the worry in his eyes, told Mila the truth before he spoke.

If calm, unflappable Dazza was worried, she should be too.

'You know we avoid sowing lentils in paddocks with a history of bad broadleaf weeds, and I thought Paddock 2 was clear. But the clovers and bedstraw are particularly resistant...' He shrugged. 'Maybe we should've delayed sowing and used a pre-emergent herbicide to ensure eradication? Regardless, we have a problem now.'

Mila had never cried in front of Dazza, despite the bad news regarding her crops that he'd delivered over the last year, but she could've easily sunk to her haunches in the dirt and bawled.

'Is there any chance of controlling the spread?'

Sensing an incoming meltdown, Dazza patted her shoulder in reassurance. 'I can try a post-emergent product to control those pesky broadleaf weeds, but I'll need to be careful as some of our lentil varieties are sensitive.'

'Do whatever it takes,' Mila said, swallowing her rising panic. The cost of running a farm was never-ending and with her finances already stretched to breaking point... Damn Phil for reneging on their arrangement.

'If it's any consolation, I've seen worse,' Dazza said, his smile laconic. 'Leave it with me.'

'Thanks, Daz. We still on for our weekly meeting later?'

He nodded. 'I've got all the updates ready. See you then.'

As her farm manager strode away, the tears Mila had been battling while Dazza delivered the bad news burned the back of her eyes.

Yet another reason to lament her aborted marriage. Over the last year or so, she'd had Phil to lean on when farming life got tough. She'd offload at the end of a hard day, and he'd never fail to cheer her up. That had been a highlight of their friendship, his ability to make her laugh, and she knew his easygoing personality had been one of the reasons she'd thought a marriage between them might work.

But with Phil off chasing a romantic dream with his new woman, she couldn't rely on him any longer. She hadn't just lost a financial solution to her problems when he cancelled their wedding, she felt like she'd lost a friend too.

Which was silly, considering they were still neighbours —but the last thing he needed was her encroaching on a new relationship.

What about Sawyer?

She ignored the thought because offloading to Sawyer about her problems, knowing he'd want to help, would only make life harder when he ultimately left.

CHAPTER TWENTY

Sawyer stepped out of the bakery and almost ran into Jack Hayes.

The man had been more of a father to him than his own. Not that he'd ever told him that. Will's grandfather could strike fear into the bravest soul and Sawyer wasn't that, always on edge that someone would see right through him. He had the feeling the old man could do exactly that.

'Good to see you, Mr Hayes.' He stuck out his hand and Jack shook it, his gaze coolly appraising as usual, catapulting Sawyer back decades when he had to stand by Will in his lies about why he'd broken curfew.

'You too, young man.' Jack released his hand. 'You came for the wedding?'

He nodded. 'Will caught Covid and couldn't travel so he asked me to attend the wedding on his behalf.'

Jack frowned. 'That young man works too hard, must be run-down.'

Sawyer didn't point out that Will could've caught the virus anywhere and it didn't necessarily correspond with his hours spent at the hospital; he hadn't seen the old man in years, no point antagonising him.

'He's just got a promotion at the hospital so he's putting in the hard yards.'

Sawyer knew he'd said the wrong thing when Jack's frown deepened. 'He didn't tell me about the promotion the last time we spoke.'

Sawyer had no intention of getting caught between his best mate and his grandfather, so he changed the subject. 'What do you think about Mila not getting married to Phil Baxter?'

'A lucky escape.' Jack shook his head, his mouth down-turned in disapproval. 'He's far too old for her.'

'Couldn't agree more. I almost punched the guy when I saw him yesterday.'

Jack's eyebrows rose. 'What did he say?'

'Nothing. It's his smarmy face I've always had a problem with.'

Jack guffawed and Sawyer managed a rueful smile.

'While they seem chummy enough, I'm not sure why she was marrying him, though the isolation affects many and they settle,' Jack said, his expression thoughtful. 'Unless they had intentions to merge the farms, build a solid financial base. Happens a bit out here, neighbours getting together for practicalities more than romance.' He shook his head. 'Hills Homestead is everything to her and I wish I'd never sold it to her.'

'She's loved that place since she was a kid,' Sawyer said, remembering the many times Mila told him she'd run the farm one day. 'I think it's pretty incredible she's bought it and is determined to make it thrive.'

Jack eyed him with grudging respect. 'Her farm-stay project is a sound idea, but it takes a lot of work to manage that and the rest of the farm.' He tut-tutted under his breath. 'She's too independent for her own good, that girl. Taking on way too much.'

Sawyer remained silent, sensing the old man was offloading.

In a moment, Jack continued. 'It would've broken her heart if I'd sold the place to anyone else though, so I went along with it when she got the loan from the bank. But having a big mortgage on your own she's tied to that place for life now.'

'It's not work if you love what you do,' Sawyer said, sounding like a motivational speaker and grimacing. 'Sorry. I agree with you, but Mila's always had a mind of her own.'

'She certainly has,' Jack said, with a wry grin. 'What are you doing with yourself these days, young man? Will said you've made a success of yourself in land sales?'

Sawyer nodded, proud when he glimpsed a glint of admiration in Jack's gaze. 'Land broking is something I enjoy, and I've been lucky enough to make a good living from it.'

'We make our own luck,' Jack said, in his own version of a motivational speaker, and held up his hand with forefinger and thumb cocked like a gun in a 'gotcha' sign.

They laughed and Sawyer marvelled at how easy it was to talk to Jack now the years had passed, and he didn't feel like the old man was judging his every move as Will's friend and finding him lacking like the rest of the town. Though that might've had something to do with his own hang-ups than any judgement on Jack's part.

Any time he visited the homestead, Jack had either been out on the farm or had his nose buried in agricultural books. A man of few words, he rarely smiled, but his presence calmed Sawyer. Jack's quiet strength was a far cry from his father's drunken, angry rants and he loved hanging around the Hayes family because of the warmth they exuded, something seriously lacking in his home.

'With the wedding not happening, how long are you staying?'

Depending on the outcome of his plan to help Mila, Sawyer could be here a week. The thought alone would've made him sweat before he arrived back here, but now he'd stepped back in time and discovered it wasn't as bad as his memories, he wanted to get his plan for Mila sorted and in place before he left.

'Not sure at this stage. A week? Perhaps longer.'

Jack nodded, approval in his gaze. 'Well, if you want to have a beer any time, let me know.'

'Thanks, Mr Hayes.'

'Call me Jack.'

They really had come a long way but the thought of calling his friend's grandfather by his first name seemed vaguely disrespectful. Like calling Mrs Knowles Shazza.

'I'm glad you're here for Mila too. She deserves to have a friend like you around at a time like this.'

With one last nod of approval, Jack sauntered down the street, still spritely for a guy who must be in his mid-seventies.

As for Jack's praise, Sawyer wondered what he'd think if he knew Sawyer had been harbouring more than friendly thoughts about Mila and how he'd like to spend his time with her in Ashe Ridge.

~

Three hours later, Sawyer had completed investigating the subdivision ruling on Mila's property and used his influence in the industry to figure out a workaround. Once he'd done that, he contacted prospective investors he knew who were always on the lookout for a sound business venture. But after another hour, he'd exhausted all his local contacts and none of them wanted to invest in a lentil farm. *'Too risky'*, *'not the right time'*, *'not interested'*, and *'economic down-turn'* were some of the reasons he'd been given.

Which left two options and neither of them appealed.

He'd tackle the first—the less palatable but easier option. As he drove along Phil Baxter's long driveway, focused on avoiding some massive potholes, he hoped he could hide his distaste long enough to get this deal done for Mila's sake.

The farmhouse came into view, a modest red-brick with a white verandah, and Sawyer wondered anew how Phil and Mila would've made their marriage work. Would they have lived here or at Hills Homestead? Would they have rented out one of the farms to make money? Would they have had kids?

He understood the practicalities of their marriage from what Mila had told him, but she was too sweet, too special, for a man like Phil not to want more from the relationship than what she might've been willing to give.

Thank goodness Phil had the decency to pull out of the wedding, but he was counting on the guy still wanting to expand his holdings and buy some of Mila's land to help her out. Which is what he assumed Mila would've done in the first place if not for that troublesome subdivision clause. It would've cost her a fair bit to resolve, money she didn't have by the sounds of it, and he was glad he could use his influence to come up with a solution.

He parked near the barn and spied Phil washing his hands at a trough. Even at a distance, the guy looked older than his forty-nine years, with baggy jeans, a faded chambray shirt, and a plaid vest.

Sawyer clamped down on his dislike as he strode towards Phil, knowing he had to play nice for this to work. If he stuffed up, Phil would tell him to piss off and he'd be down to his last option to save Mila's farm, something he really didn't want to do.

Rather than walk towards him when Phil caught sight of him, the smug prick thrust his hands into his pockets and waited until Sawyer reached him.

'What are you doing here?' A deep frown grooved Phil's brow. Sawyer didn't miss the slight back step, as if he thought Sawyer had come here to punch him.

'I came to apologise,' he said, mustering his best subservient tone. 'I was out of line when you popped into Mila's yesterday. Your relationship is none of my business.'

Phil gaped for a moment, before he shrugged. 'Yeah, well, things got complicated and as I called the wedding off, I thought I'd do the right thing and take the blame.'

How magnanimous of the dickhead, Sawyer thought.

'Actually, there's another reason I'm here,' Sawyer said, eager to get to the point so he could leave, unwilling to spend two seconds longer than necessary in this dweeb's presence. 'I was wondering if you were still interested in acquiring some of her land and expanding your farm?'

Phil's eyes narrowed slightly, assessing him, probably wondering why he was interfering, so Sawyer continued. 'I'm a land broker and I've been able to get the subdivision issues sorted.'

'You're a land broker?' Phil's brows shot up and the hint of amusement in his tone made Sawyer's fingers curl into fists. 'Considering the way you goofed around as a kid, I never thought you'd make anything of yourself.'

Sawyer mentally counted to five so his fists wouldn't connect with Phil's jaw. 'Many of us change over the years.'

Though in Phil's case, he doubted it. Sawyer had a sneaking suspicion the offer of Mila's land had only been part of the attraction in marrying her. If he refused now, it would prove what Sawyer suspected.

Phil had wanted to get into Mila's pants and thought he'd wear her down with time once they were married.

'So, what do you think?'

Phil rocked back on his heels, his expression contemplative. 'Why isn't Mila here?'

'Because I'm her friend and I'm making enquiries on her behalf.'

And he didn't want this sleaze anywhere near Mila if he didn't have to be.

Besides, he knew she'd be furious he'd interfered—but he hoped that once Phil agreed and he presented her with a solution to her problems, she'd be grateful he'd intervened on her behalf.

Phil shook his head. 'Unfortunately, it's not that easy. Even with the subdivision clause sorted, I don't have the funds to buy the land outright. We had an arrangement worked out for the financial stuff, so our marriage would've been mutually beneficial.' He grinned. 'In all regards.'

Sawyer clamped down on a surge of fury so potent he could've happily taken a swing at Phil and not given a damn.

He'd been right.

The prick had been interested in Mila romantically.

'Are you reneging because you can't get your hands on Mila?'

Shock widened Phil's beady eyes, but Sawyer saw the truth before the prick had a chance to deny it. 'Mila's a lovely woman, so of course I hoped our marriage would become real over time. What guy wouldn't want that?'

What guy indeed, considering Sawyer had lain awake most of last night, reliving the feel of her in his lap, the twinkle in her eyes as she admitted having a crush on him in her teens, the spark between them as they sparred.

'So your answer's no?'

Phil hesitated, as if sensing Sawyer's underlying anger. 'If I could help Mila I would, but my financial constraints are real, so I can't.'

Mustering every ounce of self-control, Sawyer managed a brief nod. 'Thanks for your time.'

'No worries,' Phil said, looking exceedingly relieved as Sawyer gave a brief salute before turning away.

But the slimeball was wrong. Sawyer had a major worry.

He now had to follow his last-resort plan to help Mila, and if the truth ever came out, it would ruin their friendship—or the hope of anything more—once and for all.

CHAPTER TWENTY-ONE

Mila's emergency meeting with the farm manager meant she couldn't drop Adelaide back at Jack's as she'd hoped, so Adelaide had to ask Jack for a lift.

He'd offered to pick her up again after her visit to Hills Homestead, but she had the feeling he'd offered out of politeness rather than any real desire to spend a minute longer than needed in her company.

So she texted him and he arrived ten minutes later, giving her time to evaluate the wisdom of staying longer in Ashe Ridge. She owed it to Mila after discovering the extent of the pain she'd inflicted on her granddaughter after leaving here fourteen years ago, and in a way, she owed it to herself.

Securing a divorce would be easier if she smoothed things over with Jack and their relationship was cordial rather than fraught. And instigating proceedings in person meant he couldn't be difficult—ignoring calls, not signing documentation—which she had a feeling might happen if she did this remotely.

Staying longer than anticipated made sense. But what

didn't make sense was the way her heart leaped as Jack pulled up beside her, slid the window down, and smiled.

'Ready to go?'

She nodded, willing her racing pulse to subside. 'Thanks for picking me up.'

'Not a problem.'

He waited until she'd clicked the seatbelt into place before making a U-turn and heading along the driveway to the highway. When she'd first moved here, she'd imagined them making this trip many times: heading into town regularly, going out for dinner at the pub, seeing movies screened at the hall, the occasional weekend away. But it never happened, because running the farm took over Jack's life, leaving Adelaide as a mere adjunct, someone he took for granted.

'How was your visit?'

'Good,' she said, sounding terser than intended courtesy of her maudlin memories. 'Mila's surprisingly chipper.'

'She had a lucky escape not marrying Phil,' Jack muttered, glancing left and right before turning out onto the highway. 'Does she need anything?'

Adelaide bit her tongue, wishing she could tell Jack the truth but not willing to betray Mila's trust just yet. 'She seems okay for now. But I'm planning on staying a little longer than first thought, just to make sure she's fine.'

An awkward silence descended, before Jack cleared his throat. 'How long are you sticking around?'

'Not sure yet. Maybe a week, maybe longer.'

'Your car should be ready in a few days,' he said, and she wasn't sure if he was letting her know so she'd be mobile again, or because he hoped once the car was ready she'd get in it and drive away, never to return.

'Great.' She took a deep breath and exhaled slowly,

summoning her nerve. 'I don't want to put you out, Jack, but I was hoping I could stay on at the bungalow? I thought I'd stay with Mila, but her spare rooms are filled with furniture for the farm-stay project, and the first cottage isn't inhabitable yet.'

'I guess that would be okay,' he muttered, sounding like he'd rather have a family of possums inhabiting the bungalow than her. 'Stay as long as you like.'

'Thanks, Jack.'

He didn't respond and they remained silent for the twenty-minute drive to his cottage. However, when he pulled up in his driveway and parked, he killed the engine and turned towards her.

'Why are you really staying longer, Ads?'

Heat crept into her cheeks as the intensity of his gaze bore into her, seeing too much, not seeing enough. 'I already told you. I want to be here in case Mila needs me.'

'You haven't been here for the last fourteen years. What makes you think she needs you now?'

The truth hurt, but Adelaide didn't want to get into an argument, not when he was being more than hospitable.

'Now that I'm here, I don't feel compelled to rush away.'

He grunted, and a frown appeared between his brows. 'I don't think you're being completely honest with me.'

She sighed, not wanting to bring up the D-word yet, but knowing she'd have to broach it soon enough. She'd hoped to make an appointment with the lawyer in town first and get the lowdown on what needed to be done before mentioning it to Jack.

But her husband had always been astute—except when it came to her feelings—and she owed him some semblance of the truth.

'How we left things hasn't done us any favours, Jack,

and I think it'll be easier if we sort out our issues in person. Don't you?'

Pain flared in his eyes before he blinked and turned away to stare out the windshield. 'Whatever you say, Addy.'

Her stomach churned as she watched the man who'd once been her world stomp into his cottage and slam the door.

CHAPTER TWENTY-TWO

It took Sawyer all afternoon to put his plan into place. Good, because he wanted to have everything in order before he told the one person who could talk sense into him if needed.

He knew Will woke at five thirty every morning so he could squeeze in a gym workout before heading to the hospital, and accounting for the time difference, now would be as good a time as any to call his best mate.

'Hey, Will, how are you feeling?'

'Better. Not exercising yet but heading back to work today because I tested negative. How did Mila like the surprise?'

'If you mean seeing me instead of you, she wasn't impressed.'

Will snickered. 'She should've been grateful one of us made it. Though she could've texted me afterwards to see how I am, but I assume she's too busy enjoying marital bliss to remember her brother.'

Sawyer shuddered at the thought of Mila, Phil, and marital bliss in the same sentence.

'About that... the wedding didn't happen.'

'What?' Will yelled into the phone. 'How am I only hearing about this now? Is she okay? Did that prick Phil do something?'

'He's a prick all right. The dickhead called off the wedding the morning of the ceremony.'

'I'll kill him,' Will growled. 'Unless you've already done it.'

'Don't tempt me. I wanted to punch the living daylights out of him, but Mila assured me she wasn't emotionally invested.'

Silence, followed by 'Mate, what the fuck is going on?'

'Apparently it was a marriage of convenience. Mila needs money desperately to keep the farm afloat and Phil was going to give her cash in exchange for land to expand his farm.'

'But why didn't he just buy the land from her?'

'Because there was a subdivision clause that would've cost an arm and a leg to work around. Though I reckon the real reason is he had high hopes of the marriage becoming real.'

Will cursed so loudly Sawyer eased the phone away from his ear a tad. 'She never should've bought that farm. It's more trouble than it's worth.'

'But she loves the place.'

Will sighed. 'Yeah, I know. It's everything to her, so I guess I understand she'd go to such lengths to save it. I just wish I had the cash to help her out.'

Here went nothing. 'Actually, that's what I wanted to talk to you about. I've got an idea.'

'Mate, if she thinks you're interfering, she'll castrate you. You know what she's like. Independent to a fault, not accepting help from anybody.'

'Yeah, well, I tackled the subdivision issue, and put feelers out to see if anyone would be interested in acquiring some of her land, but it was a no-go. I even approached Phil to ask if he'd buy the land, but he said he hasn't got the money, which pretty much confirms that he was only interested in the land if Mila was the prize attached to it. So I've come up with another idea I wanted to run by you.'

Will had been his mate since they sat next to each other the first day of Year 5, so it didn't surprise him his friend guessed his plan before he could articulate it.

'You want to buy the land to help her out.'

'Yeah, but she'd never accept my help, so I'm doing it through a subsidiary company I run. I've acquired land all over Victoria through the company, making sound investments, so this would be one more.'

'But is it a sound investment? If Mila's desperate for cash, the farm could be running at a loss, so you'd be throwing away your money.' Will paused. 'I know you're a good mate, but losing money because you want to help my sister? That's going above and beyond.'

'Actually, she has a sound business plan for a farm-stay project she's undertaken. Profits will increase, but she needs the equity upfront to make it happen.'

Will remained silent, thinking. 'If you do this, you know you can't tell her you're behind it, right? She'd never go for it.'

'I know, but I hate lying to her.'

'Consider this. She was willing to marry Phil Baxter rather than ask family or friends for money. Do you honestly think she'll accept your help?'

Sawyer had known the answer all along, which is why he knew if Mila ever found out the truth, it would be the end of them.

'I know she won't. But lying to her '

'Mate, you're withholding the truth for her own good, not lying deliberately.'

Sawyer knew there was a fine line between the two and Mila wouldn't see it that way. 'So you think I should do it? Bail her out?'

'Absolutely.' Will's tone softened. 'She's my sister and a major pain in my arse, but she's one of the good ones and she deserves to follow her dream.'

Will didn't have to add, *just like I've followed mine*. Sawyer knew his friend harboured guilt for leaving town the day after their final exam and not returning. He mentioned it occasionally, usually after a few beers on a late-night call. Sawyer hated talking about the past, especially his life in Ashe Ridge, so he often changed the subject. But Will lamented walking away from his family—especially Mila—without looking back.

'You can't say anything,' Sawyer said, knowing if the time ever came to tell Mila the truth, it had to come from him.

'What do you think I am, an idiot?'

Sawyer paused, and Will chuckled. 'Don't answer that. Seriously, mate, like I said, you're going above and beyond. Thanks.'

'Any time. You two were closer to me than my family growing up.'

Spending every day with the Hayes family, surrounded by the tranquillity of Hills Homestead, kept him sane back then. They eased the edginess in him, the urge to go wild and do crazy stuff, like sneak into adjoining farms and pilfer fruit, or jump into the dam in the dead of winter. Mila and Will calmed him, and it wasn't until years later when he'd been diagnosed had he understood the extent of their influence. He owed them, big time, and helping Mila out with money he could spare was the least he could do.

'Man, being back in that town has you going soft.' Will sniggered. 'Stop the sentimental bullshit and let me get to work.'

'Are you sure your eagerness to get to the hospital isn't to do with a certain orthopaedic surgeon resident rather than the outpatients lined up to get their backs manipulated?'

Will snickered. 'I'm a dedicated physiotherapist and my patients need me.'

'Yeah, right. Like that hot ortho resident needs you to—'

'Got to go, bozo. Thanks for the call. And for helping my sister out. Your secret's safe with me.'

Will hung up, leaving Sawyer bemused. His friend had never been backward about talking about conquests in the past, but he clammed up any time Sawyer asked about the new surgical resident in the orthopaedic ward where Will worked. It had to be serious. Who knew, maybe he'd be attending another Hayes wedding sometime soon?

In the meantime, hearing Will reiterate he was doing the right thing, and getting his blessing, meant Sawyer had to formalise an offer from his company that would be too good for Mila to refuse.

And ensure she couldn't trace it back to him.

CHAPTER TWENTY-THREE

If Mila's earlier emergency meeting with Dazza made her frazzled, the usual weekly update from her farm manager didn't help.

This year's crop prices were lower than expected, meaning she'd be struggling to make mortgage repayments let alone have anything left over to progress the farm-stay cottages.

She'd hated lying to her grandmother about the first cottage being uninhabitable, but if any good could come out of her shambles of a wedding—namely, her grandparents sorting out their crap—she was all for it.

She had no doubt Gramps would let Gran stay on at the bungalow. He'd actually been smiling when he picked Addy up earlier. Not that Mila had been spying from the living-room window— not much, that is. But seeing her gruff grandfather who rarely had a smile for anyone beaming at Addy vindicated Mila's decision to push the two of them together.

If only she could solve her financial crisis as easily.

Whenever she needed to solve a problem, she worked.

Keeping busy with her hands meant her mind didn't have time to wander, so after donning overalls, sticking her earbuds in and cranking up a rock playlist, she tackled the next task on her farm-stay to-do list. Painting the interior of the second cottage.

She'd already prepped with tarps and masking tape, so after popping the lid on the shade she'd chosen—a pale blue —and pouring the paint into a tray, she dipped the roller and got to work. The simple up and down action of the roller against the wall soothed her mind as she'd hoped, and she soon found herself singing along to an eighties ballad.

It took eight songs to cover an entire wall. She stood back to admire her handiwork, pleased with the result, when a tap on her shoulder made her scream and whirl around to find Sawyer grinning at her.

She plucked the earbuds out and slipped them into her pocket, glaring at him. 'That's the second time in as many days you've scared the living crap out of me. Don't you have anything better to do than sneak up on me?'

His grin widened, smug and infuriating and too gorgeous. 'Maybe if you weren't intent on auditioning as lead singer for one of those eighties bands you love so much, you might hear when others are around you.'

'I like to sing. Sue me,' she said, embarrassment heating her cheeks as his gaze roved over her and she wished she wasn't wearing her oldest, tattiest overalls. 'What are you doing here anyway?'

'Can't an old friend pop around to say hello?'

'I suppose,' she muttered, wishing he didn't make her feel so damn flustered all the time.

She'd been doing just fine, not seeing him for fifteen years. Out of sight, out of mind. But having him waltz back into her life when she'd least expected it had thrown her, and she hadn't recovered since.

He'd always had this way of looking at her, like his deep blue eyes flecked with green could see right through her, and now she'd been stupid enough to blurt the truth about the crush she'd once had, it made her want to crawl under the nearest rock.

But there was nothing but kindness in his eyes and she knew his teasing never held malice. He'd made her feel safe growing up, protective like Will but without the whole 'pain in the arse big brother' vibe.

'What are you thinking?'

'About how nice you were growing up.' She paused, her smile cheeky. 'What happened?'

He chuckled. 'I'm still nice. In fact, I have a feeling you'll think I'm the nicest guy in the world when you hear what I have to say.'

She couldn't get a read on him, not when the glimmer in his eyes shifted between excited to wary. 'Okay. Spit it out. What's going on?'

'I took the liberty of using my influence in the industry to sort out your subdivision clause, so if you're agreeable, I have a buyer for the land you were willing to give to Phil. At a good price too.'

For a second, Mila wondered if she'd had the music up too loud earlier and she was having an auditory hallucination, because she could've sworn Sawyer had just solved her monetary problems.

'How... When...' Overwhelmed, she swallowed to ease the tightness in her throat courtesy of his consideration. 'I never asked you to do that.'

'I know, but if you were willing to marry Phil to save the

farm, I thought selling the same land would be an easier solution.'

'I don't know what to say,' she murmured, his thoughtfulness making tears well in her eyes.

'You don't have to say anything now. I'll get the contract drawn up once you tell me the precise amount of land you're willing to sell, you can have your lawyer look it over, and if you're happy with it, sign on the dotted line and you'll have the cash in your account soon after.'

Those damn tears prickled harder, and her chest expanded with emotion until she thought it would burst.

'Thank you,' she said, barely above a whisper, the enormity of his gesture hitting her all at once and she flew at him, almost knocking him over as she flung her arms around his neck. 'Thank you, thank you, thank you.'

'You're welcome,' he said, his tone gruff as he tightened his arms around her.

She buried her face in his chest, inhaling the faintest vetiver, wondering if he always smelled this good before realising she'd never got this close in the past. They'd hung out as friends, and she'd been very careful to hide that she wanted to be more. They'd camped under the stars together, they'd swum in the dam, they'd made cookies, a solid threesome with Will always around.

But her brother wasn't around now, and they were all grown up, two single adults with an underlying attraction. Or was that only one-sided? Did Sawyer feel this zing between them?

Only one way to find out. As she eased back to look him in the eye and saw an answering glint of lust, she did the one thing guaranteed to change the status quo between them.

She kissed him.

CHAPTER TWENTY-FOUR

One minute Sawyer felt like a god, with Mila staring at him with gratitude in her eyes, the next he lost his mind as she kissed him.

Correction, devoured him. Mila kissed like she did everything else in her life—with passion, gusto, no holds barred—and he couldn't believe his luck.

Their mouths fused, a hungry, frantic moulding of lips and tongue that left him breathless and wanting more. A hell of a lot more.

Her fingers threaded through his hair, tugging his head closer, as she hooked a leg around his waist, and when she started writhing against him, he lost it.

With a groan, he picked her up and backed up against the nearest wall, mindless with wanting her. He couldn't see straight let alone think and it took a full five seconds to register he'd kicked the paint tray.

'Put me down,' Mila yelled, pummelling his shoulders with her fists, and he obliged, thankful the tray hadn't been filled with paint and only held dregs.

Splatters covered the floor but not enough to do much

damage and he squatted alongside Mila and grabbed a rag. 'Got any turpentine lying around?'

'Yeah, but don't worry. Floating floorboards are going over this concrete so the paint will be hidden.'

Yet she continued to scrub at the paint spill like her life depended on it, unable to meet his eyes.

'Hey, slow down.' He placed his hand over hers, not surprised when she yanked it away.

She regretted the kiss.

Though calling what they'd just done a kiss was like calling a summer deluge a drop of rain.

'Mila, look at me.'

After an eternity, she dragged her gaze away from the paint-splattered floor and looked at him. His breath caught at the depth of emotion in her wary gaze.

That kiss had affected her as much as it had him.

His heart still pounded so loud it reverberated in his ears, and he could barely think. But he knew he had to smooth this over; otherwise, she mightn't want to go through with the deal. Not that she suspected he was behind it, but as the broker she'd have to see him again and if she felt too uncomfortable...

'We got caught up in the moment, that's all,' he said, hating that he had to downplay what had been a phenomenal kiss—the kind of kiss to get him going in a way he hadn't for a long time, if ever. 'It's okay.'

'Okay,' she echoed, still looking as shell-shocked as he felt. 'I got swept up in gratitude.' She made circles at her temple. 'It sent me a little loopy. Won't happen again.'

'That's a shame,' he said, the blush staining her cheeks adorable. 'Because you can thank me like that any time.'

He expected her to fire back with a quip like she usually

would, so her silence unnerved him more than if she'd kissed him again.

'Want to stay for dinner? It's nothing fancy, reheated lasagne, but it's the least I can do.'

'Sounds good,' he said, happy to spend more time with her.

Being back in Ashe Ridge mightn't be high on his list of all-time favourite activities, but reconnecting with Mila made him feel like he'd been missing out by staying away so long.

A few hours later, Sawyer sat opposite Mila, the flames low between them as the stars twinkled overhead. He'd travelled extensively for work, but no sky came close to the Wimmera, the stars dazzling on a clear night.

'Sorry I don't have marshmallows,' she said, holding up her beer. 'But at least I have these.'

'Cheers.' He raised his bottle. 'Remember that time Will had the flu and your gran wouldn't let him come outside and sit around the fire with us? He was a grump for a week.'

She laughed. 'We had some good times around this fire pit.'

'We did. Solving the world's problems. Talking shit about kids at school.'

'Speaking of kids at school, have you run into Shazza at the motel yet?'

He grimaced. 'Yeah, this morning. Let's just say she has a long memory.'

'I swear I laughed so hard after you got caught with Simone at the motel, I had a stitch for hours.' He didn't understand the cunning glint in her eyes. 'Though I have something to confess.'

'I'm intrigued.' He sipped at his beer, more content than he'd been in ages.

When was the last time he sat by a fire after a hearty meal, enjoying casual conversation with someone he liked being around, and taking time out to look at the stars? Too long, and he intended on making the most of his time in Ashe Ridge, with Mila, no matter how brief.

'I was the one who tipped her off that you were in a room with Simone.'

Shock made him sit bolt upright. 'No way. You dobbed on me? Why?' But the moment he asked, he knew. 'Because you had a crush on me?'

She winced and nodded. 'Not my finest moment. But I was young and stupid and jealous as hell, so I called the motel asking to speak to you, saying you were in a room with Simone, knowing full well Shazza would go ballistic.'

'You cramped my style,' he said, feigning outrage, barely able to contain his laughter at the lengths she'd gone to. 'Though I guess I should be flattered.'

'Don't get an inflated ego. Like I said, I was dumb back then.'

'Smitten, more like it.'

And the feeling had been entirely mutual. Guess they both did a good job of hiding it.

'That too.' She laughed, and he joined in, thankful they'd moved past that kiss and managed to have an enjoyable evening.

It had been a tad awkward at first, but after she'd showered and they ate, they slipped into their old camaraderie. He'd been relieved, because if she freaked out over one kiss, what would Mila think if she knew how badly he wanted a repeat? And more?

Not that he had any intentions of having a fling with his best friend's sister, but if he felt the pull between them so strongly after two days in town, how much harder would it be to keep his hands off her the longer he stayed?

That was the other thing. He'd be hanging around until the deal went through to acquire her land and she had the money in her bank. He couldn't rush it, because it would raise her suspicions, so that meant he had to stick around. Who knew, maybe he could broker some other deals while he was in the area? He'd avoided the Wimmera because of its connection to his past, but the area was thriving, and he'd be a fool not to explore business opportunities while he was here.

'We had some fun growing up.' Mila tilted her head back and looked up at the sky. 'It's why I could never leave this place. Once my folks dumped me here, I fell in love with Hills Homestead because it signified home for me.'

Back then, Sawyer had been envious of Mila and Will. He would've loved to be raised by cool grandparents, not his deadbeat dad and browbeaten mum. Adelaide and Jack had given Mila and Will far more freedom than parents ever would've, and he'd loved being here, a welcome respite from his shoddy home life.

'How often do you hear from your folks?'

'Try never.' She sat up straighter and swigged at her beer. 'But I gave up caring a long time ago. I'm more pissed at Will moving all the way to London.' She waved her arm around. 'I'm so in debt with this place I can't afford to fly over to visit, and he's so busy at the hospital he never comes home.'

'Yeah, that twenty-four-hour plane trip is a killer, which is why I've only been over there once.'

'What's London like?'

'Eclectic. Busy. Cosmopolitan. Great to visit for a holiday, but I don't think I'd like to live there.'

'Why not?'

Because he needed his routines. Because the bustle of the place messed with his head. Because he needed structure and order in his life, not chaos, to function.

But he couldn't tell her any of that, so he settled for, 'It's like Sydney. Glamorous to look at, fun to play with for a while, but after a few weeks you crave the peace of home.'

She nodded, thoughtful. 'Yeah, I get that. I love my annual weekend in Sydney with Gran. The social stuff around the harbour is amazing, and Bondi has a distinct vibe, so we do a bunch of touristy stuff, but nothing beats coming back here.'

She sounded content with her life, and he wondered what it would be like to be so enraptured with a place you'd sacrifice your own happiness—namely, marrying someone you didn't love—to save it.

'I ran into your grandfather in town this morning. Did he have regrets moving away from the farm?'

Worry flickered in her eyes. 'Did he say something?'

'No, I just wondered. Hasn't this place been in his family for generations? I just assumed it must've been hard for him to relinquish control.'

'Not really. He made up his mind to move and that was that. He didn't want to sell to me because of the debt I'd be in, but I convinced him, and he finally agreed. I thought he'd still spend a lot of time here, to be honest, but he doesn't, apart from checking in with me occasionally. It's like once he made a clean break he didn't want to look back.'

'Do you think your grandmother leaving him had anything to do with that? Wanting to forget?'

She shrugged. 'Maybe, though he seemed determined to build the sandstone cottage and threw himself into it so wholeheartedly that I don't think he missed the farm at all.' She rolled her eyes. 'Not that he'd tell me. No prizes for guessing where I get my independence from.'

He smiled, buoyed by the intimacy of their conversation. They'd been friends growing up but had never confided in each other about the deeper stuff. Lucky, because he had a lot to hide back then.

'I think you get some of that from your gran too. Have you ever visited her besides catching up in Sydney?'

Mila shook her head. 'Tally Bay sounds amazing and the pics I've seen from Gran and online are gorgeous. But I can't afford to leave the farm for too long, so I've never made the trek to northern New South Wales.'

'How did she end up there?'

'Honestly? I think she just drove until she didn't feel like driving anymore. Plus there's a thriving art community there and she loves to paint. Makes a living from it too. I've got three small canvases of hers I want to frame and hang in the cottages once they're done.'

'I don't remember seeing her paint when I was around?'

'That's because she rarely did. I think she sketched a bit during the night and in the mornings before we got up, but I never saw her paint.'

'I guess farm life is time-consuming.'

Mila nodded, lost in thought. 'It is. And it's not for everyone. I love it and it's still tough, so imagine how hard it would be for someone who didn't have their heart and soul invested.'

'Is that why she left?'

'I think so. Gramps isn't the easiest person to live with because he rarely says more than two words on any subject, and Gran's outgoing, so it must've been tough for her, stuck here as a farmer's wife. She came from money too and left it all behind when she married Gramps.'

'That's romantic.'

'Considering how they ended, not so much.'

The mouth he'd happily kiss again curved into a cheeky smile. 'Which is why I think it's great Gran's staying in Gramps's bungalow.'

Sawyer's eyebrows rose. 'How did that happen?'

'She wanted to stay in the first farm-stay cottage, but it's conveniently not ready, so I gave her a gentle nudge back to Gramps's, where she happened to stay last night.'

'Are you playing matchmaker? Because it might blow up in your face and then they'll blame you.'

Mila pressed a hand to her heart, all wide-eyed innocence. 'I can't help it if my cottage isn't ready, and Gran chooses to stay at Gramps's place rather than the motel.'

He laughed and waggled his finger at her. 'You're playing with fire.'

'I'd rather be playing with you,' she whispered, so softly he thought he'd misheard.

Their gazes locked across the flickering flames and Sawyer knew he'd walk across hot coals for this woman.

She'd been the only person in his entire life who'd seen beneath his joker exterior, who'd given a damn about him. Even Cheraline, who set him on the correct path to manage his condition, had viewed him as something to fix. They may have been in a relationship, but she had a compulsion to rescue things—from cats to birds to kids—and he'd known deep down she saw him as another thing to save.

Mila had never done that. She'd been a staunch support when he needed it—and considering his home life, he'd needed it often— but she'd never judged or given unwanted advice. She'd listened and observed, and he'd been eternally grateful.

Which is why he could never hurt her, and that's what indulging this attraction between them could do.

'I thought we agreed that kiss was a spur-of-the-moment thing, not to be repeated,' he said, wishing he could get a better read on her expression. But with the flames casting shadows on her face, he couldn't tell if she was joking or not.

'We did, but that doesn't mean I can't have a little fun at your expense.'

'As I recall, you kissed me.'

'Moot point,' she said, with a coy smile that made him want to leap across the fire pit and drag her into his arms. 'Logically, I know we should forget it, but let's just say that kiss was something else and will probably keep me up tonight.'

He admired her honesty and it rammed home the fact that he wasn't being completely honest with her. What would she think of his underhanded attempt at helping her?

Will knew his sister better than anyone and he'd advised to keep Sawyer's involvement on the lowdown. Sawyer agreed, but it wouldn't hurt to test the waters, see what she said if he offered help.

Because that's the only way he could see them starting something beyond friendship, if she knew the truth.

'We're close, yeah?'

She nodded.

'And you trust me, yeah?'

'Of course. I'd say you're like another big brother to me, but that would be plain weird considering our lip-lock.'

'Then what would you say if I offered to help you financially?' He held up his hands, palms showing. 'No strings. Just a loan. Or however you want to structure it—'

'No.' She shut down, her expression blank and her brows grooved in disapproval as she shook her head. 'It's lovely of you to offer, but I don't want to mix business with pleasure.'

Before he could say anything, she continued. 'And I'm not talking about pleasure in the sense I'd like to continue beyond that kiss. I mean that we're friends and when money enters a friendship, it never ends well.'

He agreed, but this was Mila, and it would be different for them. And it irked that she'd been happy to marry Phil, her *friend*, with money a big part of their union.

'But we've known each other a long time and there'd be ironclad contracts, not me slipping you an envelope of cash under a table.'

Her hard expression softened. 'You're sweet to offer, but my answer is no. You said you had a buyer interested in some of my land; I'd rather stick with that.'

Hell.

Now would be a good time to come clean, to tell her one of his companies would be acquiring her land, so to make the transaction easier they could cut out the middleman and deal directly with each other.

But Mila had closed off the moment he'd mentioned helping her and he knew that if he told her the entire truth now, she'd end up hating him and not getting the money she so desperately needed.

She yawned. 'On that note, I'm going to call it a night. Let me know when you have confirmation from that buyer and we'll get the ball rolling, okay?'

He nodded, the guilt at deceiving her sitting like a rock in his chest.

She stood and stretched, giving him a tantalising glimpse of stomach, and he wished he could bury his face there and wrap his arms around her.

But their relationship was muddy enough thanks to his quest to help her, and he needed to get the hell out of here before he did something foolish.

Like stay.

CHAPTER TWENTY-FIVE

Adelaide missed her morning walks along the beach, missed the briny sea air that seemed unique to Tally Bay. It had been strange at first, trading the dry country air for the ocean, but she'd soon grown to love it.

She'd changed a lot of things when she'd first moved away from Ashe Ridge. She'd stopped drinking coffee, swapping to fruit-filled smoothies. She enjoyed the occasional BLT or steak but became predominantly vegetarian. And after several years, she stopped thinking of herself as married and went on the occasional date.

None of them went beyond a kiss goodnight until a decade after she'd been in Tally Bay, when she finally let Raven into her bed. She'd done it out of loneliness rather than any grand passion and their lovemaking was comfortable rather than spectacular.

That's one thing she never understood about Jack. They'd been dynamite between the sheets, rattling the headboard regularly. And while the sex had been amazing, she cherished those moments afterwards, when he'd hold her close and they'd share a laugh or a chat or say nothing at all, content to just be together.

When he stopped wanting sex, she blamed herself. Did Jack not find her attractive anymore? Had he grown tired of her?

She'd tried asking him about it once, the first time they'd gone weeks without making love, and he'd shut her down, citing fatigue and stress. So she'd waited, and when it hit the two-month mark since they'd last been intimate, she initiated it. She'd showered, shaved, moisturised, even ordered some new lingerie online. He'd taken one look at her, removed her hand from his hip, grunted, and rolled away from her.

She'd never tried again.

Instead, she bottled up her resentment and started second-guessing herself to the point she became miserable. They both had, coexisting in polite exchanges and silence behind closed doors. They'd faked it for the grandkids, of course, because poor Will and Mila had been through enough, having their parents virtually dump them before leaving without a backward glance.

While she never blamed them, Will and Mila were the only reason Adelaide stuck around so long. They gave her life purpose, and she didn't regret her part in raising them. But the day after Mila's final exam was when she knew it was time.

Time for her. Time to start fresh. Time to start living again.

The irony that Will had fled town a year earlier a day after his final exam hadn't been lost on Mila, who'd said at least one of them would stick around for Jack. But Adelaide had given up enough of her life for Jack and couldn't stand another day of existing rather than living.

Lost in her musings, she stubbed her toe on a tree root and pitched forward, managing to slam her palms against the trunk to break her fall. It took a second for the pain to register and she let out a loud yell as she glanced at her shredded palms. The sight of blood didn't bother her as much as the stinging and she bit her lip to stop from dropping a few expletives.

She heard a twig snap behind her and turned to find Jack eyeing her with concern.

'I was taking a walk and heard you yell. Are you okay?'

'Apart from these, you mean?' She held up her palms and he winced.

'Those need some antiseptic.'

She swallowed her first response, *Well done, Mr Obvious*. Pain always made her snarky, as he well knew. 'I don't have any.'

'I do. Come on.'

It was a short stroll back to the main cottage and her man of few words didn't say anything. No great surprise.

As they entered the kitchen, the smell of baking—something savoury, with tomato, basil, and onion—made her stomach rumble. Embarrassed, she pressed a hand to it, only to realise she'd left a bloody handprint on her favourite white top.

'The first aid kit is in the bathroom,' he said, and she followed him, casting a surreptitious glance at the oven, to see a quiche with a cheesy top bubbling nicely.

If her morning stumble hadn't put her in a bad mood, the delicious aromas that were evidence of Jack's cooking would have. She shouldn't be annoyed, because she'd changed over the last fourteen years too, but she couldn't help it.

Where was this man who cooked when she'd been married to him?

'If you're hungry, I've made a quiche and it should be ready soon.'

Great. He'd heard her traitorous stomach. She could be a stick in the mud and refuse, but she'd only be hurting herself, considering she'd planned on having a piece of toast after her walk.

'That'd be great. Thanks.'

She followed him down a small hallway to the bathroom, yet another room he'd modelled on what she'd once wanted. Large pale grey tiles, standalone bath, a shower big enough for two, circular vanity, and black fittings. Modern. Classy. Gorgeous.

She gritted her teeth against the urge to ask him why he'd done this. Had he thought she'd return one day, and wanted to torture her? To show her what she'd been missing out on? To punish her?

But she needed Jack onside for their divorce to proceed smoothly and antagonising him would only result in more hurt than it was worth.

'You should rinse your hands before I apply the antiseptic,' he said, turning on the taps and testing the water temperature before giving her a nod. 'Though it'll probably sting like hell.'

Adelaide didn't respond, because it took all her willpower not to cry when she slipped her hands under the water and her palms burned like the devil.

'That should do,' Jack said, turning off the taps and gathering her hands in a soft towel.

She didn't know what was worse, the stinging of her palms or the stinging in her eyes, as he gently patted her hands dry, his tenderness almost undoing her.

'This is going to hurt,' he murmured, as he poured anti-septic onto some cotton wool, and dabbed it on the cuts on her palm before blowing on them.

She blinked rapidly to stave off tears, overwhelmed by his solicitousness, and when he clasped her hands in his once he'd finished, his touch lingering, she wanted to bawl.

'There. All better,' he said, clearing the gruffness from his throat. 'Probably best to leave them open for a while rather than bandage them.'

She managed a 'Yeah, thanks,' as she followed him back to the kitchen, wishing it wasn't too early for a drink. A strong manhattan would go down very well right about now. Not that she drank often, but for the first few years after she'd left, she had a drink or two every night to take the edge off her restlessness.

She'd second-guessed herself a lot in those early days—had she done the right thing, had she been selfish, had she given up too easily—but once she started meditation and learned to release her residual tension, she never looked back. No good could come of regrets.

'I'll dish up the quiche. Orange juice okay?'

'Perfect,' she said, content to watch him bustle around the kitchen, a man comfortable in his own skin.

He poured the OJ, then slid his hands into mitts before getting the quiche out of the oven, cutting it into wedges and placing two on plates. There was something riveting in watching him take control in a way he never had. Jack had always deferred to her in all aspects of their life bar the farm. He'd been so consumed by his work that he didn't seem to care about anything else.

It made her curious. What else had changed about this man she once thought she knew better than herself?

'Tell me what you've been up to,' she blurted, sounding

nosy but not caring. For some unfathomable reason, she wanted to know everything.

'For the last fourteen years, you mean?'

His droll response held no malice and as he placed a plate and glass in front of her, she glimpsed amusement in his eyes.

'Yeah.' She pointed at the delicious smelling quiche in front of her. 'I'm guessing your newfound culinary expertise isn't the only thing that's changed over the years.'

He sat opposite and took his time answering—sipping at his juice, rearranging his cutlery. 'I guess the biggest change is that I'm not wound so tight anymore. I don't sweat the small stuff. I take time out to do things I enjoy, like gardening and popping into the Men's Shed in town weekly.' He shrugged, bashful. 'You leaving gave me a wake-up call I needed. So I guess I should thank you for that, even though I didn't see it that way at the time.'

She didn't know whether to be affronted or flattered. 'I'm glad you've found peace.'

'What about you? What's your life like?'

She had nothing to hide but revealing her new life to the man who'd been the centrepiece of her old left her feeling oddly vulnerable.

'Tally Bay is like Byron, only more chill, less touristy. I have a small studio I rent from a rich couple who are never around, that's cluttered and artsy. I paint and earn money from what I sell and subsidise my income by working part time in a juice bar.'

His eyebrows rose and she laughed. 'Yeah, I work alongside hip young things who think they invented blending ginger and turmeric with fruit for health benefits.'

His cautious smile made her think it would be okay to push for the real answer she wanted.

'What about significant others, Jack? Is there anyone in town I should be worried about who may get jealous and stab me in my sleep while I'm staying here?'

His smile faded, replaced with a frown. 'I've dated over the years, if that's what you're asking. But no one in town. Can't stand the gossip.'

He managed a rueful chuckle. 'Not from a lack of trying by the local women, mind you. Turns out, being abandoned by your wife makes you appear very attractive to the ladies.' He patted his stomach. 'I reckon I put on twenty kilos the year after you left because they kept dropping off casseroles, pasta bakes, jelly slices, and cakes.'

Not an extra ounce of weight graced Jack's body; Adelaide should know, she'd been checking him out. It wasn't fair that he still looked as trim as ever, while she carried an extra ten kilos. Then again, she viewed that weight as an indication of a good life. She didn't have to please anyone but herself these days and ate whatever she wanted when she wanted.

'What about you?'

She knew asking Jack about his dating life would mean she'd have to reveal hers and she hoped it wouldn't make things awkward between them. She wasn't finalising their divorce because of Raven, but the closure wouldn't hurt.

'I've enjoyed being single over the years, but there's a man who's been persistent and we catch up when the mood strikes.'

Jack was many things, an idiot wasn't one of them, so his glower meant he'd read between the lines and knew what she was saying: Raven was a friend with benefits.

'Do you love him?'

Hell no. She'd given her heart to only one man in her

lifetime and having it shattered meant she'd been more circumspect since.

'This quiche is getting cold,' she said, picking up her knife and fork, wincing as the stainless steel came into contact with her cuts, and hacking off a giant chunk and stuffing it into her mouth.

Thankfully, Jack didn't push the issue, but she felt his glare on her as she devoured the quiche, amazed by how good it was.

'You should enter this in the Ashe Ridge Show,' she said, after she'd finished every last crumb. 'You can bake, my man.'

She'd meant it as a flippant comment, but as their gazes locked across the table, his quizzical, hers confused, she wondered why it felt so good to claim Jack as hers, even in jest.

CHAPTER TWENTY-SIX

Mila rarely wore makeup but after another sleepless night —courtesy of replaying that sizzling kiss with Sawyer repeatedly—she slathered on concealer to hide the dark shadows under her eyes and finished with a dusting powder.

She did it out of practicality rather than vanity because a trip into town looking like she hadn't slept would invite a host of pity.

'Oh no, poor Mila is heartbroken over being dumped at the altar.'

'Mila's not sleeping. It's tough when love leads you down the wrong path.'

'The insomnia must be dreadful when your fiancé ditches you for another woman.'

The gossips would have a field day and she couldn't stand it. But she had to go into town because she wanted to meet with Freddie, her accountant, to inform him of the upcoming deal in the works to sell off some of her land. He'd been diligent when outlining the tax ramifications of combining assets and the like when she'd consulted him before marrying Phil, so she wanted to get ahead of the game in the hope Sawyer would contact her soon with a proposal.

It had been so tempting last night to accept his offer of help. They'd been cosy around the fire pit, their bellies full, and relaxed in each other's company despite that incredible kiss.

How she'd been able to act nonchalant while she'd reheated the lasagne and they'd shared half a bottle of wine, she'd never know. Her body had been hyperaware of him moving around her kitchen with ease like they hadn't been one step away from getting naked in the cottage. If he hadn't kicked over the paint tray...

Even now, her cheeks heated at the thought. She'd kissed him on impulse, unable to curb her growing attraction to the guy who'd once consumed her world. The way he responded indicated the attraction wasn't one-sided and she'd been so tempted to invite him to spend the night.

But his offer to help her financially couldn't have come at a better time because it reminded her that she shouldn't mix business with pleasure.

She intended on having the latter, with Sawyer, for however long he was in town. Accepting his offer would muddy their relationship and she didn't need the complication. Much easier for him to broker a deal, so if they ended up in bed together— though she was hoping it would be when, not if—they could part as friends, without a loan tying them together and making things potentially awkward.

After a brief stop at the bakery, where she picked up two vanilla slices and coffees, she walked the short distance to Freddie's office. He worked from home most days but twice a week he rented a room from Samuel Nobil, the lawyer, for those who preferred a more 'official' meeting place. Considering the way Freddie flirted with her, she conducted business from his town office.

She'd called ahead to tell him she'd be dropping in around ten and as she entered the musty offices just off Main Street, Samuel's door was closed but Freddie's was wide open. Samuel had a part-time receptionist, but Gwen was nowhere in sight, so Mila popped her head around Freddie's open door, to find his forehead scrunched as he studied his laptop screen.

'Hey there. Got a minute?' she called out, not surprised when his frown cleared and he grinned as she entered his office.

'I always have time for you,' he said, standing and moving around his desk to pull out a chair for her. 'Nice to see you, Mila.'

With his wavy auburn hair, hazel eyes, and ready smile, Freddie was easy on the eyes and nice to boot. But there was no spark despite his many attempts to manufacture one over the years, and when she'd announced her whirlwind engagement to Phil, he'd been surprised. But considering his eagerness now, he must've heard about her aborted wedding like the rest of the town, and probably saw himself in the role of comforter.

'Thanks for making time to see me today,' she said, handing over one of the cups. 'I brought you coffee as a thank you.'

'That's kind of you.'

Their fingers brushed as she handed over the coffee and... nothing. It would be so much easier if she fell for a local guy, someone decent and respectable who understood her love of farming in the Wimmera. But there was a vast difference between entering into an arrangement with a friend who understood the status quo, like Phil, and encouraging someone who could have genuine feelings, like Freddie.

Phil understood the rigours of farming. The isolation. The loneliness. Freddie was a townie—even if Ashe Ridge was a small town—and he'd expect a relationship to be real from the beginning. Something she couldn't offer anyone, not with the constant financial stress of keeping Hills Homestead afloat consuming every waking moment, and most sleeping ones too.

'I'm sure you're sick of people saying they're sorry about your wedding not going ahead, so I won't say it.' He perched on the edge of his desk and raised his coffee cup. 'Here's to you being single again.'

'Some things aren't meant to be,' she said, smiling behind her cup as his eyes lit up when she didn't chastise him for his lack of sympathy. 'Now that I'm not marrying Phil, I'm looking into selling a tract of land to an investor.'

'Sounds like a plan if you can tackle that tricky subdivision clause. Who's the buyer?'

'I don't know yet. Sawyer Mann's broking the deal and he has the power to render the subdivision clause void apparently.'

A tiny furrow appeared between his brows. 'Sawyer's back in town?'

'Yeah. My brother couldn't make the wedding, so Sawyer came instead.'

'Uh-huh,' Freddie mumbled, and she knew why.

Freddie had been a year behind her at school and even then, he hadn't hidden his crush well. He'd asked her out once and she'd said no, using Sawyer as an excuse—that they were almost dating and Sawyer wouldn't like it—and she'd caught him casting Sawyer death glares at school afterwards.

After Sawyer left town, Freddie had joked she was free to date him, but she'd shut him down again and he hadn't pushed the issue since. But many years had passed, and it looked like Freddie still wasn't Sawyer's biggest fan.

'Make sure you have Sam look over any contract,' Freddie said, sounding like a disapproving parent.

'Absolutely. Though I trust Sawyer. He's a friend.'

'Friendship and business don't mix,' Freddie said. 'Get everything in writing.'

'I will. Though I assumed selling to an investor would be easier for the accounts. Less complications than dividing assets with a spouse?'

He nodded. 'It is. I can forward you some information on deals of this kind. And once Sam's looked over the contract, I'll go over it too, check out the financial ramifications.'

'Thanks, that'd be great.' She handed him one of the bags. 'Almost forgot. I got you a vanilla slice to go with that coffee.'

He smiled his thanks and took the bag. 'You sure know the way to my heart.'

She refrained from rolling her eyes, just. 'Email me that info and I'll make an appointment with Sam as soon as I get the contract.'

'That's wise.' He stuck his nose into the bag and inhaled. 'These vanilla slices have to be the best in Victoria.'

'You won't get any arguments from me.' Mila rattled her own bag. 'I swear they put some secret ingredient in the custard.'

They laughed and once again Mila wondered how much

easier her life would be if she could spark with a nice guy like Freddie.

'I'll walk you out,' Freddie said, placing the bag on his desk but hanging onto his coffee.

She wanted to say, *'No need'* but she'd said it in the past and Freddie walked her out regardless. He came across as the wisest thirty-one-year-old she knew with his old-fashioned manners, unless he reserved his chivalry for her in a never-ending attempt to impress her.

When they reached the door, Freddie placed a hand in the small of her back and she tensed. But his expression was guileless as he said, 'Take care, Mila.'

'You too.'

A trite response, but by Freddie's beaming grin, he really thought she meant it.

Increasingly uncomfortable under his unwavering stare, she looked away, only to lock gazes with Sawyer, gawping at her from across the road.

CHAPTER TWENTY-SEVEN

Sawyer had woken at dawn after another crap night's sleep. It didn't sit well with him that he'd lied to Mila but what choice did he have? If he told her the truth about who was buying her land, she'd send him packing.

So to ease his conscience, he started proceedings to acquire the land not long after he woke. Work always kept him focused. He thrived on routine, the exact opposite of the scatterbrain he'd been growing up. Back then, he couldn't concentrate for longer than a few minutes and he'd acted out accordingly. To this day, he couldn't believe not a single one of his teachers had picked up on why he couldn't focus in class. Instead, they'd labelled him as the class clown and dismissed him, shifting their attention to the smart kids.

That was the kicker in his education. He *was* smart, they just hadn't cared enough to notice.

These days, he didn't dwell on the past. No good came of it, other than to undermine his self-esteem, which had taken a long time to build. With every land deal he brokered, he gave an imaginary finger to everyone who ever doubted him.

His biggest nemesis at school had been Mr Zavi, who taught science and maths, Sawyer's worst subjects. Numbers blurred before his eyes most days and he couldn't think straight when faced with convoluted problems. Rather than offering him help, Mr Zavi would torture him, picking on him to answer questions every chance he got. When Sawyer couldn't respond that sadist would get a smug look on his face and move on to a classmate guaranteed to answer correctly, leaving Sawyer feeling lower than a grass snake.

He'd hated that prick. Who was now walking towards him, leaning heavily on a cane.

Too late to cross the road, Sawyer squared his shoulders, noting the exact moment the teacher caught sight of him. His eyes screwed up for a moment, as if trying to place him, before the guy actually beamed.

What the...

'Sawyer Mann. Good to see you.' He held out his hand and Sawyer struggled not to gape at the teacher's overt friendliness when he'd been nothing but a condescending prick to him at school. 'I heard you were back in town after all this time.'

'Hey, Mr Zavi.' Sawyer shook his hand out of politeness, thoroughly bamboozled by the older man greeting him like a long-lost son.

'Call me Dave. I heard you're a land broker now. Good for you.' He chuckled. 'No thanks to me. I was hard on you in high school.'

Sawyer struggled not to gape for the second time in as many minutes as 'Dave' continued. 'Some of us older teachers were clueless back then. The young ones coming through now are much more up to date with learning diffi-culties and the like.'

All Sawyer could do was mumble 'Yeah' in agreement, considering an unexpected lump of emotion stuck in his throat. He'd harboured resentment towards so many in this town after he left—a major reason why he never returned—so to have Mr Zavi articulate how badly he let him down, and to acknowledge he'd missed the fact Sawyer had learning difficulties it inexplicably made him want to bawl.

'Are you busy right now? A bunch of us old-timers, plus quite a few young guys, get together at the Men's Shed every week. We have a cuppa, stuff our faces with baked goods, and have a yarn.' Dave jerked his thumb over his shoulder. 'We're about to meet in about ten minutes if you want to pop in and say hello?'

The last thing Sawyer felt like doing was seeing any of his old teachers, but hearing Dave apologise had been cathartic and it couldn't hurt to drop by for a few minutes. Besides, it might take his mind off Mila for all of two seconds, especially as he'd just seen her looking awfully cosy with Fred McInnerney.

That's the Freddie she'd been referring to when they talked a few days ago. If he'd known it was the same Fred who'd trailed after her at school almost panting, he would've questioned her further. And by the proprietary way Fred had his hand in the small of her back, it looked like Fred wasn't averse to stepping in and comforting Mila after her aborted wedding.

What was it with slimy pricks in this town? 'Sure. I can pop in.'

'Great. I'll see you there in a minute.' Dave grimaced and used his cane to point to his knee. 'Just going to the chemist to grab some painkillers. Had an arthroscopy on this bung knee last month and it's still giving me hell.'

Sawyer made a sympathetic noise and said, 'See you there.'

Mila had seen him staring at her and Fred a few minutes ago and he'd gawked like an idiot before coming to his senses and rushing off. But now he'd be retracing his steps to the Men's Shed and if it gave him a chance to run into Mila and suss out the real deal with her Fred it'd be worth it.

As Dave limped away, Sawyer turned back and headed towards the annexe to the Town Hall which must be the Men's Shed. He thought it was a great initiative, giving men a safe space to hang out, men who would otherwise avoid a trip to the doctor or psychologist. Similar programs ran in many towns and cities around the country, with men's book clubs and the like. There'd been nothing like that when he'd been at school, suffering in silence. The sole counsellor who served teens in the entire Wimmera area only made it to Ashe Ridge High once a month for a morning and was booked solid with kids who had 'serious' issues like eating disorders or self-harming.

Little did they know that what he went through at school was deemed serious enough in the grand scheme of things. If he hadn't been diagnosed after he left town, he'd still be drifting through life, unable to stay at one job for long, clueless as to why he couldn't stick at anything like other people. Jobs, relationships, friendships, they'd been transient for him—which is why he valued Will and Mila so much. They were the only ones who stood by him regardless and he'd never forget it. He owed them, big time, so he'd rescue Mila if she wanted him to or not. It's the least he could do.

As he neared the shed, he saw Mila perched on the bonnet of her car, like she'd been waiting for him.

'Where did you run off to?' She tipped an imaginary cowboy hat. 'The least you could've done is say hello to Freddie.'

He gritted his teeth at her flippancy. 'You didn't tell me your accountant Freddie is Fred McInnerney, who followed you like a lapdog.'

'Didn't I?' She tapped her bottom lip, pretending to think, before bursting into laughter. 'You should see your face. Jealousy isn't a good look on you.'

'I'm not jealous,' he muttered, hating that he was. 'I just don't like guys pawing you when you're vulnerable.'

Anger sparked her eyes. 'I can take care of myself. Especially with the likes of Freddie.'

Just like that, his indignation faded. He had no right to tell her how to handle any man. It wasn't his place. And his reaction to seeing Fred's hand on her back should be enough of a warning that he hoped for far more than friendship with Mila for however long he was in town.

'I saw you talking to Mr Zavi. Was he welcoming the prodigal son?'

'He invited me to pop into the Men's Shed, which is what I'm about to do.'

She waved her hand at the annexe. 'Knock yourself out. It's popular with the local blokes.'

'Can we catch up later?'

She quirked an eyebrow. Damn, he loved her sass. 'Only if you've got good news for me.'

'I might.'

'Then come over for dinner. I'll make my famous chicken curry.'

Sawyer would love nothing better than to have dinner

with her again. But the memory of that kiss had kept him up all night and the thought of spending time alone with her again at Hills Homestead, the one place in this town he'd considered a sanctuary more than his own home, meant he could be headed for trouble.

When he took too long to answer, she said, 'You don't have to.'

She sounded hurt and he silently cursed.

'I'd love to.' But he had to be honest so they were under no illusions. 'Though after that kiss yesterday, and despite our protestations it didn't mean anything, aren't you concerned we may not be able to keep our hands off each other?'

She winked. 'I'm counting on it.'

He laughed, loving her sense of humour as much as her sass. 'I'm serious.'

'So am I.' Her expression turned sombre. 'I'm not usually impulsive. I can't afford to be, living in this town. But we're friends, Sawyer. And I'm closer to you than most. Then there's the attraction between us, which, if that kiss is any indication, is pretty damn sensational, so how about we don't second-guess anything and just go with the flow?'

He admired her honesty. Wish he could say the same about himself. Because whatever happened between them, she'd ultimately hate him for withholding the truth from her.

But he swallowed his reservations because this was Mila and he cared about her, more than was good for him.

'Going with the flow sounds good to me,' he said, and he saw relief in her eyes. 'We're really going to do this? Because you know there's an unspoken rule about mates and their sisters.'

'But Will's a million miles away.' She widened her eyes

in faux innocence. 'And what my overbearing, bossy brother doesn't know won't hurt him.'

They laughed in unison, but Sawyer knew he was toying with trouble, and Will finding out about them would be the least of his worries.

CHAPTER TWENTY-EIGHT

Jack offered Adelaide a lift into town when he headed to the Men's Shed, and she'd agreed. It would give her time to do what she'd aimed to do by sticking around for more than a few days.

See a lawyer.

As fate would have it, Samuel Nobil's office was almost directly across the road from the Men's Shed, held in an annexe adjacent to the Town Hall, and she hoped Jack wouldn't see her entering. She wanted to be fully informed before she sprung the idea of a divorce on him, especially after how nice he was being.

She'd been amazed by his thoughtfulness this morning: patching her up after her tumble, serving her breakfast, their casual conversation. They'd been discussing fraught topics, like their dating life over the last fourteen years, and even though she'd sidestepped his probing question about whether she loved Raven or not, he'd still been civil after they'd finished eating and had offered to take her into town.

They'd made small talk in the car too. Was it a good

year for crops? Who would win the most prizes for the biggest vegetables at this year's fair? Did the bakery still make the best snot-blocks in western Victoria? He'd hated when she called vanilla slices by their slang name, so she'd bought him one whenever she went into town when they were married. It had been their in-joke.

Chatting with him in the car, hot on the heels of their breakfast, made her think. She'd never thought people were capable of change, but it looked like Jack wasn't the man she married. When she'd left, he'd been taciturn and inflexible. Now, he seemed to be communicative and open-minded, and was treating her better than she deserved. So for a fleeting second, as she pushed open the door to Samuel Nobil's office, she wondered if she was doing the right thing in divorcing Jack.

Not that she'd ever consider moving back to Ashe Ridge —she valued her artistic life by the ocean too much—but seeing the new improved Jack filled her with regret. The main one being that she hadn't been around to see Jack change. She couldn't help but wonder: if she'd stayed, would she have been happy when Jack became the man she thought he could be?

A young woman she didn't know, thank goodness, sat behind the receptionist's desk, and glanced up when Adelaide entered.

'Can I help you?'

Adelaide nodded. 'I'd like to make an appointment to see Mr Nobil, please.' She glanced at the open door with his nameplate. 'He wouldn't happen to have any free time now?'

The sooner she got the ball rolling, the better, before she lost her nerve.

The receptionist glanced at a computer screen and

shook her head. 'I'm sorry. He's all booked for the rest of the week and the earliest appointment I can offer you is next Friday at eleven. Does that suit?'

Not really. It meant she'd have to stick around for another ten days. But she'd come this far, and she had a comfortable, rent-free place to stay courtesy of Jack, so she'd have to do it. Besides, it would be foolish to leave before they got divorce proceedings underway. Doing everything in person would be much easier than organising the signing of paperwork remotely, even though she assumed it could be done digitally these days.

'That's fine. Adelaide Hayes,' she said, entering the appointment into her phone and adding a reminder. Not that she'd forget something as important as instigating her freedom officially.

'We'll see you then,' the receptionist said, with a cool smile, before returning to her computer screen.

As Adelaide left the lawyer's office, she intended on heading to the bakery for one of those famous snot-blocks. However, when she glanced across the street and glimpsed Jack through the open doors of the annexe, holding sway in front of a group of men, she hesitated. It was called Men's Shed for a reason—women weren't welcome.

But seeing Jack so animated, talking with his hands and throwing his head back and laughing, captivated Adelaide. She'd never seen him like that.

Drawn towards the annexe against her will, she stood near the door, just out of sight, and eavesdropped. She couldn't quite hear what Jack was talking about, but the regular laughter from the other men warmed her heart.

It looked like the reserved man she'd married had found his tribe. Unexpected tears burned her eyes, and she knuckled them away. She'd immersed herself in a new life and felt blessed she'd found herself after losing much of her identity after marrying, becoming a mother, and a grand-mother. It had been a struggle initially, dealing with the guilt of walking away from Jack, but as the years passed she thought of him less and less, imagining him mired in the drudgery of the farm.

To find him living in her dream house, cooking up a storm, surrounded by friends who obviously cared about him, made her equal parts happy and sad. Happy that he'd been living a better life than the one she'd envisaged for him and sad because the man he was now was the man she'd always wished he could be.

As she turned away, her foot caught on a crack in the pavement and she stumbled, grabbing the door to steady herself. It moved fractionally and creaked, drawing Jack's attention.

Heat flooded her cheeks in embarrassment as he caught sight of her. But rather than his gaze radiating disapproval as she expected, Jack winked, and she raised her hand in a half-hearted wave before scurrying away.

CHAPTER TWENTY-NINE

Mila made the chicken curry by rote. Sautéed the onion, garlic, and ginger, threw in the diced thighs, added cumin, coriander, turmeric, and chilli powder, added half a tin of coconut milk, brought the lot to the boil before turning down the stove to simmer. This had been her comfort meal for as long as she could remember, ever since she'd had dinner at her first Indian restaurant as a ten-year-old with her parents in Melbourne.

She'd never forgotten it, as it had been the night her parents had told her and Will they'd be living with their grandparents while Cam and Julie headed overseas to work. Will had asked how long for and when her parents had given a vague answer, Mila had known deep down it could be indefinitely. Will didn't want to leave Melbourne, but she couldn't wait to get to the farm where she'd spent all her school holidays. Living with Gran and Gramps would be a dream come true—and it had been. Her folks were rarely home anyway, so she'd practically raised herself.

Thankfully, Will adapted to life in Ashe Ridge quickly.

He'd already made friends with Sawyer years earlier during the summer holidays and Mila didn't know who was more rapt they'd moved, her or Sawyer. He spent more time at Hills Homestead than he did at home and the three of them became a tight unit. She'd never taken their friendship for granted, which made her hand tremble slightly as she diced coriander to garnish the curry when it was done.

Because tonight, she planned on moving out of the friend zone and into the bedroom.

She'd seen the wariness in Sawyer's eyes when she'd flirted with him earlier today. He'd been conflicted and she understood. But he didn't live here, and he didn't know loneliness had plagued her for a long time. Getting physical with her friend would be special and more enjoyable than the meaningless hook-ups she'd had over the years. She worked hard and was shouldering a tonne of stress. Why shouldn't she have a little well-deserved fun?

A short rap sounded at the back door before Sawyer opened it. 'Hey. Hope it's okay I'm early?'

Her pulse raced as she drank in the sight of him in jeans and white T-shirt, casually delectable. 'You know you're welcome here any time. Come in.'

He sniffed as he closed the door. 'Wow, something smells amazing.' He brandished a six-pack of her favourite beer. 'These are chilled, but I'll pop them in the fridge.'

'Thanks.'

Heat scorched her cheeks as she watched him bend over and slide the beers to the back of the fridge. His butt could tempt a nun. When he straightened, she quickly turned back to the stove, needing a ready excuse for her burning cheeks.

'Anything I can do?' He crossed the kitchen to stand behind her, too close.

'All good. The rice cooker should click off any second and the curry needs to simmer for another fifteen minutes, then we can eat. Hope you like it spicy, because I may have overdone it with the chilli.'

Heck, she was babbling, and he laid a hand on her shoulder before gently spinning her around.

'I'm just happy to eat a home-cooked meal so anything you dish up will be fine with me,' he said, his palm branding her through the thin cotton of her top. 'I don't cook very often. Seems like too much trouble doing it for one person, so I grab a pre-prepped salad from the super-market or heat up a frozen meal.'

'I like to cook. It soothes me.'

Almost as much as his touch, so when he removed his hand from her shoulder she stifled a groan of disap-pointment.

'Well, if your curry is as good as that lasagne I had last night, you better be careful, because I might just move in.'

His flippant comment warmed her more than it should. What would it be like to have someone like Sawyer as her partner? Some-one to shoulder the burden of running a farm? Someone to offload to at the end of a long day? Someone to hold her in his arms and reassure her that everything would be okay?

She'd never been interested in living with anyone, hadn't cared enough about anyone to contemplate it, then her friendship with Phil had deepened over the last year and she'd come to depend on their evening chats.

But living with someone like Sawyer... her pulse raced at the thought, because Sawyer was different. Sawyer was the guy who'd stolen her heart as a teen and, by her reaction to him now, still held it in the palm of his hand after all these years.

'You'd hate living with me,' she said, picking up the ladle to stir the curry. 'I like my condiments in orderly rows in the fridge, I like my pantry neat, I snore, and I hog the doona.'

The corners of his mouth kicked up in a sexy smile that made her heart skip a beat. 'Who said I'd be sharing your bed if I moved in? We could be roomies.'

She loved the twinkle in his eyes almost as much as their banter. 'You wouldn't be able to resist this.' She gestured at her casual outfit of denim skirt ending just below her knees and blue short-sleeved top and cocked her hip.

She expected him to laugh, but as his eyes darkened to indigo and his gaze travelled over her like a slow caress, her skin pebbled.

'You are pretty irresistible,' he said, his voice husky, and he cleared his throat. 'But by the look in your eyes, I think you should feed me first, because I have a feeling I'm going to need all the energy I can get.'

They laughed and continued to laugh all through dinner. After Sawyer had demolished two servings of rice and curry, and the last pappadum had been eaten, they took their beers through to the living room.

Sawyer hadn't mentioned business over dinner and Mila hadn't asked. He was doing her a favour in securing a buyer for her land and she didn't want him to think the only reason she wanted him around was because of that.

She sat and propped her bare feet on the coffee table, wriggling her unpainted toes. When Sawyer sat beside her, close enough she could rest her head on his shoulder, she did exactly that.

They didn't speak as he slid his arm around her so she could snuggle closer, and with her stomach full and her heart at peace for the first time in a long time, she closed her eyes.

The comforting familiarity of his crisp vetiver after-shave and the warmth from his embrace lulled her, and she sighed, more content than she'd been in ages.

Guys liked to talk—about themselves, mostly—so having Sawyer remain silent, as if sensing her need to decompress, meant a lot.

She could get used to this.

CHAPTER THIRTY

Sawyer had never had a woman fall asleep on him. But that's exactly what Mila did after dinner. And she hadn't been wrong about the snoring. A chainsaw had nothing on her.

He stifled a chuckle as she let rip with a particularly loud snort, knowing she'd hate him for not waking her but enjoying the unexpected comfort of having her warm and pliant.

He never did this. Have a homemade meal with a woman, then sit on the couch and just... be. When he dated, he had dinner at a restaurant and usually went back to the woman's place. He valued his privacy and his space and didn't want either intruded upon by someone he wouldn't see more than a few times, if that. He liked his life uncomplicated, the antithesis of what it had been growing up.

But he knew that spending time like this with Mila was one giant complication waiting to happen.

She hadn't pushed him about the land deal, and he hadn't volunteered the information. Time enough after dinner. If she ever woke up, that is.

It didn't sit well with him, withholding the truth that his company was acquiring her land. But Will knew her better than anyone and if her brother insisted that Sawyer keep his involvement in this acquisition a secret, he'd do it.

Not that he was a complete idiot. Getting Will's blessing might soothe his conscience, but it didn't change facts.

He was lying to Mila.

A woman he cared about.

And it would be an absolute shitshow if she ever found out.

Earlier today, when he'd been finalising the paperwork to present to her, he'd convinced himself that even when he eventually told her the truth, she'd be grateful he'd stepped in to save her dream. One friend helping out another. What was so bad about that?

But when he'd arrived here for dinner, seen her comfortable in the kitchen, independent and loving it, with fire in her eyes as she pushed the flirting boundaries, he knew he was kidding himself.

She'd flay him alive.

Mila stirred and he instinctively tightened his arm around her.

Rather than snuggle into him as he hoped, she stiffened.

'I'm assuming it was a full stomach that put you to sleep and not my scintillating company,' he murmured, as she eased away and he reluctantly let her go.

'I can't believe I fell asleep. Hope I didn't drool on you.' She patted his chest to check and he didn't mind a bit.

'No, but you were right about the snoring.'

She grimaced. 'Sorry about that. I'm not sleeping well at the moment.'

He'd like to think he had something to do with that—that he invaded her thoughts as much as she invaded his—but in reality, it probably had more to do with the financial stress she was under.

'I might be able to help with that.'

She quirked an eyebrow. 'That's awfully presumptuous of you. Dinner doesn't mean a sleepover, you know.' She winked. 'Not that there'd be much sleeping going on.'

The image of the two of them in bed together had him biting back a groan. He'd like nothing better than to spend the night if she meant it. But he'd been the king of deflection growing up, using humour to distract from how he was feeling, and he recognised Mila doing the same thing now.

'Nice to know how your mind works,' he said, earning a playful whack on the arm for his wolfish grin. 'But I was actually referring to the deal I've brokered for your tract of land that will enable you to finish your farm-stay project.'

Mila squealed so loudly he winced and covered his ears. 'Are you serious? I didn't want to push you earlier and ask about it, but this is really happening?'

'It's happening,' he said, the joy on her face making his deception a little easier.

Not that he was deliberately deceiving her. He just wasn't telling her the entire truth about who was acquiring her land.

'You're amazing,' she said, launching herself at him so hard that they tumbled back on the couch, with her lying on top of him. 'Thank you.'

'My pleasure,' he murmured, his arms sliding around her to anchor her, the weight of her making breathing difficult. Though that had more to do with her breasts pressed against his chest and her pelvis flush against his.

He should sit up, laugh off her exuberance, and suggest they have a coffee to wind down the evening.

But as Mila's gaze focused on his mouth and her tongue darted out to moisten her bottom lip, he knew he had as much chance of stopping this as coming clean on the land deal tonight.

'Mila, if we start something now, it's going to end with me staying the night. Are you sure you want that?'

'I'm very sure of what I want.' The corners of her mouth kicked into a naughty smile that made his heart sing. 'And that's you.'

CHAPTER THIRTY-ONE

'It's been a while since I've had dinner at the pub,' Jack said, raising his glass. 'Thanks for inviting me.'

Adelaide raised her wine glass and clinked it against his. 'It's the least I can do, shout you dinner after you're letting me stay in your bungalow rent-free.'

'Who said it's free?'

For the second time today, Jack winked, and Adelaide had no idea if her husband was flirting or making a joke.

Her husband... Since when had she started thinking of him in those terms? For years now, she'd labelled Jack as her ex, to herself and anyone else who asked. And after her visit to the lawyer's office today to make an appointment, she'd taken the first step to make sure the 'ex' label became a reality.

But she'd been so flustered after seeing Jack in his element at the Men's Shed—and that cheeky wink after he'd caught her spying— that she hadn't told him about making an appointment with Samuel Nobil and invited him out to dinner instead.

She'd been surprised he'd accepted so readily, even

more so when he'd knocked on the bungalow door to pick her up and she'd opened it to find him dressed in black pants, burgundy shirt, and polished boots that looked new. He'd never worn anything other than flannelette and jeans in winter, work shorts and singlets in summer. On the rare occasion they went out, he'd grumble about having to wear his one good pair of jeans and a button-down shirt.

It looked like this new and improved Jack extended to his wardrobe too, and she wondered if his better dress sense had something to do with a woman. He'd already told her he'd dated occasionally out of town, but would he tell her the entire truth? She didn't want to answer questions about Raven, so she shouldn't expect him to tell her everything despite how badly she wanted to know.

'What are you thinking about?'

She blinked and refocused, to find Jack staring at her so intensely heat flooded her cheeks. 'How much I miss my painting. It grounds me.'

He didn't believe her and to his credit he called her on it. 'What are you really thinking about?'

'You,' she blurted, before she could censor her response. 'And how much you've changed.'

His eyebrows rose but he didn't say anything, his scrutiny increasingly unnerving.

'What are you thinking?' she asked, putting the onus back on him, not sure if she really wanted to know.

After a long pause, he said, 'I'm thinking how nice this is.' He shook his head. 'When I found you on my doorstep a few days ago, I didn't know what to expect. But this...' He waved his hand between them. 'It's better than I expected.'

'That's because you've been extremely generous and accepting, rather than angry like I deserve.'

A tiny dent furrowed his brow. 'I let go of my anger a

long time ago. It serves no purpose, other than to give me heartburn.'

Adelaide was tempted to dig deeper, to ask how he'd coped in those initial months after she fled, but the pub wasn't the place to have a deep and meaningful conversation, not when they were already drawing curious stares from every patron in the place.

Sensing her discomfiture with being the centre of attention, he leaned forward and lowered his voice. 'Let them look. Nothing to see here.' He raised his glass again. 'Yet.'

She laughed, unsure what he intended to do to shock the gossips but sorely tempted to find out. 'What did you have in mind?'

He tossed back the rest of his wine in two gulps before placing the glass on the table and holding his hand out to her. 'I reckon we give them something to really talk about.'

She eyed his hand warily. Was this some kind of joke? Why would the man whose heart she'd broken want to touch her let alone hold her hand?

But the amusement in his eyes reassured her and, before she could second-guess, she placed her hand in his.

'I don't bite,' he said, with a chuckle. 'Do you trust me?'

She'd once trusted this man enough to abandon a life of luxury and the only home she'd ever known to move to a lentil farm in the Wimmera and marry him. She'd trusted their love would be enduring and get them through anything. She'd trusted in the life they'd built.

But that's the thing about blind trust. When the blinkers are ripped off, you realise you believed in a fairytale that could never come true.

Quashing the hurt of the past blossoming in her chest, she forced flippancy. 'Whatever you're thinking, Jack Hayes, that glint in your eyes tells me I should be worried.'

'I'd never do anything to hurt you, Ads,' he murmured, a moment before he lifted her hand to his mouth and did the most shocking thing of all.

Pressed a kiss to the back of it.

A soft, lingering kiss, his lips warm and firm as they brushed the skin just above her knuckles, setting her pulse racing in a way it hadn't since... the last time he'd touched her, years ago.

Their gazes locked, and she hoped he couldn't see how badly she wanted him to do it again.

And this time, not stop at kissing her hand.

CHAPTER THIRTY-TWO

As the first streaks of dawn stole over the horizon, Mila headed for her favourite thinking place.

The biggest eucalyptus on the farm.

She'd been drawn to this tree alongside the small dam since the first time she visited the farm as a five-year-old. It had been her parents first visit to Hills Homestead since her dad left his family home where he'd grown up and she'd been wide-eyed at the extent of the farm and the paddocks of lentils Gramps had shown her. He'd been the one to introduce her to the dam too, lecturing her about the importance of never coming here alone until she was old enough.

Turned out, that had been eight, when she'd bolted from the homestead in tears and headed for the dam after her parents calmly announced they wouldn't be staying for Christmas, but she could spend the entire school holidays here. They'd thought it would be a consolation prize and they'd been right, because for those six weeks at Hills Homestead she'd learned the only people she could depend on were her grandparents and Will, and that her parents were the two most selfish people on the planet.

She'd been gutted that her family wouldn't spend Christmas together for the first time and she'd sought refuge under the eucalyptus at the dam. She loved rubbing the leaves between her fingers and inhaling the pungent fragrance, she loved pressing her cheek to the smoothness of the bark, and she loved the warbling magpies that perched on the branches high overhead.

That day, not even the soothing sounds of the birds could comfort her, and she'd been sobbing her heart out when Sawyer found her. He'd come over to play with Will and seen her tearing from the homestead like she had a demon on her tail, so he'd followed her.

She'd been mortified he caught her crying, but rather than teasing her as expected, Sawyer had sat next to her on the ground and didn't say a word. He waited until she stopped crying and when she did, he handed her a crumpled tissue from his pocket.

Looking back, that was probably the first time she fell for him a little, and when he'd plucked a gumnut from her hair and presented it to her like a diamond ring, she'd fallen even more.

He didn't know she kept that gumnut and that she only pretended to hate it when he called her Gumnut from that moment, when in fact she loved having a nickname born from a special moment.

Because that moment beneath the eucalyptus had been special, for no other reason than she realised she could be herself in front of him and he'd be understanding. Will teased her mercilessly at that age, but Sawyer never did, as if sensing she needed people to depend on.

And in the ensuing years, she'd come to this spot whenever she needed comfort. Not that she needed comfort now, per se. But after the incredible night she'd spent with Sawyer, she needed to think.

Where did they go from here?

She knew what would happen. Their 'morning after' would consist of them reverting to their flippant best, maybe laughing off what they'd done. They'd share an affectionate hug, attribute what they'd done to two consenting adults having fun, and move on. Once Sawyer helped broker the deal for her land, he'd leave town, and she'd be left...what? Lamenting that she hadn't spoken up and told him the truth? That last night had solidified what she'd known since their teens: they were great together.

She sighed and closed her eyes, images of the two of them instantly replaying: their frantic hands practically ripping off clothes in their desperation to get naked, his skill in adoring her body with his mouth and hands, the sensuality that made her feel wanton in a way she never had. Sex in the past had been fun but forgettable. Sex with Sawyer... surpassed every single fantasy she'd ever had.

The best part had been the intimacy afterwards, how he'd cradled her in his arms and they'd made small talk, laughing over shared memories. They had history and that meant getting physical last night changed everything. Sawyer wasn't some short-term fling she could happily walk away from. Being with Sawyer had her craving more and that wasn't good, because he'd leave all too soon and she'd feel lonelier than ever.

Everyone in her life left eventually. Her folks, Will, Gran — even Gramps had moved away from the farm. She knew it wasn't fair, lumping Sawyer in with those who'd hurt her by their abandonment. He'd left a long time ago and was only in town on a fleeting visit as Will's proxy at her wedding, but with the boundaries of their relationship changed, she'd feel just as sad when he walked away.

'Thought I'd find you here.'

Her eyes snapped open to find Sawyer with bed-rumpled hair and a lopsided smile that twanged her heart. She'd been so caught up in mulling she hadn't heard him approach and didn't have time to assemble a game face, so she momentarily gaped at him.

He placed a finger under her chin and gently pushed. 'I don't look that horrific first thing in the morning, do I?'

'You look amazing and know it,' she grumbled, making him laugh. 'Did you sleep okay?'

'No,' he murmured, their gazes locking, the latent heat between them instantly flaring to life.

'That was some night,' she said, wrapping her arms around her middle so she wouldn't be tempted to reach for him, drag him over, and pick up where they'd left off.

'Sure was.'

They lapsed into awkward silence and Mila could see the confusion in Sawyer's gaze matched hers.

'When do you move in?' she deadpanned, noting his shock a second before she winked and their laughter defused the tension.

'Hey, I've already offered to do that, but you wouldn't have me.' He clutched at his heart. 'Which wounded me deeply, I'll have you know, that you'd consider marrying Phil and not me.'

'You're welcome here any time and you don't have to be a groom,' she said, meaning it.

He knew it too because his smile softened. 'This place was my second home. Better than my own, most days.'

He'd never revealed too much of his home life to her and Will and they'd never pushed. She respected his need for privacy because she feared if she probed he'd ditch her, and she'd liked having him around too much. But they were all grown up now and she was curious.

'You never spoke about your family much.'

'That's because I preferred to forget how damn lousy things were at home.' He sounded resigned rather than bitter. 'Dad was a mean drunk. Mum was a doormat. And once my sisters left they didn't give a shit about me.'

'I heard your dad died in Melbourne. Is your mum still there?'

He shook his head, sadness clouding his eyes. 'She met some guy from Christchurch and moved there a few years ago. She seemed happy enough the last time I saw her, but her new bloke has the same narcissistic, bossy tendencies as Dad. I hate to think she finally escaped Dad's clutches only to get attached to another prick.'

Mila winced. 'Sorry to hear that. Have you seen Allison yet?'

His guilty expression answered her question before he spoke.

'Will you think less of me if I say no?'

'I'd never judge you,' she said, taking hold of his hand, an instinctive gesture to comfort that felt way too right. 'We've all got crap in our lives and families are complicated.'

He stared at their joined hands for a moment before turning his over and intertwining their fingers. 'You always had the ability to do this,' he said, his tone wistful.

'Do what?'

'Make me feel better no matter how bad things got.'

'It's a gift.' She smiled, but there was no levity in his gaze.

'I mean it, Mila. You were the only person back then

who got me, and I've never forgotten. Which makes what we did last night...' He shook his head and looked away. 'Last night was incredible but I'd never want to hurt you intentionally and—'

'Hey, nobody's getting hurt. We had an amazing night, we're still friends, so let's leave it at that, okay?' She squeezed his hand, relieved when he squeezed back.

But he hadn't lost the tension in his shoulders, his back ramrod straight, and when he looked back at her, she could see he was conflicted.

'I know we joke around a lot, but I want you to know you're special to me.'

Her chest tightened and tears inexplicably sprung to her eyes, so she did what she did best: deflect with flippancy. 'Right back at you, lover.'

CHAPTER THIRTY-THREE

Sawyer managed to sound engaged by asking questions as Mila took him on a tour of her farm-stay project. *What's the rate of occupancy required to break even? How long until you turn a profit? Who's your competition in the area?* He asked all the right things but barely registered her answers, because all he could focus on was the curve of her neck, the line of freckles below her right ear, the way her ribbed singlet clung to breasts he'd explored at length last night . . .

Man, she'd blown his mind.

He'd had enough one-night stands in his life and knew what to expect. Once the initial attraction got sated with sex, the awkwardness set in, and he couldn't wait to extract himself and get away.

But that hadn't happened with Mila. Not that he'd expected to treat her as a one-night stand, but he'd thought things could get messy afterwards and he'd find himself bolting for the motel. Instead, they'd spent an incredible night talking and cuddling and snoozing between three bouts of memorable sex, and now strolled around the farm, back to their usual banter.

He couldn't get enough of her.

Which meant he was screwed, considering he'd be leaving some time in the next week.

'Are you even listening to me?' She snapped her fingers in front of his face. 'I know I kept you up all night but come on, a guy like you should have stamina.'

Another thing he loved, her ability to make light of their time together and not tiptoe around it like something to be avoided. He wasn't a complete idiot and had thought having sex might change their friendship, but he should've known Mila wouldn't let that happen. She'd always been there for him, had this way of propping him up when he needed it most.

'A guy like me?'

'Now you're just fishing for compliments.' She snorted and punched him on the arm. 'I was asking what you thought about the idea of getting a few animals to keep the kids entertained.'

'Kids? But we've only had one night together. Aren't you thinking too far ahead?'

Shock widened her eyes for a second before she groaned. 'You are such a pain in my arse.'

'And what a fine arse it is.' He grinned and she slugged him again, but this time they ended up play-wrestling until they were breathless, her hands pinned behind her back, her body pressed against his. 'Now this is more like it.'

He heard her sharp intake of breath, felt the exact moment she relaxed into him. 'I thought last night was a one-off?'

'Do you want it to be?' He didn't.

He wanted her, all of her, for as long as he could have her. Seeing her passion for the farm-stay project, how she came alive, vindicated his choice in helping her out. He'd done the right thing, even if he couldn't tell her about it.

But last night changed everything.

He wasn't just investing in her business; he'd become invested with his heart too.

He couldn't see a future for them—or maybe he didn't want to think that hard right now—but for however long he was in town, he wanted to be with Mila.

'What I want is for us to christen the first cottage.' Her eyes darkened with passion as she arched a brow in provocation. 'You up for it?'

Sawyer didn't have to be asked twice.

'Should I ask why you have a blanket and pillow in this cottage, or will I hate the answer when you tell me you bring all your men here?'

'Only the special ones.' Mila tucked the blanket tighter over them. 'Aren't you lucky?'

Sawyer growled and nuzzled her neck until she squealed. 'Okay, okay, the truth is I work late in here sometimes and I get really tired, but if I have a power nap I can keep going until all hours, so that's why I stashed the blanket and pillow here.'

'I can live with that,' he said, savouring the feel of her in his arms. 'The thought of you entertaining faceless men I'd like to pummel, not so much.'

'Jealous?'

'Hell yeah,' he said, surprised by how much he meant it. He had no right to be possessive—they were friends indulging a mutual passion—but the thought of Mila with any guy made his blood pressure rise.

'Let's just say out of the two of us, I'm pretty sure your record with the ladies must far outweigh the occasional fling I've had.' She patted his chest. 'But please don't tell me about them, because I'll want to claw their eyes out.'

'Now who's jealous?'

They laughed and snuggled into each other, and he never wanted to let her go. A crazy thought, because he couldn't live in this town and she was too heavily invested in the farm to ever leave.

'I've got a question for you,' she murmured, tilting her head back to look at him. 'I know you won't be sticking around much longer, but do you want to stay at the homestead for however long you're in town?'

Her invitation had him equal parts stunned, elated, and wary. Stunned because he knew that meant she wanted to continue the physical side of their relationship for however long he was in Ashe Ridge, elated because he'd like nothing better, and wary because the closer they grew the harder it would be when he walked away.

'Or you could continue staying at the motel and hanging out with Shazza in the hope Simone is still pining for you and will come back?'

He pinched her butt and she giggled, the innocence of it shooting him straight through the heart.

'Thanks, I'd love to stay,' he said, terrified by the adoration in her eyes.

Would her feelings turn to condemnation when she learned the truth? Because Sawyer knew if he moved into the homestead, even for a few nights, their relationship would deepen and that meant ultimately telling her the truth before he left.

It was the right thing to do.

CHAPTER THIRTY-FOUR

Unlike many of Tally Bay's inhabitants, Adelaide didn't fit into the cliche of an artist. She didn't smoke or ingest weed to spark creativity, she didn't join in their sound circles, and she didn't only paint when the urge hit.

She believed picking up a paintbrush daily honed her craft. Even the odd day when she couldn't express herself, she still painted something, anything. Which meant she'd never gone this long without painting, and it made her feel out of sorts.

Her excuse and she was sticking to it.

Of course her restless night and constant edginess this morning had nothing to do with Jack's demeanour over dinner at the pub last night, or that kiss on the back of her hand. Nothing at all. It had been Jack play-acting for the gossips who'd watched them keenly throughout dinner.

But no matter how many times she dismissed that kiss as meaningless, she couldn't stop thinking about it. Or the way it made her feel.

Since when did a harmless kiss on the back of her hand

jolt her libido? So she did the one thing guaranteed to snap her out of day-dreaming about her ex.

She called Raven.

Perching on a log, she tapped the icon on her phone and it barely rang before his face popped up on her screen.

'Hey, beautiful, it's good to hear from you. How's things?'

The familiarity of Raven's smile, the creases fanning from the corners of his brown eyes, the wisps of grey hair escaping from his ponytail, should've comforted Adelaide. They didn't, and she knew her accelerated heartbeat had more to do with how she'd have to fake it for him rather than the low-key attraction they shared.

'Good. Though my granddaughter's wedding didn't go ahead.'

His smile faded. 'Is everything okay?'

'Yeah. Long story. I'll tell you when I get back.'

'And when's that going to be?' Raven wiggled his bushy eyebrows. 'I'm missing my favourite gal.'

Raven said that to every woman over the age of eighteen who entered the juice bar. An outrageous flirt, he made her laugh most days, and she knew that was a major attraction after the fraught silences of her marriage. Their occasional coupling suited her. Scratching a physical itch and keeping the doubt demons at bay, the ones that whispered in her ear she was lonely and selling herself short.

'Probably another two weeks. I'm enjoying catching up with Mila and I think she needs me right now.'

'Gotcha.' He winked and peered closer at the screen. 'I must say, that country air suits you. You're glowing.'

Adelaide blushed, wondering if her glow had more to do with Jack's attention last night than the air.

'You're gorgeous, woman,' he said, his grin salacious.

'Get back here ASAP, so I can prove in the best possible way how much I've missed you, okay?'

Usually, Raven's overt antics entertained. Today, he came across as sleazy.

'I'll let you know when I'm back,' she said, ignoring his blown kiss and ending the call.

So much for a distraction. She thought seeing Raven's handsome face, hearing his voice with the faint Irish lilt, would take her mind off her wayward thoughts about Jack. Turns out, not so much. In fact, she couldn't help but compare the two men. How easy things had been between her and Jack last night despite their tough history, how he'd made her feel relaxed, whereas Raven's interest came across as slimy rather than funny as she usually found it.

She knew no good could come of acknowledging her growing attraction to Jack, which is why she'd embarked on this long walk at the crack of dawn. But not even a two-hour round trip had helped, and as she stood and dusted off her butt before striding towards the final bend, she knew she might have to leave sooner rather than later. Once her car had been repaired, she'd see if the lawyer had any cancellations, so she could finalise what needed to be done and head off.

As the cottage came into view, an unexpected peace descended over her. She shouldn't be getting too comfortable but in a short space of time, the cosy bungalow had become a refuge. It probably had to do with the sandstone walls she'd coveted forever, and the feel of the place She really hoped she wasn't getting too attached because of the man who lived a hundred metres away.

Sighing, she opened the door, and stopped. Her mouth hung open as she saw what someone—had to be Jack—had propped by the window flooded with morning light.

A wooden easel with a blank canvas, and a caddy filled with brushes and tubes of paint.

How on earth... Why... Then she remembered mentioning to him yesterday how much she missed painting. It had been a throwaway comment, something she'd thought he hadn't paid any attention to. Why would he, when he hadn't taken any interest in her painting in the past?

But to find this...

Overwhelmed by emotions she had no hope of interpreting, Adelaide burst into tears. Loud, racking sobs that had snot streaming out of her nose and made her chest ache.

She couldn't believe he'd done this.

The man she'd hurt, the man she'd abandoned, the man who should hate her, had given her this thoughtful gift.

When her tears petered out, she cleaned herself up in the bathroom and made a beeline for Jack's cottage. Nerves made her stomach churn as she knocked on the back door, though what she had to be nervous about she had no idea. Jack had done something incredibly thoughtful so she'd thank him, then go explore those paints. Nothing grounded her like staring at a blank canvas and imagining it come to life, and she couldn't think of anything else she needed more right now.

Jack didn't answer so she knocked again, louder this time, and when he finally opened the door, wearing a towel and a bashful smile, she did an impulsive, crazy thing she knew she'd regret.

She flung herself into his arms and kissed him.

CHAPTER THIRTY-FIVE

Phil's ute pulled up shortly after Sawyer left and Mila quashed her annoyance at him showing up without letting her know first.

She wanted to tell him off, but regardless of what had happened, Phil was still her neighbour and friend, and they'd be seeing more of each other whether she liked it or not. Besides, with Sawyer coming through for her and securing a buyer for her land, she should be happy she'd had a lucky escape and hadn't had to marry for money.

'Howdy, neighbour,' Phil said, raising his hand as he got out of the ute.

'You're not a cowboy,' Mila muttered, earning a grin.

'Can't you give a guy a break? I'm still feeling awkward around you.'

'And whose fault is that? You ditched me, remember?'

Phil grimaced. 'Actually, that's why I'm here.'

If Phil thought she'd marry him now, he had rocks in his head. 'My image in town has taken a battering after I called off the wedding, so I'm hoping to get back in the good books by hosting a B & S ball on my property.'

Mila cared about Phil so she knew it must be tough, being judged and found lacking. Nothing like small-town gossip to make you feel like a fly under a microscope. After lunch with Sawyer at the pub where she'd braved a confrontation with Anne, she'd felt the curious stares every time she ventured into town. She hated the pitying glances almost as much.

'Sounds like a plan,' she said, wondering what him hosting a ball to salvage his reputation had to do with her.

'I was hoping you'd help me plan it?'

She barked out a laugh. 'You've got some nerve, Phil Baxter. Why don't you ask your new girlfriend to help?'

He had the grace to look sheepish. 'She's from the city and doesn't have a clue about Bachelors and Spinsters balls.'

'Too bad,' Mila drawled, almost laughing out loud at Phil's hangdog expression. 'Besides, I don't have the time.'

Not with getting the farm-stay project finished now she had the funds and spending her nights with Sawyer. She'd blurted that invitation for him to stay at the homestead in a moment of post-coital brain fade, immediately regretting it when he'd appeared shell-shocked.

But then he'd agreed, and she couldn't help but imagine the nights ahead... the two of them sharing dinner, their usual banter making everything seem better, then slipping between the sheets...

'Hey, you drifted off for a second,' Phil said. 'If you can't help, maybe your gran can? I saw her last night at the pub looking awfully cosy with Jack. I think it's great they're back together. How's that for romance? Anyway, I assume she's staying here and might be able to help plan the ball?'

Gran and Gramps had been having dinner at the pub?

And were cosy enough that Phil thought they were back together? Interesting.

That's when an idea shimmered to life and Mila suppressed the urge to do a jig.

Addy and Jack had met at a B & S ball. It had been love at first sight, with Addy so enamoured of Jack she left her cushy life in Melbourne behind and moved to the farm to be with him. While Mila could never imagine making such a huge sacrifice for a guy, she'd always found their tale incredibly romantic.

With Gran back in town, and Gramps amenable to having her around from what Mila had seen and heard, what would happen if Cupid gave them a nudge in the right direction?

She wasn't averse to donning wings and slinging arrows if it meant her grandparents could reunite for real. What better way than reminding them of how they first met?

'Actually, Phil, I can rejig a few of my commitments and help with the ball.'

'That's great.' Phil beamed and held a hand up for a high-five. 'I want the ball to happen sooner rather than later, because I'm tired of the angry glares and cold shoulders already. So I was thinking of holding it next week?'

Her eyebrows rose. 'That soon? What about the marquee, permits, music, and the rest?'

He waved away her concerns with a smugness that grated. 'I've got friends in high places, so the permits are taken care of. Marquee is booked. I'm waiting to hear back from three bands. And four food trucks are on board.'

Before Mila could ask what he needed her help for, he said, 'If I'm still in the bad books, people might not come. But if you spread the word, show you're supporting this, I reckon we could get a good crowd and bring the town together again.'

Meaning, encourage townsfolk to forgive him. She understood. She'd gotten off lightly in their aborted wedding—and so she should, considering he'd called it off—but Phil had shouldered all the blame, knowing how people talked. The least she could do was help him regain favour.

'I'll do whatever you need me to,' she said. 'It's been a while since this town had a big shindig to attend. This could be fun.'

'Absolutely. Gail, my girlfriend'—he blushed, and Mila stifled a laugh—'is a graphic designer so she's done an amazing flyer. I'll email it to you and perhaps you can get it printed and distributed through town?'

'Not a problem.'

'Thanks, Mila, you've been a real sport about all this. We've been good friends for a long time, and I hope that will continue.'

'Of course,' she said. 'Our bonfire chats kept me sane the last year or so.'

'Same.' His arm swept wide, encompassing the farm. 'This life isn't for the faint-hearted.'

'You got that right.'

They laughed and, thinking about their friendship and how close they'd got to marrying, she felt obliged to tell him about her new housemate. 'By the way, Sawyer's moving in here while he's in town.'

Surprisingly, his lips thinned, and he frowned. 'Won't that get people talking?'

'No more than they're talking about you moving on after ditching me.'

'Touché.' His laugh sounded forced. 'It's your business, Mila. I'm just looking out for you.'

'I appreciate your concern, but it's unwarranted.'

He nodded before heading to his ute, so she turned away and strode towards the homestead, grateful they were still friends and relieved he'd called off their sham wedding.

She now had an investor providing her with funds for her project and she had sexy Sawyer for as long as he was around.

Win-win.

CHAPTER THIRTY-SIX

After leaving Hills Homestead, Sawyer wanted nothing more than to speed back to the motel, pack, check out, and head back to Mila.

But she'd pricked his conscience when she'd asked if he'd visited Allison yet and he knew what he had to do.

He'd put off visiting his sister since he'd arrived in town for the simple fact they rarely spoke anymore. He saw Phoebe and Jocelyn annually, but that's only because he moved around the country for work and they caught up for a quick drink.

But the last time he'd seen Allison had been at their dad's funeral five years ago, and even then it had been awkward. Faking grief didn't lend itself to bonding, and his sisters had been as relieved as him when the wake ended so they could all go back to their lives.

With the big age gap between him and his sisters, he wondered if their father had always been a prick, or if it had been his unexpected birth that set Henry off.

The thing is, his sisters weren't close to their father but that could be because Phoebe and Jocelyn moved away as soon as they turned eighteen and, like him, they never returned. Only Allison had stuck around, and he had a feeling that's because she'd made the mistake of marrying a man like Henry.

He thought they might talk about it at the wake, but they'd made small talk mostly, stilted conversation centring around their respective careers while nibbling on stale cucumber sandwiches and drinking watered-down alcohol.

Their mother hadn't attended the funeral and none of them blamed her. Bernadette had called them on the day, a group chat where she offered her condolences for losing their father but hadn't wanted to accept any in return. At least his mother had finally grown a backbone and put the past behind her once and for all.

Jocelyn and Phoebe didn't have kids, but Allison had two, Brett and Aimee, who he sent digital gift cards to on their birthdays and Christmas. They were ten and eight, but he'd never met them. They hadn't come to the funeral, staying at home with Alli's husband Mick instead, and his sister didn't seem to care. During their occasional text or phone call, she never asked when Sawyer might visit. Like everyone, she assumed once he left Ashe Ridge he'd never return. Which had been his intention, until Will had coerced him into attending Mila's wedding.

Life had a funny way of kicking him up the arse when he least expected it. Returning to town had been shocking enough without adding falling for Mila to the mix.

Not that he was stupid enough to fall in love, but she'd captivated him in a way he'd never expected, and he couldn't get her out of his head. If their night together had been spectacular, this morning in the cottage... he got hard just thinking about it.

Not the best when he intended on visiting his sister, so he stopped by the motel for a quick shower—a cold one—before packing and checking out. Thankfully, Shazza wasn't around, and Maggie didn't care he was leaving earlier than expected. With his bags in the boot, he made a stop at the bakery and toy shop before heading to Allison's, keen to get this obligatory visit out of the way so he could head back to Hills Homestead.

He should've called to alert his sister, but he didn't, for the simple fact he wanted to see if she was okay. If his suspicions were correct, and Mick resembled Henry in the husband stakes, knowing anyone would be dropping in meant putting on a show.

He'd seen his parents do it countless times—usually when one of his sisters' friends were coming over, even a teacher on the odd occasion. Henry would be on his best behaviour, acting like a solicitous husband and a caring father, when nothing could be further from the truth. During those visits, his mum would be more chatty than usual, but her laughter would be forced and he often wondered if anyone saw beneath his family's brittle surface to the festering wound beneath.

In reality, Henry was an abusive drunk who despised his wife and loathed his kids, and Bernadette put up with it for the sake of the family. Sawyer hated himself, wondering if he hadn't come along when he did would his mum have escaped Henry years earlier. Sawyer loathed his father.

Ironic, considering he was the only one at his father's bedside in that nursing home in Melbourne as Henry drew his last breath. He'd done it because he had been in the city at the time and couldn't see the point in Jocelyn and Phoebe flying in or Allison making the long drive, when Henry wouldn't have recognised them anyway. Dementia had ravaged him at the end and his passing made it easier on everyone.

As Allison's house came into view, a pang of guilt made Sawyer grip the steering wheel tighter. Rundown to the point of dilapidation, the weatherboard cottage with a tin roof had seen better days. Though the garden appeared well kept, and the kids' bikes propped against the side wall looked newish. An older SUV sat under a listing carport and he could've sworn it resembled his mother's old car.

He parked under the shade of a towering eucalyptus, grabbed the apple tea cake and the newest handheld video gaming devices. The gifts for the kids were excessive, and Allison would probably chastise him for trying to buy his way into her kids' good graces, but he didn't care. He hadn't given his niece and nephew much thought over the years beyond the obligatory gifts and now that he was here, it didn't sit well with him.

What kind of a selfish prick hadn't met his sister's kids after a decade?

Dread settled in his stomach as he knocked on the front door. This visit could be a disaster and he braced for a confrontation. Of his three sisters, he'd been closest to Allison, but that had been a long time ago and if she didn't appreciate him lobbing on her doorstep, she'd let him know.

The door opened and he smiled at his sister's open-mouthed shock. 'Surprise, Alli.'

'I was wondering when you'd show up.' She folded her arms and glowered. 'Brett said he thought he saw you in town the other day, but I said he had rocks in his head.'

Sawyer grimaced. 'Sorry. I should've popped in earlier but there's been a bit going on.'

She arched a brow. 'Like?'

'If you let me in, we can demolish this apple cake and I'll tell you all about it.'

She huffed out an annoyed breath, but her expression softened. 'Fine. But if you say one thing about the mess, I'll clobber you with a cricket bat like I did when we were kids.'

He laughed at the memory, even if he'd bawled at the time. She'd been painting her toenails, probably to impress a boy at school, and he'd snuck up on her with a frog in his hands. She'd screamed, smeared her polish, picked up the closest weapon—his cricket bat— and whacked him on the arse, hard.

As he followed her into the house and down a hallway towards the kitchen, he noted the faded wallpaper, the peeling cornices, the dusty skirting boards. But contrary to what Allison had said, the rest of the place was tidy, and as they entered the kitchen, the simmering casserole in a slow cooker filled the air with tempting aromas of garlic, rosemary, and onion.

'Dinner's on because the kids always want me to help them with their homework when they get home.' She glanced at her watch. 'They'd love to meet their uncle, if you want to stay for dinner.'

The last thing Sawyer felt like doing was spending the entire afternoon talking to his sister, but he didn't want to hurt her feelings, so he said, 'I've got other plans for dinner, but I'd love to meet Brett and Aimee.' He brandished the bag in his hand. 'I've got something for them.'

'Bribery will get you everywhere with those rascals. Want a cuppa?'

'Yeah. Coffee. Black please.'

Guilt swamped him again that he'd stayed away so long his own sister didn't know how he liked his coffee.

'I'm assuming you came to town for Mila's wedding?'

He nodded. 'Will got Covid and couldn't travel from London, so he asked me to attend in his stead.'

'London, huh?' She picked up a knife and started slicing the apple tea cake. 'The last time I made it anywhere near a city was when I was in Melbourne for Dad's funeral.'

He didn't know what to say to that, so he changed the subject. 'How's Mick?'

'Good,' she said, a little too quickly, as she deposited the sliced cake and saucers on the table. 'He's doing handyman work these days.'

'Uh-huh.'

Henry hadn't been able to hold down a steady job and took on odd jobs when he could, calling himself a handyman. The only thing their father had been handy with was a beer bottle.

Sawyer would hazard a guess that's why Allison had dinner cooking too. Mick would breeze in, asking *'What's for dinner?'* before scoffing the lot and abandoning the family to plonk himself in front of the TV. Of course Alli would be the one to help the kids with their homework. Mick would be too 'tired' to help, despite probably spending more time at the pub than he had doing actual physical labour.

'So what happened with Mila's wedding? I heard it got called off.'

'Yeah.' Though it wasn't his place to elaborate. 'Heard from Phoebe or Jocelyn lately?'

Sadness clouded her eyes, and she shook her head. 'We all lead very different lives these days and the few times we chat, we've got nothing in common anymore.'

He understood. It's exactly how he'd felt about all his sisters his entire life.

'What about Mum?'

Allison shrugged. 'She calls occasionally, and she sounds happy, so that's enough for me.'

Alli didn't have to add, *'after all she put up with'*. If anyone in this world deserved happiness, their mother certainly did.

'What about you? Anyone special in your life?' Allison placed steaming mugs of coffee on the table and sat opposite him. 'Please tell me something, anything, that's more interesting than my part-time job at the supermarket or navigating parent–teacher interviews at the school.'

'No one special,' he said, unwilling to reveal a snippet about his burgeoning relationship with Mila. She'd be living in this town long after he left and the last thing she needed was more gossip about her romantic life. 'Not that I'd tell you if there was.'

She laughed at his wink. 'I assume you're staying at the motel? Unless Shazza chased you off for that stunt with Simone.'

'This town has a long memory,' he said, with a smile. 'As intimidating as it was running into her again, I have been staying at the motel.'

'Have been? You're leaving?'

Damn, maybe he should've lied to his sister about his new lodgings, but how would that look if she found out?

'Actually, Mila said I could stay at the homestead.'

'I heard she's getting a farm stay off the ground. It's great you get to test out the cottages firsthand.'

To his mortification, heat surged to his cheeks at exactly how he'd tested out one of those cottages with Mila.

But he managed a sedate, 'Uh-huh,' not correcting his sister's assumption that he wouldn't be staying in the main house.

'You spent so much time at Hills Homestead I always

thought you had a thing for Mila, but then you left town without a backward glance the day after your final exam.'

'Will and Mila were my best mates and I hated being at home.'

If his blunt honesty surprised her, she didn't show it. 'I know it must've been tough on you after I moved out.'

He nodded. 'The age gap between us sucked, because after you left, I was the only one left to bear the brunt of Dad's crap.'

'He was a mean son of a bitch sometimes.'

'Try all the time.'

With his sisters gone, Henry turned his special brand of hatred on to him and Mum. She'd tolerated so much—because of her kids, he always suspected—and that's something Sawyer had to live with every day.

Allison grimaced. 'I hate to speak ill of the dead, but the speed with which the dementia took him was the best thing that ever happened.'

'You'll get no arguments from me.'

Sawyer hadn't come here to rehash the past, so he said, 'You've got a few hours before the kids come home, yeah? How about we stash this tea cake for later and head to the pub for a drink?'

Allison's eyebrows rose. 'I can't remember the last time I had a drink in the afternoon.'

'Well, you're a big girl, Alli, and this is the first time I've been back in this godforsaken town in fifteen years, so let's go out and celebrate.'

The cheeky expression he remembered well—usually alerting him to her teasing him mercilessly about something—lit up her face. 'You've twisted my arm. I can definitely go an espresso martini.'

'Then what are we waiting for?'

CHAPTER THIRTY-SEVEN

Adelaide didn't have time to second-guess her decision to kiss Jack, because the moment her lips touched his, she combusted.

All rational thought left her brain as his lips commanded hers in a familiarity that snatched her breath. Her mouth opened beneath his, their tongues duelling, their hands everywhere as she couldn't get enough of her soon-to-be ex-husband.

Her palms skated over his damp skin, exploring, savouring, remembering old dips and ridges, discovering new ones. And when his hands slid over her butt and pulled her flush against him, the evidence of how much he wanted her made her devour him anew.

They kissed until breathless, dragging in great gulps of air before going back for more, making out like a couple of teenagers. Lost in their passion, they staggered and bumped into the kitchen bench, resulting in a pot clattering to the floor with a resounding crash.

It didn't stop them. They clung to each other, frantic

and desperate, and Adelaide knew she'd never felt more alive.

As her fingers toyed with Jack's towel, he stilled and wrenched his mouth from hers. They stared at each other, wild-eyed, as reality crashed over them.

'What the... I mean... You... ' He trailed off, lost for words, and she didn't blame him. She could hardly form a coherent thought, let alone an explanation for the way she'd launched herself at him.

Finally, after what seemed like an eternity, she managed to engage her brain and mouth to work in sync. 'I wanted to thank you for the easel, canvas, and paints. I guess I got overwhelmed by emotion and a little carried away.'

'Uh-huh,' he mumbled, still appearing shell-shocked, so she aimed for levity.

'Then again, who can blame a gal if you answer the door wearing nothing but a towel?'

He glanced down, his expression horrified as he belatedly realised the cotton towel with frayed edges had seen better days and still sported an impressive tenting.

'I just got out of the shower. Back in a minute,' he said, all but running from the kitchen, and she stifled a laugh.

What the hell had she done?

Mauling her husband before she divorced him hadn't been on her agenda. What they'd just done... what she would've done if he'd let her whip off that towel... a giant complication she hadn't anticipated.

Considering their lack of intimacy for the last few years of their marriage, she'd long ceased to equate Jack with sex in her head. The two were poles apart. But their passionate interlude a few minutes ago seriously messed with her logic.

They'd spent fourteen years apart.

She'd walked away from him, and he hadn't come after her. She had to finalise their divorce and stop skirting around it.

So how could she explain their make-out session? She might've lost her head in the heat of the moment, caught up in her gratitude for his thoughtfulness.

What was his excuse?

She paced the kitchen and eyed the back door. She could make a run for it. But what would that achieve other than staving off the inevitable? She couldn't avoid him forever—she had no car, was taking advantage of his hospitality, and he lived about a hundred metres away.

When Jack hadn't appeared five minutes later, she filled the kettle and flicked the switch on. A nice chamomile tea would be perfect right about now to calm her nerves, but she settled for English Breakfast.

She'd just poured boiling water into two cups when she heard Jack clearing his throat behind her. She didn't know what to expect when she turned around. Would he be able to look her in the eye or would mortification set in? Would he make light of what they'd done or avoid the topic altogether?

The old Jack would've chosen the avoidance method, but when she turned, the vulnerability in his eyes slayed her.

'I fancy a cuppa,' he said, crossing the kitchen, and she bit back her first flirty response, *But do you fancy me?*

'I made it extra strong.' She handed him a cup, and as their fingers brushed a sizzle shot up her arm. So much for forgetting their lapse in reason. Looks like her body hadn't got the memo.

'Thanks.'

He didn't sit and she didn't either. No point getting cosy. They needed to confront the elephant in the room before she escaped, never to come out of the bungalow ever again until her car was fixed and she could zoom out of town. After that one important meeting with the lawyer, that is.

Adelaide inwardly groaned. What would Jack think when she told him about making an appointment with Samuel Nobil to get divorce proceedings underway? After their kissing session, he'd probably think she'd been buttering him up, and that didn't sit well with her. She'd never do something like that. Underhanded wasn't her style. Then again, Jack probably already thought the worst of her, considering she abandoned him years ago.

She took a deep breath and exhaled slowly, gathering her nerve. 'Jack, we probably need to talk about what happened.'

'Let's not,' he mumbled, staring into his teacup as if the leaves would tell him his fortune. Pity she'd used tea bags.

This was the Jack she knew. Recalcitrant. Guarded. Non-communicative.

But she'd learned a lot the last fourteen years—particularly never put up with shit—so she confronted problems head-on.

'I like how we've been getting on. Dinner at the pub last night was great, best time I've had in ages, so I don't want what we just did to ruin the tentative friendship we've re-established.'

He raised his head and eyeballed her. 'Is that what we're doing here? Becoming friends?'

'Honestly? I haven't got a clue what we're doing but I'd like to think we're friends.'

He snorted and gestured at the bench where they'd

knocked the pot off in their stumbling around while lip-locked. 'Friends don't do that.'

'Friends with benefits do.'

His eyebrows rose so high they almost reached his hair-line. 'Is that what you want? A quickie for old times' sake before you hit the road again?'

She winced at how crass that sounded. 'I don't know what I want.'

But that was a lie.

She wanted him.

And that confused her more than ever.

She'd walked away from this man because she didn't want him. Because he'd morphed into a stranger over the years. Because he didn't love her anymore. Because their marriage had become a trap rather than a haven.

So why on earth did she want him now, in every sense of the word?

Jack sighed and pinched the bridge of his nose. 'I think it's pretty obvious we're attracted to each other. But I'm not screwing around here, Ads. If we do... this '—he waved his hand between the two of them—'it's going to mean some-thing. At least, it will for me, and I won't have my heart broken all over again when you leave.'

Her jaw dropped at his honesty.

'What? Is that too blunt for you? Well, here's another dose of reality. I know I was a shitty husband to you. I know running the farm consumed me and maintaining my family legacy became all-important.'

Pain shadowed his eyes as his mouth twisted into a self-deprecating sneer. 'And I also know I should've come after you when you left but I was too damn hurt to see straight.'

He thumped his chest. 'Have I missed you? Hell yes.

Have I grown accustomed to living on my own? Yes. And I'm doing okay. But then you strut in here all gorgeous and friendly and I can't see straight let alone think'

He sighed and shook his head. 'I haven't got a bloody clue what's happening here, Ads, and it terrifies me.'

That made two of them, and as she laid her hand on the table palm up, and he placed his over hers, she had no idea where they went from here.

CHAPTER THIRTY-EIGHT

Mila wanted to enlist Adelaide's help in planning the B & S ball, so she headed to her grandfather's place. It would be nice seeing the two of them together for the first time in forever.

Not that she expected them to be cosying up. Gramps would be hiding out in the cottage; Gran would be keeping her distance in the bungalow. But the fact they were both on the same property could only bode well. She hoped.

As she neared the front door, movement inside the front window caught her eye. More precisely, the movement of her grandparents strolling into the living room.

Holding hands.

Mila gawped, stunned by the sight of the two people she loved most in the world holding hands when they hadn't communicated in years after Gran broke Gramps's heart.

So much for her matchmaking plans with the ball. Looked like her grandparents were doing a fine job themselves of rekindling an old flame.

Not wanting to interrupt, she took a step back, and trod

on a rake Gramps had left propped beside the verandah. It clanged against the railing and alerted her grandparents to her presence, leaving her no option but to knock on the door. It opened quickly and she struggled to hide her surprise.

Gramps sported a grin the likes of which she'd never seen before. He looked... happy.

'Hey, kid, nice to see you.'

'You too, Gramps.' She hugged him and glanced over his shoulder in time to see Gran smoothing her hair. Heck, what had these two been up to? On second thoughts, Mila didn't want to know.

'Your grandmother is here.'

'Great. I need to talk to her about something, but thought I'd drop in here first and say hello.' She paused for emphasis. 'It's good to see the two of you together.'

'We were just talking.'

To her surprise, her stoic grandfather blushed, and Mila knew they'd been doing more than talking.

'That's good,' she said, squeezing his arm before walking into the living room. 'Hey, Gran. How are you?'

'Fine.' Gran's response came too quickly, and when a faint pink stained her cheeks too, Mila couldn't help but smile. 'I was just heading back to the bungalow after a cuppa. Nothing like it to get the blood pumping.' Addy's blush deepened. 'Anyway, thanks, Jack. I'll see you later.'

For the second time in as many minutes, Mila gaped. She'd never seen her poised grandmother so flustered.

'We'll talk more then,' Gramps said, sending Gran a pointed look that couldn't be misinterpreted as anything other than *Running away now won't solve anything*.

Whatever they'd been discussing must've been big for them to be holding hands. That's when it hit Mila.

Maybe they'd been discussing formalising their divorce?

Rather than reconnecting as she hoped, they might've been talking about the past and getting nostalgic or saddened by the prospect of divorcing and had been comforting each other.

Whatever had gone down, she hoped the B & S ball might spark memories for them and give them a gentle nudge in the right direction: towards reconciliation.

'Gramps, I need to talk to Gran, but I'll stop by when I'm leaving.'

He shook his head. 'I'm headed out. I might drop by the farm tomorrow and we'll catch up then?'

'Sounds good.' She pressed a kiss to his cheek. 'If I'm out in the paddocks, Sawyer will be around.'

Gramps's eyebrows rose, and she continued. 'He's staying in town a bit longer and the motel isn't conducive to comfort for more than a few nights, I've got the room, so I invited him to stay.'

As expected, Gramps frowned. She may be thirty-two and capable of making decisions, but Gramps still treated her like a teenager at times.

But before he could say anything, Gran said, 'I've got a fair bit on today, Mila, so if you want to chat, we'll have to do it now.'

She shot her intuitive grandmother a grateful look. 'Okay. Bye, Gramps.'

With that, she all but bolted from the room into the kitchen and out the back door with Addy. Only after the door closed did they slow down and take one look at each other before bursting into laughter.

'You should've seen the expression on your face.' Addy

chuckled. 'It was exactly the same when we had the period talk.'

Mila smiled. 'Gramps looked like he was going to launch into a spiel about the inappropriateness of having boys sleep over.'

'He loves you. He's protective. Nothing wrong with that.'

Considering the dynamic of what she'd just witnessed, Addy leaping to Jack's defence didn't surprise Mila.

'You two looked awfully cosy when I arrived,' Mila said, fishing for information. 'Hope I didn't interrupt anything.'

'Don't be silly.' Addy snorted, but the colour in her cheeks deepened again. 'Your grandfather and I had dinner at the pub last night, because I wanted to thank him for letting me stay here, and we were just discussing that.'

'Right,' Mila said, stifling a giggle at the blatant lie. 'So talking about dinner at the pub makes your cheeks blaze the same colour as a fire engine.'

Addy made a pfft sound and Mila couldn't contain her laughter. 'Gran, I think it's great you and Gramps are on speaking terms, let alone able to coexist in the same room. I was incredibly nervous at the thought of you two seeing each other at my wedding after not speaking for so long, so being civil is nothing to be embarrassed about.'

Addy didn't speak as she opened the bungalow door and after they entered, Mila spied the easel and paints in the corner by the window where natural light streamed in.

'That's great you bought some supplies—'

'Jack did it,' Addy blurted, her voice quavering, and for a second Mila thought her grandmother might cry. 'I never expected him to be so welcoming, let alone thoughtful, when I don't deserve it.'

Mila had a feeling where this was heading—her gran

playing the blame game—so she headed her off. 'We all make mistakes, Gran. And if it's not a mistake, we make choices we think are right at the time. So whatever happened between you and Gramps in the past, I think it's incredible you're both big enough to acknowledge it and move on, without animosity.'

Addy sniffed and dabbed at the inner corners of her eyes with her pinkies. 'I don't want to hurt him again.'

'Is there a risk of that happening?'

Because that meant her grandparents had moved beyond friendship and Mila shared Addy's concern. Gramps didn't deserve to have his heart broken again, but if he'd opened himself up to Addy, and she left as intended, that might be a distinct possibility.

'There might be.' Addy sighed and sank onto the sofa. 'There's still a spark between us.'

'Wow.' Mila sat beside her. 'If you want my opinion, Gran, it's this. Tread carefully. Gramps is living his best life these days. He's come to terms with you leaving him. So if you start something up... it could get complicated.'

'Don't you think I know that?' Addy snapped, instantly remorseful as she reached out and clasped Mila's hand. 'Sorry, sweetheart. I'm edgy and confused.'

This is why Mila didn't do relationships. What she had with Sawyer was two friends indulging in some fabulous benefits, without the complication of feelings. They'd have fun, Sawyer would leave, and she'd throw herself whole-heartedly into making the farm-stay project a success and making a dent in her sizeable mortgage.

Gran and Gramps didn't just have a relationship, they were married, and with age came supposed wisdom. But now that she'd seen Gramps happy and Gran flustered, should she be dabbling in matchmaking? She'd thought reminding them of the past might rekindle feelings, but what if they'd already done that and were reeling from it?

'I'm not surprised you're edgy, Gran. It must be hard dealing with what happened in the past and everything that's now being dredged up. But for what it's worth, I think it's great you and Gramps are getting along after all you've both been through, and I reckon just play it by ear for now.'

Gran tweaked her nose, like she used to when Mila was a kid. 'Who made you so wise?'

'You did, considering you raised me.'

The twinkle in Gran's eyes faded. 'Have you heard from your parents recently?'

Mila shook her head, quelling the familiar surge of resentment that surfaced whenever she thought about her folks—which wasn't very often, by choice. 'Nope. It's been a few months. You?'

'About the same.'

Addy never badmouthed her son, but Mila thought Cam was lousy with family. He might not acknowledge his kids very often, but his parents were ageing, and he should keep in touch more often.

Keen to change the subject, Mila said, 'Anyway, what I wanted to talk to you about was giving me a hand planning a B & S ball.'

Addy brightened, before her excitement faded. 'I'd love to, but I won't be around long enough.'

'Actually, Phil's hosting it on his property next week.'

'Next week?' Addy's eyes widened in surprise. 'How on earth does he expect to pull together a ball on such short notice?'

'By coercing others, like you and me, to help.'

Astute as ever, Gran said, 'Is this because his reputation is in tatters after he ditched you at the altar?'

'It wasn't quite at the altar.'

Addy waved away the clarification. 'Regardless, I bet townsfolk can't stop pointing the finger at him and he's sick of looking like the bad guy.'

'Yeah, that's about right. So, will you help?'

'Sure. It'll give me something to do while I wait for...' Addy trailed off, her gaze oddly guilty as it slid sideways.

'For?' Mila prompted.

Addy blinked rapidly. 'For my car to be fixed.'

Once again, when Addy couldn't look her in the eye, Mila had a feeling her gran was lying.

CHAPTER THIRTY-NINE

Sawyer had never seen his sister drunk.

He'd been six when she'd finished school and moved out, the last of his sisters to abandon him. Though that was unfair. With the large age gap between him and his siblings, what had he expected? All the Manns couldn't wait to escape the overbearing presence of their father and the tolerant silence of their mother as soon as they finished school.

He hadn't missed Jocelyn and Phoebe as much as Allison, because they'd been sixteen and fourteen when he'd been born and already firmly entrenched in teen life: boys, boys, and boys. At twelve, Alli had more patience and had mothered him all through toddlerhood and beyond. He'd been distraught when she'd left home, a six-year-old all alone with parents who existed in frigid silence—when his father wasn't abusing his mother, that is.

So to see Alli grinning like a loon after three espresso martinis made him equal parts happy and wary: happy she'd had an opportunity to relax, wary that Mick wouldn't like coming home to a tipsy wife.

'The kids should be home any minute,' she said, ending on a hiccup, and giggled. 'Lucky, I got a friend to drop them off.' She held up two fingers in front of her face and squinted. 'I think I'm hammered.'

'Maybe you should've had more espresso, less martini?' he said, with a grin, and she giggled again, a girlish sound at odds with the weary expression she'd worn earlier.

'I never cut loose.' She snorted. 'I'll have a coffee now. Want one?'

He shook his head. 'I'm good. But I'm guessing I'll be helping the kids with their homework tonight?'

'Considering when I held up two fingers a moment ago I saw four, I think that's probably wise.' She paused at the sink, kettle in hand. 'Thank goodness Mick will be home late tonight.'

Sawyer stiffened, knowing it wasn't his place to pry into his sister's marriage, especially when he'd been lousy with keeping in touch, but concern driving him to ask, 'Why's that? Wouldn't he approve of you having a few drinks?'

She rolled her eyes. 'The running of the household is my domain, and he likes everything shipshape.'

Code for, he's a controlling prick.

Treading carefully, Sawyer said, 'He treats you well, yeah? And the kids?'

'He's a good provider most of the time. And he loves us.' She turned her back on him, effectively shutting him out, as she filled the kettle with water. 'But let's not talk about my mundane marriage. You're killing my buzz.'

Yeah, there could be problems in his sister's marriage, and he hoped she'd confide in him by the time he left town. Then again, what could he do? He had a feeling Allison, like many women, had resigned herself to a lacklustre marriage for the sake of her kids and wouldn't leave Mick, no matter how much of a bastard he was, sacrificing her sense of self to provide her kids with the illusion of a happy family.

That's what his mother had done for him, and he blamed himself every damn day for tethering her to Henry for far too long.

A tooting horn, followed by loud voices yelling 'bye', heralded the arrival of Brett and Aimee. Alli's face lit up in a way he hadn't seen until now as the kids barrelled into the kitchen, dumping their bags at the back door and skidding to a stop when they saw him.

'Hey, it's Uncle Sawyer from our chats on your computer, Mum,' Aimee said, eyeing him with blatant curiosity. 'We haven't seen you here before.'

'Yeah, you've never visited,' Brett muttered, his frown and puckering brow so reminiscent of Alli's that Sawyer had to stifle a smile.

'That's my fault, kids. I've been too busy with work when I should've been making time to visit my favourite niece and nephew.' He picked up the bags he'd stashed beside the dresser. 'I've brought you something I hope you'll like.'

He knew he'd gone overboard with the latest handheld video gaming console and two games each, but he felt bad for waiting so long to meet them face-to-face and hoped a little bribery might buy him forgiveness.

Both kids were rendered mute as they looked inside the bags, then back at him before peering into the bags again.

'Wow,' they said in unison, looking at each other with wide eyes like they couldn't believe their luck.

'What do you say?' Alli prompted.

Aimee said, 'Thanks, Uncle Sawyer,' a moment before Brett did.

'Perhaps once you get your homework finished, we can set up the systems and play a few games?'

'That'd be awesome,' Brett said, eyeing him with grudging respect. 'Do you know how to play the games, though?'

'You can show me if it's too hard.'

He'd said the right thing, because Brett beamed, and Aimee said, 'Let's do our homework super-fast so we can play with Uncle Sawyer.'

'Sounds like a plan,' Sawyer said, casting a glance at Alli who nodded in approval.

'Go wash your hands, get changed, then you can have a snack while you work,' Alli said, already slicing strawberries, rockmelon, and watermelon and arranging them on a platter.

The kids scrambled from the kitchen so fast they jostled for position through the doorway.

'They're cute,' he said, earning another smile of approval, this time from Alli.

'They're my world,' she said, the simplicity of her statement underscored with love. 'I'd do anything for them.'

Which virtually proved his theory: she was stuck in a dead-end marriage to a bastard for the sake of her kids.

'I've made you a coffee even though you said you didn't want one.' She handed him a mug and placed a plate of choc chip cookies on the table, along with the fruit platter. 'You're annoyingly sober.'

'One of us had to be the designated driver, and with you guzzling those martinis...' He made a skolling motion with his hand to his mouth, and she laughed.

'Thanks for this afternoon, little brother. I had a great time catching up.'

'Me too.' He squeezed her shoulder, and she leaned her

head against his hand for a moment, before straightening.

'Now, I hope you've got the patience of a saint because Brett can't sit still long enough to solve maths problems and takes forever to complete any English tasks.'

Sawyer froze, his blood turning to ice. He could be jumping to conclusions. There could be any number of reasons why a ten-year-old boy couldn't sit still to do his homework: he hated school, would rather be outside playing sport, he'd had a rough day and was tired.

He should know. He'd used all those excuses and more. But there could be another, more serious reason his nephew couldn't sit still or took a long time to problem-solve. A learning difficulty. Or ADHD.

After all, it ran in the family.

Before he could ask a question, Alli continued. 'Then again, it's not just confined to homework. I hear the same thing at parent–teacher interviews. 'Brett's a great kid but can't sit still in class. Brett's a daydreamer. Brett prefers to be outdoors than confined inside. Blah, blah, blah.' Her smile was that of an indulgent mother. 'As long as my kids are happy and healthy, I don't care. We can't all be brain surgeons, right?'

'Right.'

But kids who have genuine learning disabilities or ADHD can be diagnosed and help was available, two things he wished he'd known growing up.

He often wondered how different his life could've been if he'd been aware of what he was dealing with earlier, and if he could help his nephew in any way, he would.

However, before he could reveal his diagnosis to Alli, the kids ran into the kitchen and the moment was lost. He'd find another time. Time when he could stand up and be the uncle he hadn't been until now.

CHAPTER FORTY

Adelaide closed the bungalow door behind Mila and leaned against it.

What the hell had happened before her granddaughter had arrived for an impromptu visit?

One minute she'd been intent on thanking Jack for his thoughtfulness with the easel and paints, the next she'd been groping him.

And the rest.

She'd never been an overly sexual person but with Jack and those kisses... she hadn't been so turned on in all her life. At her age, the occasional sex she had with Raven was more about intimacy than the physical act. Truth be told, she enjoyed the snuggling afterwards a hell of a lot more than the actual mechanics.

But with Jack kissing her, his damp skin beneath her exploring hands, his erection pressing into her... she'd been obsessed with taking it all the way, the two of them naked, skin to skin.

At least they'd had a chance to talk about it, but if Mila

hadn't shown up when she did, who knows what might've happened?

Because the way she'd been feeling, Adelaide would've happily insisted they move their discussion into the bedroom.

Back home, when she was this rattled, she'd paint. And now, thanks to Jack, she could.

Taking a deep breath and blowing it out, she pushed off the door and crossed the room. Just staring at the blank canvas evoked peace, and after changing into the oldest shirt she'd brought with her, she picked up the piece of wood serving as a palette and squeezed blobs of paint onto it. Even the squelch of paint out of the tube comforted her and by the time she picked up her brush, she knew what she'd paint.

A calming mix of blues and greens slashed across the canvas with broad strokes became more precise as the picture she imagined in her head came to life. She lost track of time through the repetition of movement—dab, sweep, swirl—grateful for the escape her art provided. It always did and she should thank Jack again for the gift he'd given her.

Though this time, with less mauling.

Adelaide had no idea if she'd been painting for thirty minutes or three hours when she heard a knock at the door. She blinked and swiped a hand across eyes, laying the paintbrush and makeshift palette down, before crossing the studio to open the door.

Her heart rate instantly sped up. 'Hey, Jack. What brings you by?'

She managed to sound saucy and annoyed at the same time, and he reacted accordingly with a slight frown. So she still confused the heck out of him. That much hadn't changed.

'I'm throwing some pasta together; thought you might like some?'

'What's the time?'

'Almost six.'

'Wow, I didn't know I'd been painting that long.' Now she'd stopped, her neck muscles cramped and the spot between her shoulder blades ached, indicating she'd been at it for hours. 'Do you want to come in while I wash up?'

'Sure.'

He smiled and she swore her world tipped on its axis.

So much for painting relaxing her. In an instant she remembered the heat between them in his kitchen and what might've happened if one of them—him—hadn't come to their senses. Sharing dinner in that very kitchen so soon after what they'd done was asking for trouble.

Though would it be so bad? Technically, Jack was still her husband. And she only had a casual thing with Raven; they were both free to see other people.

But Adelaide wasn't a complete fool, and she knew having sex with Jack would change the dynamic between them. Not to mention make securing a divorce a tad more complicated.

'Are you going to let me in?' He cocked an eyebrow, and she gave a nervous laugh as she stepped back.

'Sorry. I'm always in a daze when I paint, and it takes me a while to come out of it.'

'I can leave you to it and see you at the house?'

'No, no, come in.'

As he entered, and she caught a whiff of his subtle soap combined with pure Jack, she gritted her teeth against the urge to bury her nose in the crook of his neck and inhale.

'I'll just rinse off the stuff I've been using and get changed.'

Rather than taking a seat on a chair, he strolled alongside her to the easel and dread crept through her. He'd never shown any interest in her art when they were married, and by a few offhand comments she'd assumed he deemed it frivolous and a time suck, which is why she'd eventually stopped sketching too.

Her art channelled her vulnerability, something that drew buyers to part with decent amounts of cash to acquire one of her paintings these days. She'd had several people say they loved the rawness of her work, the emotion behind it, and that was the highest compliment they could've paid her.

Now, she held her breath as Jack stood alongside her, hoping he wouldn't tear down the camaraderie they'd rebuilt with an ill-meaning critique.

She'd painted a beautiful cove at Tally Bay, the view from her favourite lookout. Craggy cliffs tumbling down to serene aquamarine waters bracketed by a white sandy beach. From a critical perspective, it wasn't her best work, but it definitely reflected her love for the spot. She could almost feel the sun on her face as she looked at it.

Jack's silence spoke volumes. He didn't like it. But when she snuck a glance at him, what she saw surprised her.

Sadness.

'Jack?' She tentatively touched his arm, and he tore his gaze away from the painting.

'You're good,' he said, his smile forced. 'I had no idea you were so talented.'

'I've been painting for the last fourteen years. It's how I make the bulk of my living.'

'I think that's incredible. It's special, being able to earn a decent wage from doing something you love.'

Was that what it had been like for him and the farm? Though from memory, every cent he'd earned had been a struggle and she'd resented his love for the farm over her.

'Thanks. That's what I think too.'

He pointed at the painting. 'Is this home for you?'

She nodded. 'The view from my favourite lookout at Tally Bay.'

'You must miss it.' His tone took on a hardened edge. 'I bet you can't wait to get back.'

So that's what his reticence was about. He thought she'd painted this because she couldn't wait to leave. That would've been true last week, but now Ashe Ridge held attractions she'd forgotten.

'I'm enjoying my time here,' she said. 'I'm in no hurry to return.'

Jack got the message loud and clear, because he took a step back, as if fearing she'd jump his bones again.

'I'll get that pasta started,' he mumbled. 'Just come across when you're ready.'

By the speed he bolted out the door, he understood why she was enjoying her time in Ashe Ridge.

So what was he going to do about it?

CHAPTER FORTY-ONE

After leaving her grandparents to their own devices, Mila stopped at the supermarket. She usually cooked sporadically, often making do with a frozen meal at the end of a long day on the farm. But with Sawyer staying, she wanted to make an effort. Not to impress him, but because it was the hospitable thing to do.

Besides, she needed to feed him so he could keep his energy levels high.

Grinning at the memory of their scintillating night together, she grabbed a trolley and headed for the fruit and veg aisle. She made a mean stir-fry, so that would be on the menu tonight, with chilli con carne for tomorrow, and grilled salmon the next night.

She usually ran through the supermarket flinging stuff into the trolley but today she took her time making selections. Maybe her inner domestic goddess had awoken. Or maybe she was nervous about heading home and finding Sawyer ready to move in for however long he was in town, and grocery shopping was an avoidance technique?

Silly, because she'd issued the invitation. And they were

comfortable around each other, even naked. That was the ultimate test for her; if a guy saw her without clothes on and she didn't feel awkward, he was a keeper. Which was precisely why she was single.

But with Sawyer, it had felt right. There'd been no 'morning after' dash, picking her clothes up off the floor and hightailing it to the bathroom. When he'd found her at the dam, they'd chatted and laughed like the old friends they were. A girl could get used to that. Not that she would. She knew their fling had an expiration date.

Part of the appeal, really. No emotions. No muss. No fuss.

She'd learned early on not to get too invested, because the people in her life left. Her folks. Will. Gran. Only Gramps stayed around, but that was only because he was too set in his ways and couldn't be stuffed leaving.

She'd been hurt by Sawyer leaving last time, even though they'd been nothing more than friends. But this time around, she was a big girl who knew the score. Zero expectations meant she couldn't get hurt.

As she perused the different brands of red kidney beans for the chilli con carne, she heard voices from the next aisle.

'Did you see Sawyer Mann's back in town? And looking mighty fine, I might add.'

'Yes, I saw him having lunch with Mila Hayes at the pub. The same day she got dumped at the altar, no less.'

Mila couldn't recognise the first voice, but she knew the second. Anne Curruthers, the notorious gossip who'd waylaid her and Sawyer that afternoon they'd had lunch at the pub. The ex-school librarian who'd made snide comments about Sawyer's lack of book smarts and it had annoyed the hell out of her.

'Don't you think it's strange that Mila and Phil were

good friends but had zero sparks between them from what I saw, and she's moved on so quickly to Sawyer, who by all reports is worth a pretty penny now?' Anne tut-tutted while Mila struggled to clamp down on her outrage. 'Gold-digger springs to mind.'

The other woman sniggered. 'She's young enough to still turn a man's head, I suppose. Though isn't she in her thirties now? Not much longer and she'll be past it. Shame, because without a husband, she's going to end up a lonely old spinster.'

'Unless she gets her hooks into Sawyer Mann,' Anne said, every word laced with disapproval. 'I'm not sure if this is true, but Babs saw him leave the motel today, bags packed, and he was headed towards Mila's farm rather than taking the road out of town.'

'Oh my. Do you think—'

'Yes, he's moving in with Mila. Which just proves what I've been saying. She's reeling him in, hook, line, and sinker.'

The women moved away, and not a moment too soon, as red spots of rage danced before Mila's eyes. She knew the gossip mill thrived in town. Most people had nothing better to talk about than each other. But to hear what those women thought of her... She had a good mind to go find them and rub it in their snooty faces that she was rooting Sawyer for his body and had little interest in his money. But it wasn't worth the angst.

Instead, she bottled up her anger, paid for her groceries, packed her car, and headed home. She'd find a felled tree and an axe to take the edge off her fury.

CHAPTER FORTY-TWO

Sawyer had just returned from a walk around Hills Homestead when Mila pulled into the driveway, a cloud of dust in her wake. She appeared to be driving too fast, her back tyres spinning a tad as she reached the house and pulled in next to his car. He'd only caught a fleeting glimpse of her expression behind the windscreen, and she didn't look happy.

Hell, had she changed her mind about inviting him to stay?

It wasn't Mila's style to throw a tantrum. If she wanted to renege on her invitation, she would've called him. No, this was about something else, and when she got out of the car and slammed the door, barely glancing his way, he knew he had to tread carefully.

He'd only seen her this mad once before, when her parents had cancelled a Christmas visit at the last minute, and he'd been the one to comfort her back then too. She'd been sobbing when he'd come upon her near the dam, and he'd been powerless to do anything other than sit next to her, hoping his silence conveyed support.

She popped the boot and started grabbing bags of groceries, and he moved to help her.

'I can do it myself,' she muttered, but he heard the slightest hitch in her voice.

'I know you're not okay, so is there anything I can do?'

She dragged in a shuddering breath, the kind of breath to stave off tears, and he'd never felt so useless in all his life. 'Just help me get these inside and packed away.'

'Not a problem.'

They worked in silence, unloading the bags then putting the groceries away. He didn't speak, giving her time to compose herself.

'Want a cuppa?'

She shook her head, and before he could make a joke about would she like something lighter, she turned to him and he saw her eyes glittering with rage but filled with tears.

'Hey.' He opened his arms, and she flew into them, bursting into tears the moment he tightened his hold.

The strong, independent Mila he knew rarely cried. She wore her tough outer shell like a cloak, rarely allowing anyone to get close. So, for her to fall apart like this... it must be bad.

For a horrifying second, he wondered if she'd learned the truth about his acquisition, but that was stupid, because if she had he'd be the last person she'd turn to.

She clutched at his shirt and sobbed, and he wondered when their friendship had morphed into something deeper. He hated seeing her this upset and would happily slay whoever or whatever had made her so sad. However, the emptiness in his chest signalled how bereft he felt at the thought of not being around for her once he left.

That was the kicker in their relationship. At some point,

he'd have to leave, and he knew it would be a billion times harder than the last time he'd fled this town.

He genuinely cared about Mila Hayes and how far he'd gone to help her financially proved it. But deep down, he had a feeling that caring could become something else entirely given half a chance, and it terrified him just as much as the thought of her discovering the truth about what he'd done.

When she quieted, he held her at arm's-length. 'You don't have to tell me what that was about, but it might help to talk about it?'

'It's nothing, really.'

He raised an eyebrow, and she barked out a laugh.

'Okay, I guess it was something. I overheard Anne Curruthers and another woman bad-mouthing me at the supermarket. They implied I was a gold-digger who'd deliberately targeted Phil, and when he dumped me, I moved on to you.'

She reddened. 'I'm upset because I pride myself on being a smart woman, yet I was stupid enough to think people in this town wouldn't judge my marriage to Phil. Just because we weren't head over heels '

She shook her head, regret clouding her eyes. 'I'm an idiot. I bet you've never done anything so stupid that you feel like a big fat dunce.'

'You're speaking to the king of dunces,' he blurted, attempting to make her feel better but instantly regretting it.

Astute as ever, Mila pinned him with a curious stare. 'Is this about school?'

Sawyer had spent a lifetime lying to everyone and he could continue now. But Mila was the only person back then who remotely gave a damn about his learning difficulties, the only one who'd suggested he might have a problem. In response, he'd run. But not anymore. Time to own what he'd gone through with a woman he trusted.

'Yeah. You were the only one who cottoned on that I might've had a problem at school.' He shook his head, remembering how utterly humiliated most teachers made him feel. 'I felt stupid all the time. Couldn't focus long enough in class to make sense of what was being taught. And even when I could sit still, I'd end up daydreaming so absorbed zero of the lessons.'

'Have you been formally diagnosed?' she asked, her tone soft and respectful as she reached out and slid her hand into his.

He nodded. 'My first girlfriend when I made it to Melbourne was a part-time tutor and had a brother with ADHD, so she recognised the signs when we talked about our respective experiences at school. I saw the right docs, got diagnosed, and put on meds.' He shrugged. 'It changed my life. Everything became clearer. I could focus for longer than ten minutes. I could actually learn rather than everything being a jumble.'

He squeezed her hand. 'You knew, didn't you? That's what you were hinting at two weeks before Year 12 exams.'

'I had a feeling, so that's why I mentioned you clowning around at school for years to hide the learning stuff.'

'And I reacted by running as far from this town as I could get.' He rolled his eyes. 'Not too mature.'

'Hey, you were eighteen. We all do dumb stuff when we're young.'

'So what's your excuse for marrying Phil at thirty-two?' he deadpanned, and she yanked her hand out of his to punch him on the arm.

'I've already explained my rationale for marrying him.'

She paused, her expression pensive. 'Phil's been a good friend to me, and it gets lonely out here. Financial security and friendship was enough for us.'

Sawyer struggled to hide his surprise. All this time, he'd assumed Mila's marriage to Phil was solely about money. But it sounds like they had a connection, albeit a platonic one. He hated the thought of her feeling so alone she contemplated marrying. Then again, he had no right to judge. He'd bolted from this town without looking back and knew nothing of farming life.

'Speaking of Phil, he's throwing a B & S ball at his place next week and asked me to help plan it.'

'I bet he did, the fucker.'

He didn't swear much, but the thought of Mila marrying Phil for comfort made him want to thump him.

Mila laughed. 'You're being too hard on him. He's a friend who's having a rough time of it, with the townsfolk hating him for ditching me.'

Just a friend? Yeah, right. Tell that to Phil.

'I know he's your neighbour, but maybe I can find someone to buy him out, so you don't have to see him ever again.'

She grinned and bumped him with her hip. 'Are you jealous?'

'What if I am?'

'I'd think you're even more adorable,' she murmured, pressing a quick kiss to his cheek. 'And thanks for trusting me enough to tell me about your diagnosis.'

'You're one of few people I trust in this world,' he said, fearing he'd said too much when confusion clouded her eyes. 'You and Will have always been there for me and I appreciate it.'

His clarification did little to dispel the sinking feeling in his gut that he'd just revealed too much. That she'd see straight to his soul and realise he was well on his way to falling for her.

But he didn't do long-distance relationships and she couldn't leave the farm, so he'd be smarter to quell his burgeoning feelings and enjoy this relationship for what it was: two friends indulging in some very sexy benefits.

'You're one of the good guys, Sawyer Mann.' She raised his hand to her cheek and rested against it. 'But for the next hour or so, I'm hoping I can corrupt you to be bad.'

She winked, and relieved they'd reverted to banter, he brought her hand to his lips and trailed his lips across her knuckles so softly she sighed.

'When you offered me a room, I had no idea I'd be expected to perform—'

'Shut up and kiss me,' she said, sliding her arms around his waist and tilting her chin up.

Sawyer did as he was told.

CHAPTER FORTY-THREE

Something had changed between Adelaide and Jack.

Ever since he'd seen her painting of Tally Bay earlier, he'd withdrawn. Sure, they made polite small talk over a simple pasta dinner he'd whipped up, and he laughed at her anecdotes, but she could see the shadows in his eyes. And it annoyed her anew.

She liked the new and improved Jack, so to see him revert to his taciturn best... not good.

'Here's your coffee.' He placed a mug on the table, but rather than resuming his seat he turned his back on her and headed for the sink.

'I said I'd clean the dishes. It's the least I can do after you fed me.'

'It'll only take me a second to rinse and stack the dishwasher,' he said, his tone reserved.

Normally, she wouldn't care they'd reverted to stilted. After all, isn't that how a couple about to be divorced should behave? But their make-out session had changed everything, and she couldn't sit here and pretend like they were two strangers tolerating each other.

'I don't need to be treated like a guest, Jack.'

He stilled and she saw his neck muscles bulge with tension. 'Isn't that what you are?'

His bland response riled her, and she stood and crossed the kitchen to stand beside him.

'What's changed?'

He turned on the taps and started rinsing crockery, carefully stacking it in the dishwasher. 'In the last fourteen years, you mean?'

'Stop being so bloody childish,' she snapped, unable to contain her angst any longer.

Jack didn't respond. He finished rinsing the cutlery and the pasta pot, wedged them into the dishwasher, and closed it before facing her, his expression thunderous.

'Childish? I'm not the one who stomped out of our marriage years ago without looking back.'

'You were supposed to come after me, you dolt!' she yelled, losing the fragile grip on her determination to keep things civil.

She didn't want to fight with Jack but maybe if they released all their pent-up bitterness they could move forward and end up in a better place.

She didn't want an acrimonious divorce. Their newfound friendship had been much better for ending things amicably.

'Come off it, Ads. Did you really want me running after you?' Jack rolled his eyes and she saw red.

'Of course I bloody wanted that! I gave up my life to follow your dreams and what did you do? End up ignoring me and treating me like a maid. I cooked your meals, I raised your kid and your grandkids, and you couldn't bear to come near me.' She flung her arms in the air. 'What the hell was I supposed to do? Wait around for another few decades while you acted like I didn't exist?'

'Calm down,' he said, his tone condescending.

She balled her hands into fists, fighting the urge to thump something—or him.

'I had a lot going on back then and not all of it had anything to do with you.'

'I was your wife. Of course it had something to do with me.' She patted her chest. 'Whatever was going on, we should've faced it together. Instead, you shut me out to the point our marriage suffered. And when I left, trying to jolt some sense into you, you didn't give a damn.'

'I gave a damn,' he muttered, scowling. 'Which is more than I can say for you.'

'What's that supposed to mean?'

'It means I'm not the one who stayed away. I'm not the one who didn't come back after they'd had time to think. Fuck, Adelaide, don't you get it?' He dragged a hand through his hair, sending it spiking in all directions. 'What the hell do you think this house is about? I knew it was your dream and I wanted to prove to you how much I cared by building it for when you came back. Tangible proof that your dreams were just as important as mine—but I just couldn't do everything at once back then.'

Her mouth dropped open at his declaration. She'd wondered if he'd remembered about the sandstone cottage on their honeymoon, and it looked like he had. But finding out like this—with harsh words and recriminations—was all wrong.

'Why didn't you reach out? Invite me to come back?'

'Because my wife shouldn't need a bloody invitation to come home.' His voice rose and anger flushed his cheeks. 'I wanted you to come home for *me*, not some fucking house.'

He strode a few steps away, his chest heaving, and for an insane moment she wanted to go to him, wrap her arms around him, and apologise. But there'd been two of them involved in tanking this marriage and this conversation was long overdue.

'Did you stop to think there was a reason, many reasons, why I couldn't come back?' She held up her hand to tick them off her fingers. 'One, my husband didn't want me, because he hadn't touched me in years. Two, my husband took me for granted. Three, my husband looked through me most days. Four, my husband didn't want to listen when I tentatively broached the subject of our marital problems.' She pushed her thumb down last. 'Five, I found the real me when I left and indulged my passion for art, and you never gave two hoots about any of that because nothing was as important to you as the farm.'

By the time she finished, a potent mix of anger and indignation tightened her chest, and she dragged in several breaths to calm down. When she risked a glance at Jack, he appeared gutted.

'Ever wondered why the farm was so important to me?'

She snorted. 'Because you were wrapped up in some fantasy of maintaining your family legacy, living up to the expectations of dead parents who never deemed you good enough, or so you said once.'

He paled, hurt evident in the slump of his shoulders. 'It was important to me because I knew you'd given up a cushy life to be with me and I wanted to provide you with the best of everything.'

Stunned by his admission, she said, 'I didn't want the best of everything, Jack. I only wanted you.'

'But I had this fear you'd leave if I couldn't provide for you and the family, and that's what drove me every day.'

His harsh laugh held zero amusement. 'Ironic, considering you left me regardless.'

'What do you want me to say, Jack? That I'm sorry?' She flung her arms wide, not proud of her theatrics but wishing she could rattle some sense into him. 'I've already apologised and it doesn't seem to have made an ounce of difference. You're still playing the blame game and I'm the baddie in all this.'

'I was lost without you!' he yelled, flushing puce as he thumped his fist on the kitchen counter. 'You were everything to me and I've never recovered...' He trailed off, his lips set in a thin line. 'So now you know. Happy?'

'You think this makes me happy?' She waved a hand between them. 'Us going at each other trying to score points?' She shook her head, tears filling her eyes. 'The thing is, Jack, I have been happy since I've been back. Happy when we had dinner at the pub. Happy when you look at me like you used to in the early days. Happy when we... you know'

His gaze locked on her, daring her to articulate what they both knew.

The happiest they'd been since she returned was when they'd been driven by lust.

'Does this make you happy, Ads?'

He stalked across the kitchen and took hold of her arms, his grip surprisingly soft, his thumbs skimming her bare skin.

'Or what about this?'

He lowered his head to nuzzle her neck, scattering goosebumps all over her.

'Or how about this?'

He trailed butterfly kisses along her jaw, seeking her

mouth, finding it, and when his lips pressed against hers, she knew what she had to do.

'You make me happy, Jack Hayes,' she murmured, against the corner of his mouth. 'And if you show me your bedroom, I'll prove exactly how much.'

Jack lifted his head to look her in the eye and when she saw the glint of desire in his steady gaze, her heart soared.

'You know, there's an advantage to all the yelling and airing of dirty laundry from fourteen years ago.' She cupped his cheek and brushed her thumb along his bottom lip.

'What's that?' he growled and nipped her thumb.

'The make-up sex.'

Jack didn't need to be asked twice.

CHAPTER FORTY-FOUR

It didn't surprise Mila that when she woke the next morning, Sawyer had already left. His note said he had to scope out some land in Kaniva and would probably need to stay overnight, but she knew better.

He was running scared.

Revealing his ADHD diagnosis to her had been a big deal and she thought it had been incredibly sweet. She'd been lamenting how stupid she'd been in trying to fool people into believing her marriage to Phil would be real, and he'd revealed how he'd felt stupid every day growing up. His admission hadn't surprised her, as she'd already guessed in their teens, but citing it as one of the main reasons he'd left town did.

Many people, some in their thirties and beyond, were getting diagnosed these days. The perceived stigma had dwindled with increased knowledge. Yet she had a feeling Sawyer still hid it, as she was one of few people he'd told. Over a snatched dinner of cheese toasties—she hadn't felt like whipping up a stir-fry—Sawyer had revealed that even

Will didn't know, and it made her cherish the trust between them even more.

They'd had a solid friendship growing up and she never would've imagined they'd share this bond so many years later. She could depend on Sawyer and vice versa. Considering she rarely let anyone get close, this was a big deal. And after another sensational night in her bed, it made her wonder.

Where did they go from here?

Because at some point during her self-talk that they were indulging in a friends-with-benefits kind of fling, she'd developed feelings. Strong feelings, the kind that made her wish they didn't have to end when he inevitably left town.

Thankfully, Gran's arrival put an end to her mulling, but when Mila opened the door and saw Addy beaming at Jack as he tooted the horn and waved, she realised she may have something else to ponder: her grandparents' relationship.

'Good morning, sweetheart.' Gran pecked her on the cheek. 'How are you?'

'Not as good as you, apparently.' Mila raised an eyebrow. 'You and Gramps look awfully chipper.'

'We're morning people, you know that.' Gran's cheeks flushed crimson as she bustled down the hallway towards the kitchen. 'Now, how can I help with planning this ball?'

As Gran flitted around the kitchen, moving between the kettle and the sink, appearing lost, Mila laid a hand on her arm. 'Gran, it's okay for you and Gramps to be happy.'

Addy visibly deflated as all the tension drained out of her. 'It's been a long while. I'm still getting used to it.'

'So you are? Happy, that is?'

Gran nodded, her eyes shining with joy. 'We had a good talk last night.'

By the second blush in as many minutes stealing into her grandmother's cheeks, Mila hazarded a guess they'd done more than talking. Ew. She didn't want to go there.

'I'm glad you're getting along so well.' Mila hesitated, not wanting to burst her gran's bubble of happiness, but needing to ask the obvious question for Gramps's sake. 'What happens when you leave?'

Gran's eyes clouded. 'I'm enjoying living in the moment, so I'll face that when it happens.'

'And when's that going to be?'

Mila persisted because she'd hate to see her two favourite people hurt when the initial euphoria of their reunion wore off.

'After the ball, I suppose ' Gran stared out the window, a small smile playing about her mouth. 'I'm looking forward to it. Your grandfather and I met at a B & S ball, you know.'

'I know.' Mila slid an arm around her gran's waist and rested her head against hers. 'Love at first sight, if I recall the story correctly.'

'He swept me off my feet.' She sighed. 'Still does, if I'm being honest.'

Mila straightened and turned her grandmother to face her. 'What are you saying? Is there a chance you two will reconcile?'

'Uh... no... I don't think so... ' Gran shrugged, her expression guarded. 'Who knows?'

'Wow, I'll take that as a maybe.'

Gran pressed her palm to Mila's cheek. 'I don't want you getting your hopes up about something that may not eventuate. But we're on good terms now and I'm happy about it.'

'That's great,' Mila said, wishing she could cross all her fingers and toes that her grandparents reconciled. That's what helping with the ball had been about, but maybe they didn't need a nudge. 'And we don't need to have all the answers, Gran, just go with the flow.'

Addy homed in on one word. 'We?'

Mila winked. 'Sawyer and I are getting pretty close too. He's staying here for the remainder of time he's in town.'

'And how long will that be?'

Not long enough, Mila thought. 'He's doing a bit of work in the region, so whenever that ends, I guess.'

'He hasn't said?'

Mila shook her head, knowing she should ask him but unwilling to change the status quo. Logically, she knew Sawyer would be leaving sooner rather than later, but emotionally, he'd only just moved in and she liked having him around. Especially in her bed.

'Like I said, Gran, we're going with the flow.'

Gran snorted. 'You young people and your casual relationships. It's all swiping left or right, or sexting, or playing hard to get.'

Mila arched a brow. 'And what would you know about swiping and sexting, huh?'

As her grandmother reddened, Mila held up a hand. 'On second thoughts, don't answer that.'

Mila paused, knowing it wasn't her business to probe into her grandparents' relationship, but concerned about Gramps. He'd already appeared happy to have Addy back and now if they'd ramped up their relationship, it stood to reason he'd be more invested.

Which meant he could be devastated all over again when Addy left if they hadn't clarified what they were doing.

'Gran, I know this isn't my place, but I was left to pick up the pieces with Gramps last time you left. If you two are starting up again and you eventually leave, I'm worried he'll get hurt.'

Anger sparked in Addy's eyes. 'And what about me? Are you concerned I'll get hurt, or am I the bad guy in all this because I was the one brave enough to call it quits when our marriage was a shambles?'

Yikes. Mila loved her grandmother, and she'd offended her when she hadn't meant to.

'Gran, I'm not prying into your relationship or what happened in the past, but I lived with you, and I tiptoed around you both because the tension in the house was so thick. Do I blame you for leaving? No. You made a decision for your own self-preservation at the time, but I'm just being honest when I say Gramps was gutted and I don't want that to happen to him again.'

Addy's shoulders slumped and she nodded. 'I don't want to hurt him again either. But I can't give either of you any guarantees.'

'Nobody's after a guarantee, but growing closer with Gramps means he'll have expectations. So I guess I'm hoping you two will talk things through this time.'

Mila half expected her grandmother to tell her to mind her own business, but to Gran's credit, she merely nodded.

'Didn't you invite me over to help plan this ball?'

As a deflection, it worked. While Addy scrolled through the list Mila had made on her computer and added a few suggestions, Mila wondered if she should follow her own advice and talk things through with Sawyer.

CHAPTER FORTY-FIVE

Sawyer didn't want to stick his nose in his sister's business, but if his suspicions were correct and his nephew had ADHD, he owed it to her to steer her in the right direction. Brett seemed like a good kid and the last thing he wanted was for him to go through what Sawyer had.

Allison was hanging out the washing when he arrived, and her face lit up as he strolled towards her.

'Wow, I don't see you for ages, then two visits in as many days. Lucky me.'

He slung an arm around her shoulder. 'I can go if you like.'

'Don't be an idiot,' she muttered, and elbowed him in the ribs. 'Want a drink?'

'I'm good, but I did want to talk to you about something.'

His tone must've alerted her this wasn't purely a social call.

'Sounds serious. Are you okay?'

'Yeah.' He gestured to the cracked outdoor furniture nearby. 'Let's sit.'

A frown furrowed her brow as they pulled the chairs into the shade. 'You're scaring me.'

'It's nothing bad, honest. But I'm not sure you'll appreciate my interference.'

Her frown deepened. 'What's this about?'

'Brett.'

Her frown cleared but confusion clouded her eyes. 'Did he say something to worry you? Because that kid's always making up stories. Has a good imagination for someone who can't focus on schoolwork for more than two seconds.'

She'd provided him with the perfect segue. 'Actually, that's what I want to talk to you about. Have any of the teachers at school mentioned reasons why Brett can't focus?'

She shook her head. 'He's energetic and rambunctious, perfectly normal for a ten-year-old used to running loose in the country. Why?'

'Because I see a lot of myself in Brett. At school, my focus wavered constantly. I couldn't study for longer than ten minutes so my homework was rushed. I switched hobbies and interests constantly. I even mixed up words sometimes.'

Recognition sparked in her eyes. 'Brett does all that too.'

Relieved he'd made the connection after hearing about his nephew's learning behaviours, he said, 'Back then, everyone thought I was stupid, so I acted out. Mum and Dad thought I was lazy, dumb, or both, so I learned to deflect their focus by being funny. And that carried over to school, because being the class clown distracted from my inability to learn. But after I left town, a girlfriend mentioned I might have ADHD, like her brother, and she was right. I was diagnosed, put on meds, and my life changed. I could concentrate long enough to study and complete a degree. I could remember stuff. Everything seemed clearer.'

'I didn't know,' she said. 'I'm sorry nobody picked up on it back then.'

'It's not your fault. It's nobody's fault. But if Brett's like me, I want the best for him, and that means getting an early diagnosis.'

She nodded. 'You're right. I'll get a referral for a specialist in Melbourne.'

'I can come with you to the appointment, if you like? I'll be heading home sometime in the next few weeks. And you're welcome to stay with me.'

He caught the shimmer of tears in her eyes. 'Thanks, little bro. I'm so glad we've reconnected, so let's keep this going, okay? Regular catch-ups, whether it be here or in the city or even halfway.'

'Sounds good.' Sawyer forced the lie, knowing he probably wouldn't return to Ashe Ridge for a long time, if ever.

Because he'd come to a realisation in the wee small hours this morning. After divulging the truth about his diagnosis to Mila, he'd been tempted to tell her everything, and that meant revealing the truth about who had acquired her land.

And he had no doubt that once she learned the truth, she'd be glad to see the back of him.

'How will Mick react?' he asked, only to hear a footfall behind him.

'How will I react about what?'

Sawyer's heart sank as he turned and fixed a smile on his face. The last thing Alli needed was her husband thinking they'd been talking about him behind his back.

'Hey, Mick.' Sawyer thrust out his hand. 'Good to see you.'

'You too, mate.' A lie, and they both knew it. Mick shook his hand quickly and released it. 'What's going on?'

Sawyer shot Alli a quick questioning glance and when she nodded, he said, 'I was just telling Alli I have ADHD. How I acted out at school because of it, how I couldn't concentrate long enough to learn anything, but I got diagnosed in my early twenties and never looked back.'

'Sounds a bit like Brett,' Mick said, his expression thoughtful. 'He can't sit still for long, especially when it comes to homework.'

'He's a great kid. Aimee too. You and Alli are lucky,' Sawyer said, relieved Mick had taken his interference in the right way and hadn't reacted defensively.

'Yeah, we are.' Mick slung an arm across Allison's shoulders and Sawyer had never been happier to see his sister lean into her husband rather than stiffening, which would've happened if they were truly on the outs and Mick was a controlling prick. 'So you think we should get Brett assessed or something?'

Sawyer nodded. 'Can't hurt.'

'I agree,' Mick said. 'How about you, Al?'

Allison glanced up at her husband and smiled. Looked like Sawyer wasn't the only one relieved by how Mick was taking the news.

'Our kids are incredible and we want to give them every opportunity in life, so if that means maximising Brett's potential if he needs help, we do it.'

Mick's fond smile at his wife made Sawyer wish he hadn't misjudged the guy. 'You're a smart woman, Allison Fogarty, one of the many reasons I married you.'

Pleased that this had gone better than expected, Sawyer said, 'Want me to pick up the kids so you two can sort out appointments?'

Mick nodded. 'Thanks, mate. And we appreciate you telling us about what you went through in an effort to help Brett. You must've had it tough growing up.' He sent a pointed stare at Allison. 'Especially with much-older sisters who were more interested in chasing after boys like me than keeping an eye on their little brother.'

'You're an idiot,' Alli said, elbowing Mick hard enough he let out an 'oomph'.

'But seriously, Sawyer, we do appreciate it.'

'No worries.'

At least, not with his family. But with his impending plan to tell Mila the truth, that was a giant worry.

CHAPTER FORTY-SIX

Knowing she would see Jack for the first time in fourteen years at Mila's wedding, Adelaide had wanted to make a good impression— equal parts *'See what you've been missing out on'* and *'I'm rubbing your nose in it'*—so she'd packed a knockout dress.

She'd grabbed it for next to nothing at a vintage market in Tally Bay. While the floor-length, layered chiffon one-shoulder dress had been second-hand, it fitted like it had been made for her. She paired the ice-blue gown with silver kitten-heel sandals, a beaded clutch, and simple diamanté drop earrings, kept her makeup to a minimum with coral lipstick, blush, and mascara, and twisted her hair into a loose chignon at the nape of her neck.

As she gave a final twirl in front of the mirror, she knew she'd never looked so good. Though the natural glow she sported might have more to do with the last few nights spent in Jack's bed than any serum regimen she adhered to diligently.

The way they'd reconnected... it's what she'd envisaged

for their future in later life but had given up on a long time ago. They talked well into the nights, they cooked together, they watched movies together, he read while she painted, they made love...

It scared her, how good they were together after all the acrimony of the past, and it made her entertain thoughts she never would've. Thoughts like, *what would happen if she stayed in town longer? Would Jack be willing to give them a second chance? Would she be giving up her independence and all she'd achieved if she moved back permanently? Was this just the best make-up sex/reunion and it would wear off if they got back together?*

So many questions she needed answers to before she made any life-changing decisions, but they could wait for tonight.

Tonight, she intended on making every moment count.

She'd planned on heading over to Jack's for a quick drink before they left, but when she opened the door, he stood on the other side, one hand raised to knock, the other clutching a bunch of daisies.

'These are for you,' he said, reminiscent of the first night he'd given her a bunch with those exact words, the night they met at the B & S ball in Nhill, when he'd run out to the nearest paddock and picked her a bunch after they'd danced for an hour straight.

There'd been no mucking around that night. Jack had declared he'd found the woman he wanted to marry, and while she'd laughed him off initially, deep down she'd known she'd found the man she wanted to spend the rest of her life with.

Until she didn't.

'Thank you.' She took the bunch and pressed her lips to

his, a soft lingering kiss that tempted her to drag him inside and tear the tux off his body. 'You look dashing.'

'And you look beautiful,' he said, taking hold of her hand and spinning her around. 'I hope those fancy shoes are comfortable though, because I intend to dance the night away.'

'Promises, promises.'

He spun her into his arms and held her tight, staring at her like he wondered how he'd got so lucky. This is how he used to look at her before their marriage went to crap. But she wouldn't think about the negative stuff, not tonight.

If Jack was intent on having fun, she'd make the most of it. She'd never seen this side to him, not after their initial whirlwind courtship, and she couldn't get enough. It made her wonder: if Jack had changed this much, was it worth sticking around and giving their marriage another shot?

She didn't have to make any hasty decisions. She could stay in town longer, spend more time with him, see how their relationship developed. She could put a halt on divorce proceedings—not that she'd got beyond making that appointment for advice, which would be easy enough to cancel—and take her time.

At her age, the type of connection she shared with Jack was unique. Not once in the last fourteen years had she been remotely emotionally invested in any of the men she'd dated, and even her relationship with Raven was lukewarm compared with the sizzle she had with Jack.

She owed it to them to give their marriage another shot and after the ball tonight, she'd tell him.

'What are you thinking about?' His fingertip traced the frown lines between her brows, down her nose, before ending on her lips.

'If I tell you, we'll never get out of here, and our granddaughter won't forgive us for not turning up to the ball.'

'Fair point.' He ducked down to whisper in her ear, 'But whatever you're thinking, I reckon we can give it a red hot go when we get home later.'

We. Home. It had a nice ring to it and Adelaide couldn't wait to tell Jack the good news that she'd be sticking around.

~

'Remind me again why I can't give Phil a mouthful for dumping our Mila at the altar for some woman he just met?'

Adelaide laughed and laid a hand on Jack's arm as he parked and turned off the engine. 'Because she doesn't need you defending her honour.' She pointed at Mila and Sawyer, their heads bent close together at the entrance to the marquee. 'She's found her own knight in shining armour.'

Jack grunted. 'Sawyer Mann's a good kid. Always respectful when he used to hang around our place.'

'Which was every day.'

Adelaide had often wondered if Sawyer knew Mila had a crush on him and chose to ignore it because of his friendship with Will, or if he was just obtuse, as most boys his age were.

The three of them, Mila, Will, and Sawyer, had been close. They loved camping out in the backyard of the homestead, stringing a few old sheets between branches of the eucalypts and sleeping underneath them in their swags. She'd provide them with food they could cook over a campfire—sausages, damper, marshmallows— and loved hearing their laughter as they tried to outdo each other with who could stay up the longest.

They'd ride their bikes around the property, play cricket in the summer, and kick the footy in the winter. Sawyer spent a lot of time at the homestead and Adelaide treated him as another grandchild. From what she heard about his fraught home life, the less time he spent there the better. He'd been too proud to discuss what he faced on a daily basis—she'd tried to broach it once and he'd changed the subject quickly—so she mothered him as best she could.

She often asked him to stay for dinner and he rarely said no. Shepherd's pie, apricot chicken, and curried lamb chops were his favourite, and he had a massive soft spot for her roly-poly pudding. If Mila and Will knew about his tough home life, they never said, and she liked that Sawyer could depend on her grandchildren. They'd been good kids and Adelaide couldn't be happier that Sawyer finally reciprocated Mila's feelings.

'I'd like her to find a decent bloke and settle down.' Jack sighed. 'She deserves happiness.'

'We all do,' she murmured, reaching across to clasp Jack's hand. 'I'll be honest, Jack, that in returning to Ashe Ridge, I never expected... this... us '

Overwhelmed by emotion, she cleared her throat. 'What I'm trying to say is, I've loved every moment with you these last few days and I hope to create many more.'

'Sounds like you're planning on staying a while.'

'If that's okay with you.'

He shrugged, feigning nonchalance, but she saw the elation in his eyes. 'Fine by me.'

'Now that's settled, you promised to dance me off my feet, remember?'

'Lady, I'm about to make all your wishes come true.'

He winked and lifted her hand to his mouth as Adelaide blinked away tears.

Jack didn't have to dance with her to make all her wishes come true. He already had, by just agreeing to give them another chance.

CHAPTER FORTY-SEVEN

'I've never seen them so happy,' Mila said, giving a subtle jerk of her head in the direction of her grandparents, who'd rarely left the makeshift dance floor all night.

Sawyer followed her line of vision and smiled. 'Romance is in the air.'

'You're not getting soppy on me, are you?' Her hands, draped around his neck as they swayed to a ballad, tightened a little, forcing his head closer to hers. 'I like my men tough.'

'You love my marshmallow core,' he said, palming her butt and tugging her closer against him. 'And my hard bits too.'

She sniggered. 'I'll remind you we're in public, and while some of the singles have hooked up and are snogging in the back of utes, we're already open to enough speculation, so let's not give the gossips any more fodder.'

'Let them talk.' He lowered his voice. 'Or we can go make out in that dark corner over there and really give them something to talk about.'

'We can do that in private later.'

And she could hardly wait. Sawyer looked incredible in a charcoal suit and black shirt that lent him a devilish edge. Though she much preferred him not wearing anything at all.

Snuggling up to him at night, waking in his arms every morning... A girl could get used to it. He hadn't mentioned leaving yet and she hadn't asked, content to make the most of their time together, however long they had.

The only instance he'd mentioned returning to Melbourne was to accompany his sister and nephew to a doctor's appointment, but that wasn't for another month. Four long weeks where she could see them growing closer and making it difficult for her to say an inevitable goodbye.

A pragmatist usually, it shouldn't bother her. She'd known the score from the start. She'd always had a thing for Sawyer and indulging her crush meant she'd have great memories to resurrect on dark winter evenings. But she had a feeling her logic would desert her when it came to saying goodbye to this incredible guy.

'Hey, Alli and Mick have just walked in. Let's go say hi.'

'Sure.'

Mila didn't know Allison well. While everyone could recognise everyone else in Ashe Ridge, if you didn't move in the same circles the only time you saw each other was if you happened to be having a meal at the pub. Besides, Mila had probably avoided the woman because she knew Allison was Sawyer's sister and if they'd chatted, she would've been tempted to ask what her brother was up to.

Allison caught sight of them as they strolled across the marquee and waved.

'I'm glad they made it,' Sawyer said. 'From reading

between the lines after hanging out with Alli a bit, I don't think they get out much.'

'Nothing wrong with being a hermit. I'm proud of my recluse status.'

'That's only because you're locking me in the bedroom these days,' he murmured, and Mila laughed.

'Maybe I should install a permanent lock on the door and throw away the key?'

While flippant, she'd thrown her comment out there to test his reaction to the hint of something long term, and disappointingly, he ignored it and thrust out his hand at Mick as they reached the other couple.

'Good to see you guys,' Sawyer said, shaking Mick's hand and giving his sister a hug. 'You know Mila, right?'

'Of course,' Allison said, with a warm smile, and Mick nodded. 'How are you, Mila?'

'Good thanks. Busy, like everyone else.'

'You must have the patience of a saint to be putting up with this one on top of your usual workload,' Allison said, pointing at Sawyer.

'He's not so bad,' Mila said, chuckling as Sawyer tweaked Allison's nose.

Allison glanced around the marquee, her eyes wide and filled with excitement. 'I can't remember the last time we got a babysitter let alone went out on our own. This looks great.'

'As long as you don't expect me to dance.' Mick grimaced. 'I'd rather do a nudie run to the dam than hit the dance floor.'

Allison rolled her eyes, but she smiled at her husband. 'In that case, brother dearest, you owe me a dance.'

Sawyer glanced at her, and Mila nodded. 'Go ahead.'

Besides, she saw Freddie incoming and wanted to ask

him if he'd finished looking over the documentation for the land acquisition.

'I'm grabbing a beer,' Mick said. 'Want anything, Mila?'

'No thanks. I need to chat with a friend, but I'll see you guys later?'

'Sure,' Allison said, linking arms with Sawyer. 'Ready to show this town a move or two, little brother?'

Sawyer winced. 'Be gentle with me.'

Mila laughed. 'I'll see you back here when you're done.'

With one last pleading look in her direction as Allison dragged him towards the dance floor, Sawyer surrendered with a shrug and Mila gave a little finger wave.

'Back soon,' Mick said, heading for the bar in the far corner, just as Freddie arrived.

'You look gorgeous, Mila,' he said, with a grin. 'Though you know what they say about purple.'

Yeah, she knew, but with Sawyer around, purple did not equate with sexual frustration. Besides, didn't Freddie ever give up? She'd made it more than clear they'd never be more than friends— acquaintances, really—but he just didn't quit.

Ignoring his innuendo, she said, 'Actually, I was going to call you tomorrow to see if you're doing due diligence, checking for any loopholes in the acquisition paperwork.'

His eyebrow arched a little. 'I didn't think you'd be worried about anything like that, considering who bought the land.'

He pointed at the dance floor. 'You two seem super cosy.'

He pulled a face. 'Sawyer's a lucky bastard.'

Annoyed that he wanted to bring up her relationship with Sawyer rather than discuss business, she said, 'We've been friends a long time. So, from an accounting perspective, the deal looks good?'

He rolled his eyes. 'Of course it does. As you just said, if you two are such good friends, why would he screw you over?'

Confusion gave way to dread as she realised she'd misinterpreted what Freddie meant when he mentioned the acquisition and her closeness with Sawyer. He hadn't been talking about two different things.

He'd meant Sawyer had been the one to acquire her land.

Oblivious to her devastation, Freddie continued. 'I've researched the other land-broking deals he's done and he's a bigwig in the industry. Highly respected, so you've done well. But I guess you already knew that? Though it always pays to research documentation and the financial ramifications thoroughly, friendship or not.'

Mila couldn't speak, anger tightening her throat. Sawyer had deceived her.

He'd swept in to save her, even after she'd rejected his initial offer. She didn't need a knight in shining armour. She needed a guy to respect her enough to let her make her own decisions, not a guy with a rescue complex.

Heck, for all she knew he'd done this for business and would on-sell the land at a profit. Maybe that's why he'd been cosying up to her from the beginning?

Her stomach churned at the thought and the hot dog she'd consumed earlier threatened to make another appearance.

'Hey, are you okay?' Freddie touched her arm, and she jerked back.

'I think I need to head home,' she managed to say, averting her gaze from the dance floor so she wouldn't be tempted to march over there and slug Sawyer in front of everyone. 'Thanks for checking over the paperwork, Freddie. I'll be in touch.'

With that, Mila hiked up her dress, and made a run for it.

CHAPTER FORTY-EIGHT

'Your girlfriend just left.' Allison poked Sawyer in the chest. 'Maybe she's seen your dance moves and they turned her off?'

'Mila likes my moves just fine,' he said, earning a groan from his sister. 'Wonder where she went?'

'By the goofy expression on your face, you're about to run after her and find out.' Allison shook her head. 'Man, you have it bad.'

He opened his mouth to refute it, but what was the point? Moving in with Mila for however long he was in town, spending every night together, jostling side by side in the kitchen as they cooked dinner, chatting over early morning coffees, merely solidified what he already knew.

He was crazy about her.

The overnighter he'd done in Kaniva had made him realise just how much.

He hadn't slept a wink that night, and it had nothing to do with the dodgy springs in the old bed at the motel. The cause of his insomnia had been a constant whirring of thoughts, centred around when was the best time to confess about buying her land.

He hadn't come to any conclusions about their relationship, but the last few days together solidified he had to tell her the truth about the land, and soon.

Namely, tonight, after the ball.

'Just go already.' Allison gave him a shove. 'Besides, if Mick's had a beer, maybe I can coerce him onto the dance floor.'

Spying Mick talking to a bunch of blokes holding stubbies, Sawyer didn't like her chances.

'Good luck with that,' he said, and she smiled.

'By the way, thanks for that referral to your guy in Melbourne. Are you sure it's okay we stay with you next month?'

'Of course. It'll be great having you in Melbourne.'

Yet the thought of returning home left him cold. Ironic that he once couldn't wait to flee this town and all it stood for, and now he wanted to linger as long as possible. Mila had addled his brain and captured his heart, and he'd never be the same again.

'Go,' she said again. 'We'll speak soon.'

'Love you, sis.' He gave her a quick hug. 'See you later.'

Starting up with Mila hadn't been the only good thing to come out of his visit to Ashe Ridge and he vowed to maintain a relationship with Alli, as well as visit Phoebe and Jocelyn more often.

As he slipped out of the marquee, he saw Mila jogging barefoot towards her ute, sandals in hand.

'Hey, Mila,' he called out, but she didn't stop, so he ran after her.

As he got closer, he yelled her name again, and this time

she heard him because she glanced over her shoulder. But she didn't stop.

Foreboding strummed the back of his neck as he picked up the pace, his long strides outpacing her shorter ones, and when he caught up to her, he laid a hand on her shoulder.

'What's wrong?'

She took several seconds before she turned around and when she did, her expression gutted him.

Fury mixed with betrayal. Her eyes narrowed and filled with accusation. Her mouth twisted in anger.

Hell.

She knew.

'I was going to tell you tonight—'

'How magnanimous of you.' Her upper lip curled into a sneer. 'When what you should've done was tell me from the start.'

Guilt lodged like a rock in the pit of his stomach. 'I wanted to, but Will convinced me not to say anything because you wouldn't accept any help.'

He could've sworn her eyes shot blue fire. 'That idiot of a brother of mine knew about this?'

'I wanted to help and acquiring the land myself was the only way I could think to do that.'

'Wrong!' she yelled, and he jumped. 'You could've brokered a deal, like you do every day of the week for clients. Instead, you rode in on your high horse to *save* me. Well, thanks a lot.' She slow clapped. 'You must think I'm an idiot. And what was you moving in all about? An easy way to survey more of my land? See what you can gobble up in the future?'

Her nose crinkled in disgust. 'Because I'm getting the

feeling you used me, Sawyer. You took advantage when I was vulnerable, and I'll never forgive you for it.'

Ice trickled through his veins as he looked at the woman he'd give his life for, who was staring at him like he was lower than the cow patties scattering the nearby paddock.

He'd thought she'd be mad when he told her the truth, but he never expected it to be this bad. For her to assume the worst of him, to doubt his motives in entering a relationship with her, however fleeting, slugged him hard.

His entire life in this town he'd felt useless. People looked down on him. They pitied him for being a joker. They thought he'd never amount to anything.

Yet the way Mila had just judged and found him lacking... he'd never felt so worthless.

'Do you have anything to say?' she spat, every word laced with loathing, and he did what he always did when confronted by anyone who looked down on him.

He retreated.

'Leave my bag outside, please. I'll pick it up in the morning.'

Stifling every instinct urging him to take her in his arms and beg for forgiveness, he turned and walked away.

CHAPTER FORTY-NINE

As dawn filtered through the plantation shutters in Jack's bedroom, Adelaide stretched, aching all over. She'd barely left the dance floor last night, with Jack matching her every move, something he'd done the night they met.

Back then, she'd admired him for wanting to dance so much when most of the guys at the B & S ball stood on the outskirts, downing beers and ogling the girls.

And last night, with every jive, foxtrot, and waltz, he'd reminded her of why she'd fallen in love with him; when Jack held her like he never wanted to let her go, she knew he was the man for her.

Not that she needed a ball to remind her of that. His every action lately had shown her how much she meant to him and these last couple of days felt like she'd never left at all.

'You're still an early riser like me.' Jack rolled onto his side to face her, reaching out to drape his arm across her waist. 'Best part of the day.'

That's what she used to think, until they started coexisting in frosty silences and he couldn't wait to down his coffee and head out onto the farm.

But that was the past and they were both older and wiser.

'It is, though I doubt I'll be able to get out of bed, I'm that sore.'

'Oh, really?' The mouth she'd kissed repeatedly last night curved into a wicked smile. 'I thought you liked it a little rough.'

'I'm talking about all the dancing we did,' she said, gently slapping her palm against his chest. 'That was some night.'

'Reliving old times,' he said. 'The good parts.'

'Does that mean you're ready to put the bad parts behind us?'

It seemed odd, slipping it into a casual conversation, but would there ever be a good time to ask the hard questions? After last night, she knew where she wanted to be: by Jack's side.

'If you're asking if I like having you around, Ads, of course I do.' He cleared his throat and his hand on her waist trembled a tad. 'I never stopped loving you.'

'Oh, Jack...' Tears sprang to her eyes and she blinked, her heart breaking as she glimpsed the tears in his. 'I can't make any promises, but I want to stay longer. Give us a chance at reconciling, with a view to moving back if you'll have me?'

'I think that's a great idea,' he said, without hesitation. 'Stay for as long as you like.' He eyeballed her. 'Maybe forever?'

She wanted to say yes. She'd love nothing better than to resurrect her marriage. But despite the amazing time they'd had becoming reacquainted, she couldn't quash all her reservations.

What if she moved back to Ashe Ridge and they ended up back where they once were, coexisting in frosty silences and bereft of intimacy? While they didn't have the farm hanging over them, Jack's manic work ethic hadn't been the only problem in their marriage. And at their age, didn't they only get grumpier from here?

'By your resounding silence, I'm assuming that's a no.' His expression closed off and his hand slid off her waist. 'So what is this? A fling before you hit the road again?'

'You know it's more than that.' She sighed and snuggled closer to him. 'I'm scared, Jack. Scared of falling back into the old routines where our marriage suffered. Scared of taking a chance on us again and getting hurt. Scared that if I move back permanently, the gloss will wear off our reunion and we'll end up back where we started.'

His expression softened. 'I appreciate your honesty, Ads, but I'm scared too. Terrified, in fact. You broke my heart last time and I can't help but think no matter how long you stay this time, you'll get bored again and leave.'

She wanted to say boredom was never the issue but she'd be lying, because that's exactly how it had been between them at the end of their marriage. She'd craved an escape, a change of scenery, anything to jolt her out of the lethargy that had been suffocating her for years. Tally Bay had provided that, and she valued the life she'd created there.

What would happen if she gave it all up for this man, her husband, and their relationship went pear-shaped again?

'Jack, I can't make any promises, but I know one thing.' She framed his face with her hands so he had no option but to look at her. 'I love you too and if I decide to stay, I'll throw myself one hundred percent into this marriage.'

'If you stay…' he said, his expression mutinous.

She sighed, releasing him. 'We need to be honest moving forward if this is to work, so yeah, *if*. I haven't made up my mind yet.'

After a long pause where he couldn't meet her eyes, he gave a brief nod. 'Okay. I'll take it. For now.'

A phone rang and, rolling over, Adelaide realised it wasn't hers. Once again, she'd forgotten to charge it and the battery had died.

'Must be yours,' she said, not averse to perving on Jack's bare butt as he rolled out of bed and shrugged into a dressing gown.

'It's in the kitchen. Be back in a minute.'

If they were to continue their confronting conversation, Adelaide would prefer to not be naked, so she slipped out of bed and pulled on a kaftan she'd left here the last time she'd slept over. Before she could splash water on her face, Jack had returned, his expression eerily blank and his mouth set in a thin line.

'What's wrong? Is Mila okay?'

'That was Sam Nobil's office.'

The moment he said who'd called, her heart sank. She'd been meaning to call the lawyer and cancel her appointment, but with all the excitement of the ball and spending every spare minute with Jack, she'd forgotten.

'They said they tried to contact you to let you know they need to change your appointment, and when they couldn't get through, they knew you were staying here so contacted me to pass on the message.'

The chill in his tone made her shiver.

'Tell me, Adelaide, would that appointment have

anything to do with securing a divorce, which is probably the real reason you stayed after Mila's aborted wedding?'

'Yes,' she said, tilting her chin up, wanting everything out in the open so they could move forward. 'I wanted to instigate proceedings while I was in town. But things have changed—'

'Actually, I don't think anything's changed. I think you've been schmoozing me to make this divorce go smoothly. I think you have no intention of staying and giving us a second chance.' His face flushed an angry crimson. 'I think you've been making a fool out of me.'

It took a lot to get Adelaide riled, but when she did, she retaliated, and Jack's stupidity in thinking the worst of her really got her back up.

'And I think you're being an idiot. How did they have your number anyway?'

His eyes narrowed to angry slits. 'Because I changed my will after you left and Mila bought the farm. Understandable, considering I didn't want a wife who'd abandoned her family inheriting a cent if something happened to me.'

'You're never going to forgive me for leaving, are you? No matter if I move back, how many times I profess my love, however many years I stay, you'll always throw it in my face when we have an argument.' Sadness tempered her anger. 'If we're to have any chance at happiness, Jack, you have to forgive me.'

He glared at her, his shoulders rigid, his hands balled into fists. 'I don't have to do anything.'

Before she could talk sense into him, because one of them had to calm the hell down before they really said something they'd regret, he whirled away, stomped down the hall, and slammed the front door.

CHAPTER FIFTY

Mila had spent a boring two hours going over crop forecasts and harvesting timetables with Dazza in the big shed, ignoring the sound of a car engine around eleven. It had been Sawyer, because by the time she finished her meeting with her farm manager, his bag she'd left at the front door had vanished.

She'd been perched on the front step since, numb, when her grandmother arrived at midday. She hadn't been expecting Addy and was in no mood for visitors, even her gran who she'd miss terribly once she left.

It took Mila a few moments to realise Addy had arrived in her car, not Gramps's, and her heart sank. Surely this impromptu visit didn't mean Gran had come to say goodbye.

She'd been thrilled by how close her grandparents had been last night. Totally smitten, they'd barely left the dance floor. They'd stared into each other's eyes like a couple of lovestruck teens, completely oblivious to everyone around them. It gave her hope that relationships do work, despite hiccups along the way.

'Sweetheart, you look rather ragged,' Addy said, enveloping her in a hug. 'Tired after the ball?'

'Tired after a sleepless night because I kicked out Sawyer's lying arse.'

Gran's face fell. 'Oh dear. Time for a cuppa?'

Tea wouldn't solve the permanent ache in Mila's chest, but she nodded. Not that she felt like talking, but the caffeine might help pep her up enough to tackle one of the cottages today. That was the annoying thing. The money from the sale had just landed in her account, meaning she could forge ahead with completing renovations and get her farm-stay project opening sooner rather than later.

But thanks to Sawyer's deception, that money would always be tainted, and he'd robbed her of the pleasure of accomplishing something on her own.

'If the wind changes, your sourpuss expression will stick.' Gran pulled a face. 'It can't be that bad.'

'Just because you're all loved-up with Gramps, don't expect everyone to be so lucky.' She stomped ahead of Gran into the kitchen and filled the kettle before flicking the switch on.

At her gran's stricken expression, she softened her tone. 'Don't mind me. I'm happy for you, Gran, truly. I'm just in a foul mood.'

'That makes two of us.'

Guilt swamped her. She'd been so self-absorbed, wallowing in her own misery, she hadn't noticed the redness bracketing Addy's nose and her bloodshot eyes that meant she'd likely been crying.

'What happened? Did you and Gramps have a fight?'

'Something like that.' Gran slumped into a chair, a good indication of how bad she felt, because she'd usually be bustling around the kitchen alongside Mila prepping the tea. 'He's gone and I have no idea where or when he'll be back.'

'Gone?'

Gran nodded. 'Vanished. We had an amazing night, then were discussing our future this morning and the possibility of me moving back to Ashe Ridge and giving our marriage another go, when he got a call from the lawyer's office.'

She shook her head. 'Damn small-town mentality. They couldn't get through to me, because my phone died, and they knew I was staying with your grandfather, so they called him to pass on a message to me about rescheduling my appointment.'

'Why would you need to see a lawyer... Oh...' Mila trailed off as realisation hit. 'You made it when you first got to town to start divorce proceedings.'

'Yes. And I forgot to cancel it these last few days. Jack got in a big huff and stormed out, so I went back to the bungalow. When I'd cooled off enough to try and talk sense into him, he'd vanished. Luckily the mechanic dropped my car off, so I gave him a lift back to town then came straight here.' She tapped her temple. 'Jack is crazy if he thinks I'm going to walk away without a fight this time.'

'Good for you, Gran. Men.' Mila rolled her eyes and placed two cups of tea in front of them before taking a seat. 'For what it's worth, give Gramps a bit of time to calm down, then he'll be rational and ready to listen.' She hesitated, before continuing. 'He's a different man to the one you left fourteen years ago. And by the look of you both, I think he'll be willing to fight for your marriage as much as you.'

Tears glistened in Addy's eyes. 'I hope so, sweetheart. Anyway, what did Sawyer lie about?'

Mila almost snapped, '*I don't want to talk about it*' but having her gran here as a shoulder to lean on was a luxury she hadn't had for years, and she'd be a fool to not take advantage of a sounding board.

'When the wedding with Phil didn't go ahead, Sawyer offered to help me financially. I said no. But turns out, he went ahead regardless and bought the land, hiding behind some company, and didn't tell me.'

Anger flooded her again, at the gall of him for going against her wishes. 'I found out because Freddie was looking into the financials, making sure everything was okay, and he told me last night.'

Gran snorted. 'Is that the same Freddie you told me about last time we met up in Sydney, the one who's persistent no matter how many times you tell him you're not interested?'

Mila nodded and Gran scowled. 'How magnanimous of him to tell you, knowing full well he might be interfering in your relationship with Sawyer. What a prick.'

'Gran!'

How was Freddie to know that Sawyer hadn't told her the truth about acquiring her land?

'You told Sawyer to leave?'

'Yes. Who knows, he might've been hanging around me with a view to gobble up more of the farm.'

'Don't be ridiculous,' Gran snapped. 'That boy is crazy about you. By the way he hung around here all the time when you were teens, I thought you'd end up together.'

Surprised by Addy's vehemence, Mila said, 'He hung around here because of Will, not me.'

'Bull. I'd see the two of you talking even when Will was off doing something else. And the way he looked at you... He admired you, Mila. He hung on your every word. You can't fake that kind of closeness, especially when you're a teen boy. So, for you to even contemplate he'd use you in this way to get more land...' Addy shook her head. 'It's ludicrous.'

'I know,' Mila murmured, well aware her fury last night had overridden her common sense and she'd flung the accusation at Sawyer in the heat of the moment.

Then again, how well did she know him? They hadn't spoken in fifteen years and maybe his goal had been to acquire as much land as possible in the region to further his career. And she'd been a bonus, throwing herself at him like some desperado.

'Whatever you're thinking, stop.' Addy took a sip of tea before continuing. 'That young man is one of the good ones and if you've been hot-headed, you need to take stock and give him a chance.'

Suitably chastened, Mila said, 'Is that what you're doing with Gramps? Giving him a chance and not leaving town again?'

'Both of you need to give me more credit,' Addy muttered, with a shake of her head. 'I'm older and wiser, and willing to take a risk despite the outcome. Can you say the same?'

'Maybe I'm not as enlightened as you?'

But her grandmother's advice hit home. Had she over-reacted last night? Using Sawyer's lie by omission as an excuse to push him away before he left town and broke her heart?

Because all her self-talk that she'd be fine moving on whenever he left had been delusional, as she found out last night when she'd driven him away for good. Her heart had shattered, and she'd sobbed for what felt like hours. A long hot shower, two shots of tequila, and half a tub of cookie-dough ice cream hadn't helped soothe and she'd known then that it would take her a long time to get over him.

Meaning she'd moved beyond liking Sawyer and into scary love territory.

'I want you to be happy, sweetheart, and if Sawyer makes you happy—which I think he does from what I've seen—you owe it to the both of you to try and move past this.'

'Thanks, Gran.' Mila reached across the table and squeezed her hand. 'I love having you around, so you better stay, okay?'

'I'll do my best.'

They shared a smile and sipped their teas, while Mila thought, if her grandparents could resolve their differences after fourteen years apart, surely the least she could do was talk to Sawyer.

CHAPTER FIFTY-ONE

'Stop making such a racket.' Alli groaned as she stumbled into the kitchen, pressing her fingers to her temples. 'You're worse than the kids.'

'Someone's hungover,' Sawyer said, stifling a laugh at his sister's bedraggled appearance: lopsided ponytail, mascara smudged under her eyes, and her complexion a sickly grey. 'I made the kids pancakes this morning but can whip you up a greasy lunch?'

She moaned and clutched her stomach. 'What time is it?'

'Almost one.'

'Fuck,' she muttered, peering bleary-eyed at her watch. 'I haven't slept this late since I drank an entire bottle of wine on graduation night.'

'Mick seemed fine when he left this morning.'

'That's because he was the designated driver for once and he foolishly let me consume one too many champers. Remind me to kill him.'

'Take it easy on the guy. He has to live with you.'

Alli flipped him the middle finger. 'If you make me a strong coffee, I'll let you stay another night.' Her expression cleared a little. 'Why are you crashing here anyway? What happened with Mila?'

'Don't ask,' he said, turning his back on his sister to make her coffee. The last thing he felt like doing was rehashing last night and how gutted he'd been by Mila's assessment of him.

How had he got it so wrong with her?

'What did you do?' Alli slumped into a chair at the dining table, her pallor improving when he placed a cup of coffee in front of her and she inhaled. 'Lovers' tiff?'

He almost responded with, *'I didn't do anything'*, but that wasn't entirely true. He should've told her he'd bailed her out from the beginning, rather than listen to Will. Though he shouldn't blame his best mate either. Sawyer was a big boy and he'd known what withholding the truth from Mila would do when he eventually came clean.

'I helped her out when she didn't want me to by buying some of her land, and I didn't tell her.'

'You idiot.' Alli gulped at her coffee as if it were iced. It must've worked because the bleariness in her eyes cleared. 'What are you going to do to make it up to her?'

Nothing, because he never wanted to feel as worthless as she'd made him feel last night ever again.

'We'll sort things out,' he said. 'We have to, considering I own some of Hills Homestead, though I'll probably take my time looking for another buyer this time and sell for the right price.'

'At the risk of repeating myself, you're an idiot.' She pointed at his face. 'Any fool can see you're in love with her.'

'Even if I am, what's the point? She can't ever leave Ashe Ridge and I live in Melbourne.'

'Ever heard of long-distance?'

'Ever heard of butting the hell out?'

She laughed, instantly regretting it as she pressed her fingertips to her temples again. 'In every relationship, someone always makes more of a sacrifice. It's what couples do if they want to make a go of it. In your case, if she can never leave the farm, you'll need to rethink where you live.' Her expression softened. 'Would it be so hard for you to move back here?'

If Alli had asked him that question any other time, he would've said hell yes. He'd never consider moving back to this town, a place that held nothing but bad memories for him.

Except the memories he'd made with Mila back then. And now... He'd convinced himself that walking away from her was inevitable. They had no future. How could they? He had to move around. His ADHD meant he couldn't stay in one place too long. He may call Melbourne home, but he could count the weeks he spent in his house in Hawthorn on one hand. Being on the road suited him. Land broking was the perfect job.

What would happen if he gave it all up to stay in one place for longer than a month or two?

Would he grow to resent her? Would he be physically and mentally incapable of staying put? Would he run again, but this time leaving her heartbroken?

'I can see you've got a lot to think about,' Alli said, draining her coffee. 'For what it's worth, you can stay here as long as you like, because we love having you around, but I think you should sort out your shit with Mila.'

She stood and moved around the table to press a kiss to

the top of his head. 'You're smart, little brother. I'm sure you'll do the right thing, for both of you.'

Sawyer was glad one of them had confidence, because he couldn't shake the terror that this life-changing decision could make or break him.

CHAPTER FIFTY-TWO

When Jack hadn't returned by six that evening, Adelaide started to worry.

She'd tried painting when she got back from Mila's, but all she'd managed to do was create a few slashes of crimson, black, and grey that matched her mood perfectly. She'd tidied the bungalow, scrubbing it from top to bottom, and had stocked up on groceries, cooking a Thai prawn curry they could share for dinner tonight while she tried to make Jack see sense.

But she couldn't do that if the man in question wasn't around and by late afternoon, she wondered if she was doing the right thing in giving them a second chance.

Jack had closed off again. Retreated to the point of disappearing, which is exactly what he did for most of their marriage. Had he really changed as much as she'd thought?

Only a fool would make the same mistake twice. If she moved back and he ran away like this every time they had a disagreement, where would that leave her?

She couldn't go through the coldness of their marriage

again. She wanted a fresh start with the man she'd grown to love again over the last few weeks, not a stroll down memory lane that would end in disaster.

'Stubborn mule,' she muttered, referring to Jack, not herself, as she paced the living room, peering out the window every now and then in the hope his car would pull into the drive.

Her gaze fell on the locked door in the corner of the studio, the one he'd freaked out over when she'd asked what was behind it when she first arrived, and it struck her that she hadn't asked him since despite her curiosity. Maybe if he ever returned, she could ask him again.

Her annoyance built as she continued to pace. This wasn't her style, waiting for a man so she could knock some sense into him. She'd left passive Adelaide behind a long time ago. These days, she made things happen. Which meant she needed to find Jack and have the talk to end all talks.

The talk that would reveal whether she stayed or left.

Now she had her car, she could drive into town and try to find him, but after fourteen years, she wouldn't have a clue where to start. When they were married, he'd always retreat to his favourite spot near the dam on the farm, where an old shed stored his fishing equipment.

She wondered... could he be there?

It was a long shot, but waiting here wasn't helping, so she grabbed her keys and headed out the door before she could second-guess the wisdom of chasing after a man who might not want her.

~

Dusk descended as she walked the last hundred metres to the dam. A kerosene lantern shone like a beacon from the shed and as she got closer, she spied a small campfire, with a figure sitting in front of it.

Jack.

She should've been angry at him for stomping out this morning rather than sticking around and talking through their issues. She should've been annoyed he'd reverted to type. She should've wanted to yell at him for being so damn immature and overreacting over a stupid phone call.

But she felt none of those things as she neared him. In fact, she felt nothing but love, a warm glow that spread through her chest and made her want to fling herself into his arms when he glanced up and caught sight of her.

'Ads,' he said, and stood; it was all he had to say before she ran to him and they embraced.

They hugged for a long time, words superfluous, as she realised she'd never felt so at home as she did in this man's arms.

When they eventually disengaged, Jack said, 'You remembered my hiding spot?'

'I remember a lot of things,' she said, with a smile. 'And I'd like to make new memories with you so I can remember those in another fourteen years.'

'You'll be eighty-seven then, and I'll be eighty-eight.' He grimaced. 'And I'll be just as grumpy, if not worse.'

'I can handle it.' She took hold of his hand. 'Now that we've both calmed down, shall we make plans for the future?'

Rather than joy transforming his features as she hoped, Jack couldn't quite meet her eyes. 'I'd like nothing better, Ads, but I've been doing a lot of thinking.'

Fear clutched her chest. 'Is that what you've been doing out here all day?'

He nodded. 'I always did my best thinking here. I needed the time out sometimes, to make sense of it all.'

'Sounds like you don't want a future with me after all?' Her voice wavered. 'You can't forgive me for walking away?'

He shook his head. 'No, that's not it. I can forgive you. I want to, as much as I want to give us another chance. But...' He trailed off, misery clouding his eyes. 'There's something I have to tell you.'

'Whatever it is, I'm right here, Jack Hayes, and I'm not going anywhere.'

He took hold of her other hand and squeezed both. 'When my parents died and I inherited the farm, I didn't have time to grieve. I felt this weight of responsibility to prove myself, even though they weren't around anymore.'

He grimaced. 'I'd never wanted to stay on the farm, and I made that clear to my folks, repeatedly. I was such a disappointment to them, so when I had to step up, I wanted to make up for it, even if they weren't around to see it. Then I met you and I wanted to be wherever you were, so I resented being tethered here. But then this miracle happened, and you gave up everything for me, and while I was ecstatic, I couldn't help but feel even more guilt, that I'd deprived you of a life of luxury you were used to and I might not live up to your expectations.'

He hung onto her hands so tight she braced for what was to come.

'I know I should've been happy. I'd married the love of my life, we had a new baby, and I was making a go of the farm. But all I felt every day when I woke was a sense of dread. A sense I wasn't good enough. A sense I'd inevitably fail and I'd lose you.'

His shoulders slumped. 'I was sad all the time and I didn't want to put that on you, so I retreated. I spent more time away from the homestead and I hid out here regularly. I saw the way you looked at me, like I disappointed you, and that made it worse because I loathed myself for putting you through it when you could've had a better life, one that you deserved. It got to the point I couldn't touch you because I was that much of a failure and it just snowballed from there.'

Tears welled in her eyes at what he'd gone through, what they'd both gone through, back then.

'When you left, you proved what I'd always thought. I wasn't deserving of you, and I couldn't inflict any more sadness on you. The least I could do was let you go. So that's why I didn't come after you, despite every bone in my body urging me to do it. And I got sadder. A lot sadder, to the point Mila started watching me like she was terrified I'd leave too. So I went to the doc and he confirmed what I pretty much suspected. I had depression and had been suffering for a long time. He put me on meds, and I started seeing a psychologist in Nhill. It took time but I eventually started feeling myself again, like it was worth going on rather than...'

Pain contorted his face. 'Rather than contemplating ending my misery every damn day. Something I'd been thinking about, even before you left.'

He blew out a breath. 'Over the years, I wondered if I should've confided in you, if telling you how bad I was feeling would've changed things for us. But I had to be thankful you'd escaped because I'd dragged you down for long enough.'

He lifted both her hands and pressed them to his chest. 'Though I never stopped harbouring this foolish hope you might come back. That's why I built the cottage. And the bungalow, which is a studio actually, where you could paint. I wanted to prove I'd listened to you all those years earlier, even if I didn't show it.'

'Oh, Jack.' She let the tears fall and he swiped them away gently, his own trickling down his cheeks.

This stoic man had endured so much and thought she'd abandoned him because he'd never been good enough. If only he'd told her, but there was no point lamenting the past now. Their future was what counted.

When they stopped crying, Jack said, 'I want to show you something back at the studio.'

A studio he'd made for her. A testament to his love, that he'd never forgotten her even if she thought he had.

'Okay. I have my car back, so I'll meet you at home?'

'Home,' he echoed, his voice filled with wonder. 'Our home.'

'For as long as you'll have me,' she said, slipping her hand into his. 'Leave your car here and come with me. I don't want to let you out of my sight.'

He chuckled. 'I'm not going to do a runner.' He paused and winked. 'Like you.'

'Too soon, Jack,' she said, with a mock frown, before joining in his laughter.

Once they put out the fire and locked up the shed, they strolled to her car.

'Thank you for opening up to me, Jack. It means a lot. I know you didn't shut me out deliberately back then, but the emotional isolation is what drove me to leave. I stayed in Kaniva a few nights, hoping you'd come after me, and when you didn't, I drove away.'

A deep frown grooved his brow, and he opened his

mouth to respond, but she pressed her finger against his lips.

'In a way, leaving was the best thing I could've done for myself. I followed my passion for art, I finally felt validated through my paintings. My whole life I'd felt like I'd been taken for granted, first by my folks who viewed me as another possession, and then by you when I thought you loved the farm more than me. So making a life for myself in Tally Bay... it's been good.'

'Are you sure you want to give that up?'

'Honestly? I'm not sure of anything, but I love you, and I want to give this marriage another try.'

'Then that's good enough for me.'

He drew her into his arms and kissed her, a slow, sensual kiss that made her cling to him. While the physical sparks they created were wonderful, it was their newfound emotional connection that turned her on more than anything.

'There is one thing,' Adelaide said, cupping his cheek. 'I'd love to show you Tally Bay. That place healed me. It feels like home.'

He nodded, his gaze never leaving hers. 'For me, home is wherever you are. And as I'm not tied to the farm anymore, what do you say we spend some of our year here, and some in Tally Bay? The best of both worlds?'

Joy unfurled in Adelaide's heart at how much her man had changed, how far he was willing to go, for her. 'I say yes, let's do it.'

He kissed her again and she melted into him, scarcely believing they were lucky enough to have a second chance.

'Now, what's this surprise you've got for me at the studio?'

'You'll see.' He made a zipping motion over his lips, and she tamped down her impatience.

Jack rested his hand on her thigh the entire drive home and she liked the feeling, like he never wanted to let her go. After she parked, they held hands as they walked into the studio and Jack headed straight for the locked door that had piqued her curiosity.

'Finally,' she said, as he unlocked it with a key from his chain. 'I was beginning to get worried about what you might have stashed in there.'

'Just this.'

He flung the door open and gestured her to come closer. When she did and saw what he'd kept in the tiny storage cupboard, her throat tightened with emotion.

'Jack,' she whispered, stepping forward to pick up the first frame, then the next, and the next, awed that he'd done this.

'After you left and I found this stash of sketches, I thought they might be important to you, even though you'd never showed them to me. So I had them framed and stored in here, on the off-chance you'd come back and I could surprise you.' With a sheepish grin, he flung his arms wide. 'Surprise.'

'I can't believe you did this,' she murmured, blown away by the proof he really had hoped she'd return one day. 'I used to sketch at midnight sometimes, or in the mornings, as a way to centre myself before the start of yet another monotonous day. Turns out, I didn't know what I had until I lost it, but by then it was too late. I'd stayed away too long, had completely broken things between us to the point of no return.'

She swallowed several times before continuing. 'If it's okay with you, I'd like to hang these in the cottage, because even though they're far from my best work, I want to look at evidence of where we started and how far we've come.'

'I'd like that,' he said, pocketing the key. 'Now, isn't there a fun way we can seal our new relationship?'

'I'm all yours,' she said, grabbing his hands and dragging him to the nearby sofa bed.

CHAPTER FIFTY-THREE

No matter how many times Mila studied weed risk in paddocks or rode around the boundaries, the extent of her land never failed to astonish.

She owned all this. Every scrap of turned soil, every legume produced, every single tree. From the first time she'd visited Hills Homestead with her parents, she'd loved the place. Loved when Gramps drove her around on the back of a quad bike, loved the unique mustiness of ripening lentils in the air, loved the striking sunsets over harvested fields. She'd never understood her father's disregard for the farm. He couldn't wait to escape it and he rarely returned.

Like Sawyer, which is why she'd invited him here today.

She'd sent him a brief text, asking him to pop over around four, at the southernmost corner of the land he'd acquired. She had a plan. And even if it didn't come to fruition, at least she could say she tried.

As his car approached, she slid from a log and dusted off her jeans, her palms clammy. She smoothed her hair, tucking stray strands into her ponytail, and tugged down her red ribbed singlet, which had ridden up. She never fussed over her appearance but she wanted to present a confident front so Sawyer took her seriously.

This had to work.

His terse response to her text, *'See you then'*, hadn't inspired her with confidence. But at least he'd arrived and that was something. She'd had her doubts after the way she'd spoken to him when she'd kicked him out two nights ago. She wouldn't have blamed him for not showing up. Then again, he owned this tract of land so perhaps he was protecting his investment.

He took his time getting out of the car and her heart kicked as he strolled towards her, long legs clad in denim, a black T clinging to his chest, but without the usual laconic smile. She'd done that, wiped the smile from his face, and she'd do anything to coax it back.

His strides slowed as he neared her and she pasted a smile on her face.

'Thanks for coming.'

'No worries,' he said, but there were plenty, and she hoped to address some of them now.

'Firstly, I want to apologise for the way I spoke to you the other night. I was way out of line.'

He gave a terse nod. 'Apology accepted.'

She took him at his word but he sounded dubious, like he didn't really buy her apology.

'I overreacted, when you were obviously trying to help me out, so thanks.'

'You're welcome.'

Yikes. The garrulous guy she loved hadn't spoken more than two words at a time since he arrived.

Loved?

Yeah, of course she loved him. She wouldn't be doing this otherwise. The emotion had snuck up on her and was nothing like books and movies portrayed it. There hadn't been an exact moment she could pinpoint when she fell for him. No instant lust. No swoonworthy meet-cute. She'd known and trusted Sawyer for over half her life and the teen she'd considered a good friend had morphed into an amazing man she couldn't help but love.

'This is the land you bought,' she said, sweeping her arm wide.

'I know.'

Still with the two-word responses. Maybe what she said next would change that.

'I want to discuss what we do with it.'

His eyebrows arched slightly. 'I'm listening.'

'This tract hasn't been used for sowing in years, so I was thinking it could be used for housing? That way, you'd make a killing on your investment and have enough money to retire now if you wanted.'

His other eyebrow joined the first. 'Why would I retire now?'

'Well, you wouldn't necessarily have to retire. But having that much money would mean you wouldn't have to work, and travel so much to do it, and you'd have to spend all your time here to oversee a project of that magnitude '

Heck, why couldn't she just come out and say it?

She didn't want him to leave.

Ever.

He took an eternity to answer, his face an impassive mask, and she knew she'd blown it.

'Never mind. It was a crazy idea from left field—'

'Is that your weird way of asking me to stay?'

The corners of his mouth twitched in amusement, giving her hope.

'What if it is? Do you think it's something you'd be interested in doing?'

He shook his head, sending her newfound hope plummeting. 'I'm not interested in housing development.'

'Oh.'

Her visions for the future, and the two of them living happily ever after, evaporated, leaving her trembling as the adrenaline that had been pumping while she'd harnessed the courage to encourage him to stay drained from her body.

'But I am interested in developing a new paediatric medical centre in town. A place where specialists could regularly visit, so kids like Brett can get an early diagnosis and the proper intervention to maximise their learning potential and set them up for life.'

'That's great, Sawyer.'

Great for the kids of Ashe Ridge, not so great for her, as he'd be pouring money into the construction and outsourcing the labour, all from afar. Leaving her alone and lamenting what might've been.

'To give a project of that magnitude my full attention, I've quit my job. I'll need to stay in Ashe Ridge for the foreseeable future. Perhaps I could help complete that first cottage of your farm stay and rent it?'

As Mila processed his startling revelation, she wondered if helping support kids like his nephew was his only motivation.

'Or I could move in with you permanently if you like?'

Daring to hope, she scanned his face for confirmation he'd just made a declaration that would change their lives.

'Are you saying you're staying in Ashe Ridge because of me?'

He pretended to ponder by screwing up his eyes. 'Well,

catching up with Alli and her family has been great, but yeah. I'm hoping my grand gesture will prove how much I love you and that no matter how hard you push me away I'm not going anywhere.'

But everyone left her eventually. It's what they did. Her parents. Will. Gran. Even Sawyer.

What if she opened her heart to him completely but he left regardless?

'What if you get tired of me?' She screwed up her nose. 'I can be hard to live with. And I'm too independent for my own good. You'll probably get annoyed all the time. And what if—'

'No more what-ifs.' He held up his hand. 'There's only one question you need to answer. Do you love me?'

'Of course,' she said, without hesitation.

Sawyer beamed, relief in his eyes, as she strode towards him, slid her arms around his neck, and pulled his neck down to kiss him.

An eternity later, Sawyer said, 'So that's a yes then?'

'It's a hell yes.' She placed her palm over his heart, the steady beat a comfort she could get used to. 'We make a great team, Sawyer Mann. Let's make it official.'

His eyes widened. 'Are you proposing, Gumnut?'

Considering how happy she was, she let the nickname slide. This time. 'No. I was thinking more along the lines of giving you a key.'

He swiped at his brow. 'Phew. Because if anyone's doing the proposing around here, it's going to be me.'

'Is that so? And do you have a timeline on this proposal?'

'It'll be a surprise,' he murmured, pulling her close again. 'Stay tuned.'

CHAPTER FIFTY-FOUR

'You have a lot of stuff,' Jack said, holding up a Himalayan salt lamp in one hand and a large tourmaline crystal in the other. 'Do these go in the keep or discard pile?'

Adelaide smiled and pointed to the ever-growing pile of things she wanted to take back to Ashe Ridge. 'Keep.'

'You know the studio I built is for your painting, not hoarding, right?'

She flung a cushion at his head. 'I'm not a hoarder. I like to surround myself with pretty things.'

'Me too.' Jack carefully placed the lamp and crystal on the floor before crossing the room to slide his arms around her waist and nuzzle her neck. 'Extremely pretty.'

'I never would've picked you for an old romantic,' she murmured, savouring the feel of being cherished by her husband. 'But I like it.'

'Good.' He nipped her neck before easing away, a wicked glint in his eyes. 'You know what I like? Taking a break from this endless packing for an afternoon nap.'

Adelaide laughed. 'When we had one of your infamous

"naps" yesterday, we didn't make it out of the bed until this morning. At this rate, we'll never finish packing.'

'We happen to be very good at *napping*.' His cheeky smile warmed her heart. 'Plus, we have to make up for lost time, you know.'

She cupped his cheek, wishing they hadn't been so stubborn for so long. 'I know. But I also want to get back to Ashe Ridge and set up our home.'

His gaze softened. 'Our home. I like the sound of that.'

'Me too.'

She pressed her lips to his, still marvelling that in the last month since the B & S ball, they'd reunited for good, and Jack had accompanied her to Tally Bay to pack up the remnants of her life here.

The last two weeks had been bliss: easy hikes, afternoon swims, impromptu picnics, and making love long into the night. Adelaide had never dreamed she could be this happy again and while they'd holiday here on occasion in the future, she knew where her heart belonged.

With Jack, in the cottage he'd built for her, in Ashe Ridge.

'I guess the faster we pack, the faster we go home?' Jack's mock huff made her chuckle.

'Exactly.' She winked. 'Besides, the faster we stuff those boxes, the sooner we can take a nap.'

'Don't have to ask me twice.' He released her and headed back to the bookcase he'd been emptying. He picked up a dreamcatcher. 'Keep or discard?'

As she studied the lines of her husband's face, the uptilting of his mouth, and the softness in his eyes as he looked at her, Adelaide knew she didn't need the dreamcatcher anymore.

Her dream of happily-ever-after had come true.

EPILOGUE

One Year Later

'If I thought farming was tough, I had no idea what I was letting myself in for with running a farm stay.' Mila moaned as Sawyer pressed his thumb into the ball of her foot. 'If I didn't have you to give me foot massages, cook stir-fries, and help manage the social media side of the business along with the bookings, I'd be screwed.'

'All in a day's work.' He grinned and increased the pressure, almost making her eyes roll back in her head from the pleasure of it. 'I like having things to do to fill my days now I'm a kept man.'

'You are so far from a kept man it's not funny.' She stuck her tongue out and winked. 'Though I do like the thought of you at my beck and call.'

'Actually, about that…' He moved her feet off his lap and slid off the sofa, onto one knee, and she swore her heart stopped. 'How do you feel about making our living arrangement permanent?'

'It already is,' she murmured, not daring to breathe as Sawyer slipped a tiny blue box out of his pocket.

'Well then, how about you make an honest man out of me and agree to be my wife?'

He popped the lid of the box and she exhaled on a sigh.

The princess-cut emerald surrounded by diamonds was breathtaking.

And a ring she'd admired when they'd headed to Melbourne for a city-cation a few months ago.

She hadn't thought much of them window-shopping in Collins Street at the time. They'd been eating spicy lamb souvlaki and struggling not to let the garlic sauce drip all over them as they passed the jewellers and the emerald had caught her eye. They'd barely paused because Sawyer had wanted to visit a bookshop to stock up on reading for Brett and Aimee. Or maybe that had been a distraction technique so she wouldn't guess he'd been wanting her to choose her own engagement ring.

'If you're taking this long to answer my proposal, I'm starting to think I've made a mistake.'

She smiled and held out her left hand, which trembled a little. 'No mistake. I'd love to be your wife.'

'Phew, you had me worried for a second.' He slid the ring onto her fourth finger and it fit perfectly. Her heart pounded as he lifted her hand to his mouth and pressed a kiss on her knuckle above the ring. 'I love you and I can't wait to marry you.'

'I love you too.' She cupped his cheek with her other hand. 'How about we do it next week?'

He gaped for a moment before laughing. 'You're serious?'

'Of course. We'll keep it small. Close friends and family only. Catering will be easy to organise. Maeve from the bakery will do the cake at short notice.' She gnawed on her bottom lip. 'And I may already have a dress.'

It had been an impulse purchase on that same weekend in Melbourne, a simple ivory strapless sheath made from silk that had been on sale in a boutique. It wasn't a wedding dress per se, and she'd bought it for when Hills Homestead hosted its own B & S ball early next year, but it would do nicely.

'In that case, I'll get the legalities sorted and I'm all yours.'

'Promise?'

He leaned in for a kiss. 'Promise.'

'This is your fault, you know.' Mila elbowed Will, who clutched his side. 'If you hadn't gotten sick at the worst possible time and asked Sawyer to attend my first wedding in your stead, we wouldn't have fallen for each other, and Gran and Gramps wouldn't have got back together either.' She bumped her brother with her hip. 'I suppose you're proud of yourself.'

'Of course.' Will grinned as they watched Adelaide and Jack dance beneath a eucalyptus, locked in a close embrace, unable to take their eyes off each other. 'All part of the grand plan.'

'And what plan is that?'

He snickered. 'Okay. You got me. It's all a giant fluke but I'll take the credit if you want me to.'

'You're an idiot,' she said, holding up her champagne flute. 'But I'm glad you flew from London to make it to this wedding.'

'My best friend and my sister marrying?' He clinked his stubbie against her glass. 'Wouldn't miss it for the world.'

They sipped their respective drinks, watching Brett and Aimee clamber all over Sawyer who pretended to hate it as he acted defenceless.

'I've never seen him so happy, sis. And I think that's because of you.'

'I'm happy too.' Her chest ached most days because of it. She could hardly believe how lucky she was. 'What about you? I know you're solo here, but that could be because of the exorbitant last-minute plane fare you had to fork out. Is there anyone special in London?'

Will hesitated before shaking his head. 'No. Been through a messy breakup recently though, so it's most unkind of you not to have any bridesmaids I can hook up with.'

She heard a hint of sadness beneath his levity and wished her brother could be as happy as she was. 'The women of Ashe Ridge aren't ready for a worldly guy like you.'

'You're right,' he said, taking another slug of beer, but she detected vulnerability in his tone. 'Looks like your groom is heading this way, so I'll leave you to it. I see a quiche with my name written all over it at the buffet table.'

Mila watched her brother as he walked away, wondering if she'd get to the bottom of what was really bugging him before he left. Like her new husband, Will hid his feelings behind humour, but she saw right through him. He couldn't hide the sadness in his eyes, and it worried her. Will deserved to be happy and if he wouldn't open up to her, she'd get Sawyer on the case.

'Everything okay, wifey?' Sawyer slipped his hand into

hers. 'Did that bozo say something to upset you? You're looking a little worried.'

'I'm fine, though sounds like he went through a breakup recently and it's affected him more than he's letting on. Has he said anything to you?'

Sawyer shook his head. 'We haven't had time to catch up properly, what with you putting a rush on this wedding because you couldn't wait to make me your husband.'

She smiled and squeezed his hand. 'I just want everyone to be as happy as us.'

'Not a chance.' He pulled her close and slid his arms around her waist. 'How lucky are we?'

'The luckiest people in the world,' she murmured, a second before his lips claimed hers.

If you enjoyed this book, please leave a review.

ACKNOWLEDGEMENTS

I love the warmth of small country towns. The history, the old buildings, the locals, so when I write women's fiction set in rural areas I get to fall in love with a small town of my own creation!

Where the Heart Is happens to be my fifth rural romance with Harper Collins/Harlequin Australia and I know we're not supposed to pick favourites, but this story is unabashedly mine. These characters strutted from my heart onto the page and I love them.

Writing is a solitary occupation and having a story reach bookshelves takes a team effort so I'd like to thank the following people: Rachael Donovan, my publisher at Harlequin Australia, for your ongoing support. I love working with you and your insights into the publishing industry are invaluable.

Julia Knapman, I appreciate your editorial guidance in ensuring my manuscript is the best it can be.

Suzanne O'Sullivan, for your insightful editing. This story is stronger thanks to your feedback.

Annabel Adair, for your keen proofreading skills.

Sarana Behan, my publicist, who devises innovative ways to sell my books.

The entire team at HQ Australia and HarperCollins

Australia, for placing my rural romances into readers' hands.

Jacqui Furlong, the Fields Sales Manager at HarperCollins, for getting my books into stores.

Tim Rethus, a grain grower in the Wimmera, who patiently answered all my questions regarding lentil farming in the region. Thanks for your invaluable help with my research.

For the bookshops, librarians, reviewers, booktokers, bookstagrammers, and bloggers who help spread the word about my books. You are appreciated!

Martin, who makes me laugh when I'm in deadline hell.

My boys, who give the best hugs when I'm juggling back-to-back deadlines. Love you to infinity.

My folks, for being the strongest support system I could wish for.

You lift me up when I need it most.

My loyal readers, I can't thank you enough for buying my books. Every review you leave, every email saying how much you love my stories, every comment you leave on TikTok/Instagram/Facebook/ Goodreads, makes this job a little easier.

Writing can be tough at times and knowing you're waiting for my next book is a great incentive to keep going.

I hope you love *Where the Heart Is* as much as I do.

Happy reading!

Nic x

FREE BOOK AND MORE

SIGN UP TO NICOLA'S NEWSLETTER for a free book!

Read Nicola's feel-good romance **DID NOT FINISH**

Or her gothic suspense novels **THE RETREAT** and **THE HAVEN**

(The gothic prequel **THE RESIDENCE** is free!)

JOURNEY TO YOU

Try the **CARTWRIGHT BROTHERS** duo

FASCINATION

PERFECTION

The **WORKPLACE LIAISONS** duo

THE BOSS

THE CEO

The **REDEEMING A BAD BOY** series

THE REBEL

THE PLAYER

THE WANDERER

THE CHARMER

THE EX

THE FRIEND

REDEEMING BAD BOYS BOXED SET BOOKS 1-4

Try the **BASHFUL BRIDES** series

NOT THE MARRYING KIND

NOT THE ROMANTIC KIND

NOT THE DARING KIND

NOT THE DATING KIND

The **CREATIVE IN LOVE** series

THE GRUMPY GUY

THE SHY GUY

THE GOOD GUY

Try the **BOMBSHELLS** series

BEFORE (FREE!)

BRASH

BLUSH

BOLD

BAD

BOMBSHELLS BOXED SET

The **WORLD APART** series

WALKING THE LINE (FREE!)

CROSSING THE LINE

TOWING THE LINE

BLURRING THE LINE

WORLD APART BOXED SET

The **HOT ISLAND NIGHTS** duo

WICKED NIGHTS

WANTON NIGHTS

The **ROMANCE CYNICS** duo

CUPID SEASON

SORRY SEASON

The **BOLLYWOOD BILLIONAIRES** series

FAKING IT

MAKING IT

The **LOOKING FOR LOVE** series

LUCKY LOVE

CRAZY LOVE

The MILITARY MEN IN LOVE duo

THE SECOND CHANCE GUY

THE NO CHANCE GUY

Check out Nicola's website for a full list of her books.

And read her other romances as Nikki North.

'MILLIONAIRE IN THE CITY' series.

LUCKY

FANCY

FLIRTY

FOLLY

MADLY

Try the **LAW BREAKER** series

THE DEAL MAKER

THE CONTRACT BREAKER

About the Author

USA TODAY bestselling and multi-award winning author Nicola Marsh writes page-turning fiction to keep you up all night.

She's published 86 books and sold millions of copies worldwide.

She currently writes contemporary romance and domestic suspense.

She's also a Waldenbooks, Bookscan, Amazon, iBooks and Barnes & Noble bestseller, a RBY (Romantic Book of the Year) and National Readers' Choice Award winner, and a multi-finalist for a number of awards including the Romantic Times Reviewers' Choice Award, HOLT Medallion, Booksellers' Best, Golden Quill, Laurel Wreath, and More than Magic.

A physiotherapist for thirteen years, she now adores writing full time, raising her two dashing young heroes, sharing fine food with family and friends, and her favorite, curling up with a good book!